I0729941

From the Ashes

REDWOOD BAY FIRE
BOOK TWO

HJ WELCH

From the Ashes
Redwood Bay Fire Book Two

Copyright © 2025 by Helen Juliet aka HJ Welch

Cover Design by Jacqueline Sweet

This book is a work of fiction. Names, places, and incidents are either products of the author's imagination or are used fictitiously. Any resemblance to actual events, locales, or persons, living or dead, is entirely coincidental.

All rights reserved. No part of this book may be used or reproduced in any manner whatsoever without written permission, except in the case of brief quotations embodied in critical articles and reviews.

The publisher, Helen Juliet aka HJ Welch, does not consent to any Artificial Intelligence (AI), generative AI, large language model, machine learning, chatbot, or other automated analysis, generative process, or replication program to reproduce, mimic, remix, summarize, or otherwise replicate any part of this novel, via any means: print, graphic, sculpture, multimedia, audio, or any other medium.

❀ Created with Vellum

Also Available

BY HJ WELCH

Contemporary small town & found family series set in the US

Redwood Bay Fire (Small town found family firefighters)

#1 Igniting His Flame

#2 From the Ashes

#3 Striking the Match (Coming Soon)

Pine Cove (Small town – six books, five short stories)

Complete Box Set

Homecoming Hearts (Found family former boy band – five books, three short stories)

Complete Box Set

Paddle Creek Daddies (Small town Daddies and kink)

#1 Heaven Sent

#2 Yes, Sir

#3 Little Pleasures

#4 Four Play

#5 Hell's Kitten

#6 Make Believe

Seasonal Daddies (International romance multi-author shared universe)

Jalen & Colby: A Daddy for Christmas

Arlo: A Daddy for Summer

Bears-4-U (Daddies and bears multi-author shared universe)

<u>Keep Me</u>

———

BY HELEN JULIET

Standalone contemporary Fairy & Folk Tale and Classic Literature Adaptations set in the UK

<u>The Fairy Tale Collection Box Set</u> (Beauty and the Beast, Cinderella, Rapunzel)

<u>Daddy's Fairy Tales Box Set</u> (Daddies and kink – Goldilocks, Little Red Riding Hood, The Three Little Pigs, Puss in Boots)

In Good Spirits (Daddies and kink, Christmas, MMMM – A Christmas Carol)

Sweet Tooth (Christmas – Hansel and Gretel)

Jacked Up (D/s – Jack and the Beanstalk)

Rise and Shine (Novella – Sleeping Beauty)

We're All Mad Here (Novella – Alice in Wonderland)

CHAPTER 1

Colt

Damn, I've missed this.

I stand on the golden beach of my hometown and inhale the salt air deep into my lungs. Sunshine sparkles on the waves as children and adults alike frolic in the water. I'm very proud of the time I've spent in Massachusetts and New York, but the West Coast will always have my heart.

Moving back wasn't in my five-year or even ten-year plan. But neither was my father's massive heart attack and subsequent triple bypass. It was always the endgame for me to inherit the family law practice that my grandfather founded. I just thought I had another couple of decades before that happened.

Another couple of decades to get my life in order.

Now I'm standing back on this slice of paradise, though, it feels less like my choices were taken away from me…yet again. Destiny intervened a little sooner than expected, is all. Redwood Bay is where I belong. This is still my beach.

Picking up my brand-new board, I march determinedly into the water. It's been a minute since I went surfing. Outside of a few vacations to Hawaii and the Caribbean, it's not really been something I could do on the East Coast. The waves at Long Island weren't half bad. It was more like the vibe didn't fit with who I was out there. But I grew up on this shore, and I have no doubt my body will remember everything it's supposed to do now.

Despite the beaming sun above, I know the water is going to be pretty chilly as it's still only early spring. Sure enough, it's bracing as soon as it hits my skin. I laugh and whistle as I wade into the surf in my board shorts, knowing that there's nothing I can do but let my body get used to it. I'll soon warm up once I get going.

The beach is busy, but as I power myself farther into the water, it feels like I'm out here all on my own. There's a peacefulness to be found under the roar of the waves.

They're not too huge today, about seven to eight feet tall, I'd guess. Just right for easing myself back into the swing of it. As it's not too crowded, I don't feel rushed as I paddle to a good spot and wait for a decent wave to hit.

The second I jump up and my feet hit the board, it's like I'm flying. I let out a primal bellow of glee that's probably not appropriate for a defense lawyer of my stature, but no one's out here to judge me. Certainly not my father. I grin and reach out with my fingers into the water as I ride the dazzling blue tunnel through to the end.

This was exactly what I needed after the stress of the sudden move across the country. My old company was very good at letting me go as fast as they could once I'd wrapped up a few major cases. But the rest I was able to hand over and seeing as they're almost three thousand miles away, the non-compete clause shouldn't affect me all that much, if at all.

It's going to be quite a change, shifting from big, corporate law to the kind of clients my family's small, elite firm usually represents. I have a feeling I'm going to be dealing with a lot of multimillion dollar divorce settlements in the not-too-distant future.

I thought I'd be more upset about that. For years, the thrill of all those cut-throat cases felt like the only thing that got me out of bed most mornings. Whenever I've thought about taking over the practice, I've been mostly convinced that babysitting couples squabbling over who gets what mansion was going to bore me to tears. But as I hop on another wave, my leg muscles straining and the salt air filling my lungs, it hits me that perhaps a slower pace of life might give me room to care about things other than work.

The beach is only a ten-minute drive from the apartment I've just moved into. The idea of getting up early and coming here for a run or a surf before heading into the office sounds like a little moment of heaven every day.

One thing that quickly became clear once I realized I had to move was that I might have had a lot of colleagues and acquaintances back in New York, but no real friends. That was pretty fucking embarrassing to come to terms with. What's the point of working that hard and earning all that money if I'm just going to find myself alone in an empty home every night? Of course I had a big farewell party, and a ton of people bitched at me for abandoning them. But how many of them will I still be texting by Christmas?

Hardly any, I bet.

Rather than jumping back into the next wave, I straddle my board for a while, letting my legs and hands float in the water. I know exactly why I keep people at arm's length. When your whole life is constructed around a lie, you're kind of forced to be cautious and not let anyone get too close. I've spent my entire career telling people that I don't date much because I'm too busy.

Nobody on the East Coast ever found out the truth. At least, if they ever suspected, they never let on to me.

But being back in Redwood Bay makes it almost impossible to ignore. My father might have pressured me to get into 'the best law school in the country,' at least in his opinion, but ultimately, I was the one who chose to run away. I've been running ever since.

It never felt like there was any other option. But now I'm home, will I be forced to stop and face some of those core, secret truths in a way I've never had to before? Am I ready to deal with all that shame of what a coward I've been?

Exhaling, I run a wet hand though my already drying hair and decide that I don't have to deal with any of that today. I arrived in town almost two weeks ago, but it's been such a whirlwind, this has been the first chance I've had to order a board and get down to the beach. No matter my past sins, I don't deserve to sabotage this experience for myself. I'm allowed to let loose and have a little downtime for a change.

Big, life-altering self-assessments can come later. Maybe on a Tuesday afternoon. Nothing interesting ever happens then. Right now, I've still got a couple of hours left of sunlight, then I can envision an enormous amount of Chinese takeout and maybe a nice glass of whiskey to see out the rest of my Friday evening.

But of course, the ocean has other plans.

I'm just about to gear up for another wave when movement in the corner of my eye catches my attention. I snap my head, not quite sure what I saw, only that it didn't seem natural somehow. However, I scan the water and don't spy anything unusual.

Until I do.

My breath catches and my heart rate picks up as I stare unblinkingly at the spot. It was almost too quick to see, but I'm sure I saw a flash of something brown. It could have been a seal, but it's not really the time of year for them to be getting close to the beach. Maybe it was an otter or a dolphin's fin or—

There!

Not any sea life.

That was a hand.

Before I really know what's happening, I'm propelling my board through the water, laying down with my arms cutting through the surf. "Hold on!" I yell. If someone's there, it's pretty obvious they're struggling to surface and probably can't hear me. But just in case they can, I want them to know that help is coming.

The current is strong, and I can feel my board trying to escape from me. But I grip on tight with my thighs and power on. I haven't seen the hand again and cold fear is slicing through me.

"Come on, come on," I mutter as I let the water pull me, hoping I'm going in the same direction as whoever's gotten caught in the riptide.

It's the hair I finally see, bobbing like a jellyfish under the surface. With a yell, I lurch forward and grab, managing to wrap my hand around what might be an arm.

A small, skinny arm.

My heart flips as I pull the young girl onto my board. She's not big, but she's completely limp and that makes her a dead weight. I don't know if she's breathing, but I have to get both of us to safety before I can stop and check. With her wedged between my chest and the board, I struggle to free us from the riptide.

One good thing about that fancy law firm I used to work for? They had an in-house gym and whenever I needed a break from a case, I'd go work my ass off on the treadmill until I had a breakthrough. These legs aren't afraid of a little kicking.

With a roar, I push and push until suddenly, the current

isn't working against me anymore. Relief bursts through me as I make a beeline for the shore. But I'm also aware of what's going on around me now. People in the water and on the beach are yelling and waving their arms. The lifeguard is swimming out to meet me. Someone is screaming with such terror, I know it has to be whoever's here with this little kid today.

"Nevaeh!" the woman is wailing, running into the water with tears streaming down her face.

If I had a second to think beyond moving forward, I'm sure my heart would break.

"I've got her!" the lifeguard calls as she pulls the girl from me. It's not until I make it back onto the sand do I realize how much my legs are wobbling. But I drop my board and stagger forward until I fall beside the girl and the lifeguard, who's already doing CPR.

"Nevaeh, please," the woman is crying on her knees, gripping onto the girl's hand as she shakes from head to toe. "Baby girl, wake up!" There's a crowd around us, but I hear the siren from the road above.

"The paramedics are here," I say to the lifeguard, assuming she or someone else called them. "Let me take over." I don't know what the safety protocols are like she will, but I get my first aid training recertified every year. I can do the repetitive task while she uses her training to coordinate with the medics and give this kid her best shot.

"Thanks," the lifeguard gasps. She keeps pumping the girl —Nevaeh's—chest but moves over so I can give the next rescue breath before swapping my hands with hers. Nevaeh looks so small as she lays on the sand, her big curly hair fanned out around her in a dark cloud.

"Come on," I snarl. No way my first day back on Redwood Bay beach is going to end in tragedy. I refuse to let it happen. "Come on, sweetheart. Come on."

A lot of people are shouting and the siren has stopped, so I assume the medics have made it down the steps from the road to the beach. They must be nearly here.

But that's the moment Nevaeh rolls over, choking up a stomach of saltwater and gasping for air.

The woman who I guess is her mom shrieks with relief and I can't stop the sob that escapes my chest as the little girl continues to retch. "Fuck," I utter, even though I probably shouldn't. There's an even smaller little boy hovering behind the woman, looking stricken.

Well, I'd rather he picks up a bad word to tell his big sister than the alternative.

"Paramedics coming through!" a woman yells and I look up as two people drop down into the sand beside us. The woman immediately takes Nevaeh's pulse. I glance at her partner, a man.

I know before our eyes fully meet what's about to happen.

It's as if time grinds to a halt. Despite all the adrenaline rushing through my system, my pounding heart, and my trembling hands, it's as if everything suddenly becomes very still.

Because I've found myself face to face with everything I tried to run away from over the past fifteen years.

"Zahir," I whisper in disbelief.

The look of absolute horror as he stares at me tells me everything I need to know.

I didn't run far enough.

CHAPTER 2

Zahir

I was prepared to treat a drowning victim.

I was not prepared to have to pick up the pieces of my shattered heart fifteen years after it last broke.

"Del? *Del?*" I blink and realize that Yara is scowling at me. "Check her lungs."

She's always so sunny, but I can't blame her for being unimpressed with me freezing up as soon as we arrive at a call. Our patient needs my full attention.

Colton Ross will have to wait.

"Is my daughter going to be okay?" the woman beside us tearfully asks as I press my stethoscope to the little girl's back. She's still coughing, so she's not out of the woods yet. However, this is a hell of a lot better than being unconscious and not breathing.

"We'll need to take her to the hospital to give her a check over," I tell her. "But the fact that she's woken up and is alert is a very good sign. I promise you we're going to do everything we can for her."

"She's a fighter, I can tell," Yara says warmly, speaking

mostly to the little boy clinging to the girl's mother. I'm guessing he's our patient's brother, but I've learned never to make assumptions in this job.

The girl appears stable enough to move. "Let's get her onto the backboard," I say, preferring to get her into the ambulance as soon as possible where we have a lot more equipment to monitor her vitals. I turn to the mom. "Do you guys want to grab your things so you can ride with us?"

"Yes, yes," the mom says, blinking and taking a deep breath as she regains some composure after her terrible fright. "Come on, Dashel. They're taking your sister to the hospital."

"I want to stay with Nevaeh, Mommy," the little boy says tearfully.

"We'll watch him," I promise the mom. She's not going to be thinking straight, and I don't want her to leave her phone or her car keys behind. "You can meet us by the ramp."

"Do you want to hold my hand?" Yara asks Dashel. He nods and shuffles to slip his palm against hers, not taking his eyes off Nevaeh.

"Thank you," their mom says, her voice still thick with emotion.

Then she turns to Colt.

"And thank *you* for pulling her out of the water. I had no idea she'd gone in that far!"

In that moment, I'm forced to look at the boy—*no*, the man—who I naïvely thought I was going to spend the rest of my life with. I'm trying to remain professional with every ounce of self-restraint I have. However, it's impossible to keep my body totally under control. My skin prickles and my uniform feels too hot and too tight.

I almost can't believe it, but he's even more beautiful than I remember. I think of the dogeared strip of photos I have pressed into my yearbook. It's living at the bottom of a box under my bed. I might not have looked at it in a very long time, but that's not necessary to recall every tiny detail in my mind's eye. Colt and I had been seventeen, and with the curtain closed on that photobooth at the shopping mall, we'd gotten brave.

In one of those little faded rectangles, I'm kissing my boyfriend, both of us smiling shyly. In another, it's obvious to anyone who might see it that we're looking at each other with nothing short of the deepest, truest love.

They're the only photos I had of us as a couple. The only evidence that we were even together at all. No one else has seen them. No one else ever knew.

Colt has been frozen in time for fifteen years to me. I memorized every millimeter of his teenage image. It doesn't matter that he's changed with age. I could pick him out of a crowd of thousands today. As it turns out, that really wasn't necessary.

As he stands there, dripping wet in nothing but his swim shorts, I feel a soul-crushing pang that I never got to see him grow into the man he's become today.

Hopefully, I haven't been staring at his body for more than a second or two. Nothing matters more than the well-being of my patient. But there's no escaping the fact that Colt is fucking gorgeous. A little paler than I remember, suggesting that wherever he's been living isn't as sunny as California. But his body is muscular, his jaw sharper, and his blond hair thicker than ever.

He's definitely a man now. Not a boy.

My heart and mind might very well remember the devastating grief I felt for months after he vanished without anything more than a note that simply said 'I'll never forget you,' but my blood is already thrumming with desire. If I'd met Colton Ross as a stranger today, I'd be very interested in getting him naked as quickly as possible.

As it is, our gazes lock briefly once more before I force my feet to do the unthinkable.

Walk away without knowing if I'll ever see him again.

It's not like *I* ever left. He's known where to find me all this time. What the hell is he even doing back in Redwood Bay now? I thought he'd left all this behind.

I thought he'd left *me* behind. Forever.

Of all the people that could have jumped into the fray and recused this young girl, of course it was him.

He always was a decent, good, and kind person.

It's a shame that honesty was just that stretch too far.

"What the *fudge* is up with you," Yara hisses as we carry our patient over the sand.

Nevaeh has an oxygen mask over her face and has mostly stopped coughing. Her brother is diligently trotting beside her, their hands clasped together as the four of us make our way back to the path where we can put the backboard onto the gurney and wheel our patient the rest of the way to the ambulance.

I sigh and shake my head. "Nothing."

She laughs hollowly. "Oh, don't think you're going to fool me with that nonsense. Who was that guy?"

I should have known better than to try and slip my unfortunate reaction to Colt past her. I shake my head again and glance at the small children in our care. "Later," I say simply.

She doesn't look happy, but she nods, and we make the rest of the way to solid ground in silence.

Thankfully, I'm driving the rig like usual, so that leaves Yara in the back with Nevaeh and her family. My partner is excellent at her job, and manages to balance monitoring our patient and talking reassuringly with the mom. It means I'm left alone with my whirling thoughts, but at least I can avoid answering any awkward questions for the time being. I try to concentrate on the traffic and nothing else.

We make it to San Clemente General in good time and without incident. It's nice to calmly wheel a patient through the doors rather than sprinting inside for a change.

"Who have we got here?" Samia Duke, the formidable nurse in charge, greets us warmly.

"Nevaeh Adams," I tell her as we move into the bustling emergency department. "Eight-year-old female, submerged for approximately three-to-four minutes, given CPR and resuscitated on site. Alert and responsive en route, although still coughing sporadically."

"The paramedics said she was going to be okay?" her mother says anxiously.

Nurse Samia nods, a hardened vet at dealing with panicky relatives. "We'll run a couple of tests and keep her in for observation for a few hours. Also get a medical history to make sure that there's nothing underlying that added to the incident. But with any luck, we'll have you all home by tonight." She smiles before glancing around the intake room. "Dr. Kidd, can you take Bay Three for me please?"

Just as the orderlies are about to wheel Nevaeh away, she shoots her hand out and grabs my wrist. Her fingers are so small they don't even make it all the way around.

"Thank you, Mr…?" she croaks through her oxygen mask.

My heart melts. "Everybody calls me Del. And it was a group effort from the One-Thirteen." I jut my chin to indicate Yara. "You focus on getting all better now."

"Thank you," her mom tells me as well.

Little Dashel waves at us. "Bye, Team One-Thirteen!" he calls after us.

I chuckle, and for the first time since we got to the beach, I feel some of the weight lift off my shoulders. Yes, it was tough coming face-to-face with the man who caused me so much heartache. But all that matters is that a little girl is still here with us to tell the tale.

I have to concede that's mostly down to Colt saving the day, no matter how complicated it makes things for me personally.

During the ride back to the station, I can feel Yara glancing at me. But she takes the hint and allows me to keep all my attention on the road. We haven't had a call from dispatch, so I'm not surprised that both the truck and the rig are parked out front when we return. It means I can get lost in the sea of people as soon as we hop out into the house.

"Hey, guys!" Lochlan calls from the dining table where most of the squad are crowding around. "You're just in time for lunch! I made enchiladas."

"You go," I tell Yara sincerely. "I'll do the restock. It won't take long."

She arches an eyebrow at me. "You sure?"

I nod. Technically, I'm the senior of us both, so it's my responsibility. Sometimes, that comes in handy when I need to be alone and decompress for a while.

She claps my shoulder and grins. "I'll save you some."

I'm not sure how much longer it is when she comes to find me. I took my time putting the bus back in order, then filled out Nevaeh's paperwork. I'm in the utility room, putting out some food for the station's slightly feral gray cat, Smokey. Lochlan's Dalmatian puppy, Rocky, is headbutting the backs of my knees, trying his best to also get fed. But I know for a fact he's already had his own lunch as well as plenty of tidbits from the dining table that probably weren't very good for him.

"So," Yara says, taking Smokey's dish from my hand and thrusting a plate of Mexican food into its place. "It doesn't take a genius to work out you knew that guy from the beach who saved our girl. Your face was lit up like a billboard on Hollywood Boulevard telling a story of shock and mild horror. You either hate him, *orrrr* you used to like him, but something happened and *now* you hate him."

Sighing, I turn around to lean against the counter, watching Smokey eating on top of the cupboard where Rocky can't reach her. I twiddle my fork between my fingers, but there's only so long I can procrastinate.

"I don't hate him," I say softly.

Yara folds her arms and leans opposite me, her expression sympathetic. "But you do know him?" I nod, unable to deny it after what she saw. "Did he break your heart?"

For a moment, I just focus on my food, even though I'm not hungry. I can't lie to her, but I can't out Colt either. That's what got us in all this mess in the first place.

"It's not my secret to tell," I say eventually.

Yara makes a whimpering noise and stomps over to me, throwing her arms awkwardly around my side. "I get it," she mumbles into my shoulder. "I know you'd never betray anyone, even if they hurt you. But I can read between the lines and assure you he's obviously an asshole for doing that to you."

I give up and put the plate down so I can return her hug. "He wasn't an asshole," I tell her truthfully. "He was just young. I understand what happened, even if it devastated me."

"How long ago are we talking here? High school?" Her powers of observation never fail to amaze me. I grunt noncommittally, and she takes that as the affirmation it was intended as. "Urgh, teenage boys suck. Believe me, I know."

I don't doubt it. Her brother is almost a decade younger than her, and after they lost their parents, she's practically raising him on her own. She loves him dearly, but, well... she's right. Teenagers can be a lot to deal with.

She jerks her head back and blinks at me. "Wait…is this guy the reason why you never date?"

I scoff and gently push her off. Unsurprisingly, my unsupervised meal has already been cleaned by a very naughty puppy. But all I can do is shake my head and admit I should have put the now licked clean plate up higher. At least he didn't swallow the fork.

"I date," I say defensively. But I don't meet her eye, instead reaching up to let Smokey sniff my fingers from where she's having a post-lunch bath out of reach of certain misbehaving dogs.

"You hook-up," Yara counters. "You take guys out to fancy places, you go home with them, then you're gone before morning with no intention of ever seeing them again."

I wince, regretting being so honest with her now. But she's not wrong. I've tried long-term in the past. But I could never trust myself to get close to anyone and it would always fizzle out. So now I keep things simple so nobody gets hurt.

"I've just never met the one," I say with a shrug.

Yara jerks her thumb toward the station's open front. "And who was the Ken doll back on the beach, then?"

I think of the faded photos pressed in my yearbook. The rivers of tears I cried. The numbness in my chest that I managed to shrink down over the years but never got rid of.

"The one that got away," I say sadly.

Yara whistles. "But he's back now?"

I shake my head. "Nothing's changed. I doubt I'll ever see him again."

My partner looks like she wants to protest that fact, but I get saved by the bell, literally. We rush back to the ambulance, this time with the rest of the One-Thirteen with us to tend to a house fire.

I know Yara's a romantic. She wants to believe the best in people. But I know myself and I know Colt, for better or worse. And what's better for us both is if we just let sleeping dogs lie. Anything else would undoubtedly be worse in the end.

My heart barely survived being broken the first time. There's no way I'm going to risk it again.

Colton Ross is going to stay in the past, where he belongs.

CHAPTER 3

Colt

I'M NOT EVEN SURE HOW I'VE MADE IT TO MONDAY MORNING. I feel like I've been in a daze since I stumbled back onto Redwood Bay Beach, a little girl in my arms as I fell at the feet of the love of my life.

Okay, it wasn't quite as dramatic as all that, but it certainly wasn't the chilled-out afternoon of surfing I'd hoped for, either.

Zahir Delacroix. All grown up into the most gorgeous man I've ever seen in all my thirty-three years. In that moment, I was faced with everything that I gave up, everything I walked away from.

Everything I lost to be the person my father insisted I had to be.

As I sit at my desk staring listlessly at the affidavit I'm supposed to be working on, I wonder what I hell I had been I thinking.

Over the years, I tried not to think about the boy I loved so desperately in secret back in high school. We were each other's firsts in all the ways that mattered most. That last summer before college was the happiest I can ever remember.

But then reality came crashing down around us. He knew I'd gotten into a bunch of schools, but I selfishly let him believe that I had options and hadn't made my mind up. Of course, my father had decided I was going to Harvard Law from the moment I was born, and I stupidly applied like the loyal son I am.

I never had a choice. So when the time came, I took the coward's way out and simply left him a note before heading east and never looking back. I was certain I could have never dealt with the pain of keeping Zahir in my life but not being able to be with him, so I just shut him out completely. I tried my best not to think about him at all, burying myself in studies and occasionally dating acceptable girls that I could bring home the odd Christmas to keep my parents happy.

But I could never bring myself to sleep with them. I might be a manipulative sonovabitch, but I'm not cruel. I'm also not a cheat. When I wasn't 'seeing' anyone, I'd feel free to find some out-of-town bar and pick up a guy for the night.

It was Zahir I tasted in every kiss, though.

And now I'm back in Redwood Bay. I kind of already appreciated that my hook-ups would most likely dwindle now. The risk of getting outed is so much greater this close to home. I could go into LA or San Diego, but now that I've seen my lost love in the flesh, filled out and even more hand-some than before, I don't think I have an appetite for strangers. All I'd do is go looking for his doppelgänger, and again, that wouldn't be fair to anyone.

Is what I'm going through fair, though? I feel like I'm stuck in an awful limbo, paralyzed and helpless. I can't even focus on a simple legal document. Nothing seems to matter other than Zahir.

Of course, the *only* thing that really matters is that the

little girl was okay. She seemed to be when Zahir and his partner took her off to their ambulance. I'd just really like to know for sure, but when I called the hospital, the nurse in charge kindly but firmly told me that if I wasn't family, she couldn't give out any information. I already knew that and sheepishly apologized. But there's this niggling anxiety at the back of my mind that wants to know for sure.

I thought about going to the firehouse to ask there.

Redwood Bay only has one. There are several in San Clemente, and it wouldn't be out of the question for Zahir to be working at one of those. But my gut is telling me that he's stayed here.

That would be a real dick move, though. Even if I really do want to know if little Nevaeh is okay. I have to be honest with myself and admit that wouldn't be the only reason for me visiting.

I want to see Zahir again so badly my insides are in knots and my head hasn't stopped throbbing since Friday afternoon. However, that would be outrageously out of order. I'm the one in the wrong with how everything ended. I should never have ghosted him the way I did, and I cannot expect anything from him now.

Hopefully, time will heal this gaping hole in my heart the way it sort of did before. I'm certain I hurt him beyond measure when I left, and I probably have no right to feel sorry for myself considering what I did. But Jesus Christ, I've never suffered like that before or since. When I got to Massachusetts, I barely ate or slept for weeks, constantly picking up my phone day and night, typing out hundreds of messages that never got sent.

In my life, I've made mistakes. I've lost cases and said dumb things, and there was that one time I invested in my buddy's cactus farm start-up when I knew I really shouldn't have.

But no regret comes close to how I ended things with Zahir Delacroix. Or the fact I ended our relationship at all. At the time, it seemed like the only option.

Now, I'm not so sure.

There has been the odd moment of drunken weakness where I've looked him up online. He doesn't appear to be on Facebook or BlueSky, and his Instagram is pretty much just nature photography of wildlife and flowers and sunsets, so it doesn't give a lot of insight into his life. But as I cave in and pull up the page on my work computer now, I can see his artistry in every shot. He always had an incredible eye for composition and finding beauty in the mundane.

Having seen the man behind the camera up close in the flesh for the first time in a decade and a half, I look at the photos in a new light. I wonder if he's hiding from the lens. If he is, I hope it's not because of me. It would be outrageously arrogant to think that I could still be affecting his life choices after all this time. But still…I still hope it's not my fault.

The world deserves to see him. All of him.

Leaving him isn't my only regret. So is hiding him and our relationship. Our love. He knew my parents weren't exactly homophobic, but they had a very set life plan for me that seemed too big and important to them to risk coming out at seventeen. I was old enough to know that *other* people being gay and queer was fine, but not Angela and Fredrick Ross's only son. Nuh-uh. It was my duty to carry on the family legacy and bloodline.

Still is.

I puff out my cheeks and wonder how long it'll take for my 'settling in' period to be deemed over. Once my father has been given a clean bill of health and I'm up to speed at the firm, no doubt that'll be the cue for my mom to start reminding me about nice young ladies and all the babies they could be having for me.

Or rather her. I'm not sure how good a father I'll ever be. Like I said, I'm selfish, and I don't think there's anything wrong with admitting that. Because looking at my own parents, I'm not sure it's such a hot idea for selfish people to reproduce.

Wow, I really am determined to hurt my own feelings this morning, aren't I? It's one thing to wonder about a different life lived where I never abandoned Zahir, but it's another thing entirely to be arguing with myself that I should never have been born. My situation really isn't that bad.

Giving myself a mental slap and reality check, I take a breath and look at Zahir's Instagram some more. There might not be any selfies, but he's still captured plenty of beauty that makes the world a better place.

I wonder idly if he still paints. He was always at his freest when he was painting. At our fancy private school, I knew he was constantly in a state of self-awareness, trying to prove to people like my parents that he'd earned his scholarship and wasn't less because his family didn't have a ton of money. He never got in trouble or drew much attention to himself. He just kept his head down and got the best grades he could.

But when he painted...oh, man. He could extract an explosion of color from the dullest of scenes. He could have gotten another scholarship to college, I'm sure. But that's wasn't Zahir. Painting was something he did just for himself, for joy. It took months for him to open up and even show me in our sophomore year. No, he always knew he wanted to help people in a much more direct way. I'm not surprised he's become a paramedic.

I just wish he'd put those paintings online as well. Perhaps it's a secret account I can't find, and even though that thought makes me sad, it also gives me hope. Maybe I don't deserve to enjoy his skill and talent anymore, but other people do.

If his work still exists, that is. His grandma's garage was constantly filled with his canvases. He never seemed concerned about keeping them, but she treasured every one of them. She always was a smart woman. Scary, but smart. And always his biggest cheerleader, even more than cowardly me. I bet she kept all the best and most important paintings.

This is the strange existence I've been skirting around for so many years. Knowing what Zahir was doing on the other side of the country without me would have been too painful. It was better to pretend he only existed when I left him at eighteen, frozen in time. But now I've been thrown back into his orbit, I need to know that he's happy, that he's loved. Then I think I can manage to keep up the strength I'll need to stay away from him.

Maybe.

My cellphone flashes with a notification that drags my attention back into the here and now. I blink away from my computer and frown, not recognizing the number. Before I can unlock my screen and work out what it is, I hear a rumbling sound.

For a second, my heart stops.

It's been a long time since I experienced an earthquake. Even though old instinct kicks in and tells me this just feels like a minor tremor, I still jump up and brace myself in the doorframe like I was taught as a kid.

I'm pretty sure this theory has since been debunked. I should have gone under my desk—it's sturdy enough—but I wasn't sure I'd fit. Besides, my father would think that undignified to cower like a panicked woodland creature. It doesn't matter what's safer, I'm sure. Only that I don't embarrass him.

Like I thought, the shaking stops before it even really begins. My diplomas rattle on the walls and one of the lamps falls onto the carpet, but all in all, it's pretty tame. I realize that the alert that flashed up on my phone was probably an advance warning system of some kind.

I puff out my cheeks and cling to the doorframe for a second, gathering my bearings.

"Living out east has made you soft," my father's voice scoffs. I sigh and look up.

"You'd prefer me to stay seated at my desk and die like a man?" I drawl with a crooked eyebrow.

My father harrumphs and smooths his tie down and approaches my office along the corridor. "Just no need to make a fuss, is there?" my father grumbles, his white mustache twitching like a disgruntled mouse on his lip. "Buck up and stop being a sissy about it."

I grit my teeth, knowing there isn't going to be any winning this disagreement. He has very set ideas about how men and women should behave so they maintain their dignity. I guess showing relief that the roof didn't collapse makes me a pussy in his eyes.

How tedious.

"I'm almost done with that affidavit," I tell him to change the subject.

I'm lying. I've barely started it. But I know it won't take long once I finally corral my brain into focusing.

"Good, good," he says absently as he continues to walk down the hall of his practice, nodding at his employees as he wanders past. Like earthquakes are nothing out of the ordinary.

Well, this is California. I'd forgotten that they aren't.

"Welcome home," I mutter to myself with a chuckle.

If there was a metaphor for how I'm feeling right now, the world falling down around me is damned on point. I look up to the ceiling as I sit back down again.

"Yeah, yeah, I get it," I grumble to the universe. "You don't need to hit me over the head with it like a hammer."

I fucked up. I knew it then and I definitely know it now. Zahir deserved a million percent better from me and I let him down. But the universe can send all the tremors it wants. I can't change the past and I don't really see what I can do about it in the present, either.

I'm not sure how I'll manage it in a town this small. But I have to at least try and stay away from the man I once loved —the man I never stopped loving, truth be told. I failed him fifteen years ago, but I can do right by him now and put my own selfish need to be forgiven aside.

He's never going to forgive me, anyway. So I should probably just dive into this document and lose myself in work like I always do.

Well, maybe just five more minutes on Instagram.

CHAPTER 4

Zahir

"YOU ARE SUCH A TRAITOR, PROBIE," LILI SAYS WITH A SNORT.

It's eight in the morning and the end of our twenty-four-hour shift. Most of us are about ready to head out. But our probationary firefighter, Teddy, is dawdling as he takes an age styling his blond hair in the mirror hanging from his locker door. So it's kind of fair game that the other guys start laying into him about the poster he's got hanging on the inside.

"What?" Teddy says defensively with a frown. "Cassius Garda is a legend."

Sawyer scoffs in mock outrage. "Who played for the Seahawks for over a decade."

"Yeah, where's your Chargers loyalty?" Lili asks.

Sawyer arches an eyebrow at her. "Uh, I think you mean Rams."

"I think you both mean 49ers," our lieutenant, Lieutenant Flores, chimes in.

Lili and Sawyer look at each other. "Nope," they say in unison. I chuckle as I tie my shoelaces, finding their banter comforting, even if I'm only observing it.

Young Teddy closes his locker door and scowls at them. "Garda still holds the record for the highest completions and had more than four thousand passing yards every season. *And* he's from right here in Redwood Bay!"

Lili softens. "We know, dude. We're just pulling your chain. But did *you* know that our very own Beast played ball with him?"

Teddy's eyes go wide and his head snaps over to where Lochlan is fussing over Rocky, who is clearly eager to get out of the station and go for a long walk. "Really?" Teddy practically squeaks.

Lochlan shoots his best friend Lili a look before nodding at Teddy. "Yeah, I did. How do you not know this already? I'm sure I've mentioned it before."

Our probie scoffs. "I would definitely remember if you had."

Lochlan chuckles. "Fair point. Well, we were in different grades, but yeah, we were on the high school team together. We're not even Facebook friends or anything, so I'm afraid I can't hook you up with an autograph."

Teddy's slightly rounded cheeks flush pink. "No, I'd never...that would be rude...I wouldn't..." He huffs in frustration. "I just think it's a shame he had to retire after that knee injury. But it's cool that a local guy made it big, you know?"

"And your admiration has nothing to do with how smoking hot he is?" Lili says with a grin, slinging her arm around his shoulders as we all start to trail out. The second watch are already out on a call, so the house feels echoey as we walk out onto the empty floor.

"Oh, screw you," Teddy grumbles, but he still lets Lili hug him and kiss his cheek.

Warmth ebbs through me. I always feel better after time with my work family. They're a handful and slightly crazy at times, but there's also an abundance of love between us all. It's hard not to take comfort from them, even when they're teasing.

The last few days have been rough on my mental health. I've tried not to let Colt's reappearance rattle me so much, but I'm only human. There have been times where I've swung from feeling angry to sad to almost hysterical about it all. The uncertainty of whether or not Colt is just visiting or is back for good has left me on uneven footing. I always assumed he went off to get his law degree as his family has a practice on the outskirts of town, catering to the more upscale clientele in San Clemente. It wouldn't be too much of a leap to think he was back to work there now.

When he was firmly in my past, I was able to push my memories of him to the peripheral of my mind. But the prospect of accidentally running into him has my nerves on edge. It's like I'm anticipating getting rejected all over again.

After a day and night with the One-Thirteen, though, I'm feeling secure in myself once more. Despite the minor quake yesterday afternoon, our shift was a relatively calm one. Even the tremors only caused some minimal structural damage around town and a few fender benders, so it gave me plenty of time to reflect on the situation.

Redwood Bay is my home. It's Colt who left. I've got nothing to be ashamed of. If he's got any sense of self awareness, I'd hope he's the one feeling anxious about coming back around.

Yes, some good company has reminded me of what really matters and where I stand. It makes me reluctant to go home to my empty apartment, but my grandma's door is always open. In fact, she likes to complain that I don't visit her enough, despite the fact that I'm there at least two to three times a week. The idea of surprising her for breakfast sounds like an appealing plan right now, and I smile to myself.

As the crew bustles toward the open front of the house, I cast my gaze across the concourse for Yara. She's in the kitchen, boxing up the cookies she made early this morning for the current shift. I adore that she often does things like this. She's a staunch believer that random acts of kindness are what make the world go round.

I wave the other guys off, then slow down and wait for her so we can walk out together. I also know that she'll have a box of cookies to bring home that I can sneak a couple out of, but I mostly wait to have another few minutes of her company.

Mostly.

"Smells good," I comment as she skips over to join me.

"White chocolate and raspberry," she declares proudly. "Want one?"

"Oh, if you insist," I say with a wink. It's still warm when I bite into it, and I moan slightly.

"No sex noises this early in the day," Yara tells me primly, and I just laugh.

"Trust me, if I were making sex noises, you'd know it, young lady."

She giggles and wrinkles her nose. "Ew, Del. No thank you."

"You started it."

"And now I'm finishing it," she says in her best, most smug mom voice.

I chuckle and shake my head. "Can I have another cookie?"

"You're so predictable," Yara says, but she's already holding the box over to me.

"Hello?"

We both stop, me with my hand halfway to my mouth as we look around. We're almost to our cars but the person who spoke is hovering by the wide entrance to the currently pretty empty house. Nancy, our administrator, is manning the fort, along with Smokey the cat. But a sense of duty draws me back to see who's come to visit the station. I can feel Yara following just behind me.

They're silhouetted by the morning sunlight, but I can tell it's an adult and two children. Before I can even clearly see their faces, I have an inkling as to who it could be.

"Nevaeh?" I say as I approach.

The little girl's face lights up like Christmas and she bursts into motion, throwing herself into my arms and knocking the cookie clean out of my hand.

"Sweetie, be careful!" her mom cries, but I shake my head as I squeeze Nevaeh tight, looking over her shoulder.

"It's quite all right. We have plenty."

"I hoped you'd both be here!" Nevaeh cries. She lets go of me and then launches herself at Yara who's slightly more prepared than I was for a hug and manages to keep a hold of her box of spare cookies.

"You're looking good!" she tells Nevaeh, and she's right. You'd never know that this little thing had almost drowned only four days ago.

"I've been taking care of her," her younger brother, Dashel, announces proudly.

"I bet you have," Yara says sincerely as she and I both stand back up. Mrs. Adams has her own Tupperware box gripped in her hands. She looks a little tearful, but she smiles at us as she holds it out for us.

"The kids baked you cupcakes," she tells us. "To say thank you. I'm not sure there are enough cupcakes in the world to thank you enough for what you did, but still..."

She sniffs and my heart pangs as I take the box with genuine gratitude. "That's very kind of you, but you really didn't have to."

"It was fun!" Dashel cries.

"They're rainbows," Nevaeh adds as if this is very important information. I happen to think she's right.

"Is that true?" I say with raised eyebrows.

She nods. "My best friend Rebecca Quick's daddy works here, and she said that the One-Thirteen would like rainbows better than unicorns or flowers."

"Your best friend is Anton Quick's daughter?" I say in disbelief, glancing at Mrs. Adams as I peel back the box lid. Inside there are cupcakes with various different colored frosting and sprinkles, but each one has a little sugar rainbow decoration as well. My heart melts.

"It seemed like fate that you guys are the one who came to the beach," Mrs. Adams says with a happy shrug.

"I'd say," Yara agrees. "Is that how you knew how to find us here?"

Nevaeh nods, but then she nibbles on her thumbnail. "The cupcakes are for the other nice man, too. But we didn't know how to find him."

I freeze, trying not to let my surprise show on my face. Of course she'd want to thank the person who literally dragged her from the ocean as well.

How would she be expected to know the guy is my ex?

"Oh, I'm sure he knows how grateful you are—" I start to say.

But Yara talks over me.

"Del knows him," she says brightly.

Mrs. Adams blinks and Nevaeh claps her hands in glee. "You do?" she squeals.

My mouth opens and closes but no sound comes out. I look in panic at Yara, but she's still smiling at me like she hasn't just put me in an absolutely terrible position.

"Uhh…" I say. But all three family members are looking so hopefully at me, I can't bring myself to let them down. "We went to school together, yeah."

Nevaeh presses her hands over her heart. "That's the best news ever!" she says with the kind of enthusiasm only eight-year-olds can muster. "Can you tell us where he works so we can visit him as well?"

"I'm afraid we're not allowed to give out that kind of information, sweetie," Yara says apologetically. "But why don't we take your mom's phone number, and then Del can give it to the other nice man for you?"

"Could you really?" Nevaeh asks me. "You can give him some cupcakes as well, but I can bake some for him too if he'd like. I owe him my literal *life*, Mr. Del! I just *have* to tell him thank you!"

I forgot how dramatic eight-year-olds can be, too. It's nothing to how sneaky my partner is, though. She knows there's lingering, unresolved crap between Colt and I, and she thinks I'm never going to get over it unless I confront it.

Or more specifically, him.

Part of me wonders if she's right. But right now, it doesn't seem like I have a choice either way.

"I can try and pass your number along," I promise with a smile that almost reaches my eyes. "And some cupcakes. He might have just been in town for the weekend, but I think I remember where his dad works. I'm sure he'd be very happy to hear from you and to know that you're all better now."

Nevaeh throws her arms around my waist. "Oh thank you, thank you, *thank you!* I'm so glad you were here when we came. It was fate again, bringing us together!"

Fate, yeah. Something like that certainly dropkicked Colton Ross back into my life. I give Yara a steely glare as she offers her cookies to the grateful family, but she just winks at me.

I know if I really didn't want to put myself through this, I could tell her the name of Colt's dad's law firm and she'd go pass the message along, no problem. In fact, if she thought she'd genuinely upset me, I know she'd be mortified. Which suggests it's possible that she's better able to see the bigger picture here.

Perhaps it's time I face my past and close the door on Colt and me for good. If I confront him, maybe I'll get some of those answers I never had when I was a brokenhearted teenager.

So I nod, and she subtly crinkles her nose at me in victory. I reserve the right to still be a little bit mad at her. However, it's hard to hold onto that with Nevaeh and her family's gratitude surrounding us.

It's a good thing I've got a bunch of cupcakes so fill me up, I guess. Because I'm sure not going to my grandma's for breakfast anymore.

I'm going to head over to Ross & Associates and get this unpleasantness over with as soon as possible.

CHAPTER 5

Colt

This office is a lot...chattier...than the firms I worked at back in New York. It's not necessarily a bad thing, but I'm still getting used to the fact that if I find myself in the breakroom, I'm expected to join in with whoever's having a good gossip session.

Most mornings, I either make breakfast at home or grab it on the way in. But today the surf was too good, and I stayed longer than I know I should have. I only just made it through the door before nine o'clock. It's not like my father is monitoring me, per se. But I'd feel shitty if I started letting my standards slip only a few weeks into the job.

So that's how I find myself waiting politely in the kitchenette for the coffee maker to produce another pot while I toast a bagel. A couple of the other senior attorneys are shooting shit, apparently either unaware that I'm waiting or not really caring.

I can't say there's been a tremendous amount of socializing since I joined the team. Judging by the way some of these people look at me, they must think I'm just going to waltz in here and step in as managing partner the second my father clicks his fingers, and no doubt some of them resent that. I'm not sure how to casually bring up over the water cooler that none of this was my idea and I don't even know if I want to be running the place.

It's certainly not something easily segued into from the discussion my colleagues are currently having about their kids and school.

"Timothy keeps whining that he wants to drop advanced chemistry and pick French back up instead," Lynda is saying scornfully. "Who speaks French, anyway?"

"At least Spanish would be useful around here," Winston agrees with a laugh.

Lynda snorts. "Well, yes, if you need to tell your house-keeper she missed a spot."

Winston gasps in mock outrage and playfully slaps her arm. "Stop, you're so bad. At least learning another language might help with trade negotiations or understanding foreign markets. Dillon is still insisting he wants to 'make movies,' whatever that means. I'm seriously tempted to delete his TikTok account. Maybe that'll get his head out of the clouds."

It's probably because I've been thinking about Zahir so much lately. But hearing their discussion only makes me think of my own parents, sneering about how subjects like art were a waste of time, knowing full well that my best friend's passion was painting. Not to mention the casual racism. I'm so disgusted at my colleague's attitudes and consumed by thinking how they're probably crushing their own children's dreams, I don't realize I make a tsking noise out loud.

I certainly realize when they both turn to face me, eyebrows raised.

"You don't have kids yet, do you, Colton?" Lynda asks in a tone clearly meant to convey to me just how much of a moral and social failing that is.

I clear my throat. "Oh, um, no. I didn't mean to—"

"But you're married, aren't you?" Winston interrupts. He's smiling. However, I can tell by the way it doesn't reach his eyes that it's intended as a dig.

And I hate it. I hate the shame that rises inside me for failing to meet my parents' expectations by my early thirties as I shake my head and laugh nervously. "Uh, no," I say, wishing I'd gotten out of the water even five minutes earlier so I could have skipped this excruciating interaction.

Why do I care so much that they're judging me right now? So what if my life is on a different timetable or trajectory to theirs? I know it's because that's what my folks want for me, and I hate disappointing them so much. Whenever I do, I can feel their love slipping a little further away from me each time.

But there's no doubt in my mind that if I'd given in and married a woman and she'd popped out a kid or two by now, we'd all be living a miserable lie.

I don't think these guys' offspring are doing much better, if I'm being honest. Perhaps it wasn't Zahir I was thinking about when they were discussing sabotaging and manipulating their kids' education and futures.

Man, it's like since that incident on the beach I've been all over the place. It wasn't just Zahir I came face-to-face with, but every life decision I've made since we parted ways. As I stand in the admittedly very nice break room of the very successful business my father and grandfather dedicated their lives to, I wonder who the hell I even am or what the hell I'm even doing.

Winston hums and Lynda chuckles like she's embarrassed for me. "Oh, you'll understand when you're in our shoes," Lynda says cheerfully, *finally* pouring some damn coffee and moving out of the way. "You're only, what, twenty-five, right?"

"Yeah, basically," I mutter, purposefully moving in front of the coffeemaker, which encourages them to shift over. I'm hoping the subtle hint will get them to forget about me again so they either leave or at least continue their inane conversation without me.

They do give me space to get my caffeine. But then my bagel pops from the toaster, black and crispy around the edges where I neglected to keep an eye on it. I sigh, wondering if I'm just not destined to have breakfast this morning.

Before anything else can happen, one of the only people I've actually formed a connection with in this place sticks his head around the door and looks directly at me.

"Colt," Preston Windward says, flashing me a perfect smile.

He's the kind of all-American guy my parents definitely wish I was. But rather than being an asshole, he's pretty much the only person who's treated me with respect since I arrived. He even went to far as to defend me when a frequent flier got uppity as we were informing him about the upcoming change in his representation due to my father's health issues.

"There's someone here to see you," he says, glancing at Lynda and Winston, like he knows he's saving me from the horrendous exchange we were just having.

I blanche as I realize what he's saying to me. I didn't think I had any appointments until noon. "A client?"

He shakes her head. "He said he was a paramedic following up on an incident you assisted with at the weekend?"

I can hear the curiosity in Preston's voice as well as feel the stares from our other colleagues. I haven't mentioned what happened at the beach to anyone. It seemed too personal to bring up in idle chatter, both with regards to mine and Zahir's history, as well as on behalf of the little girl who almost drowned.

Not that many people are including me in idle chatter, as Lynda and Winston have just illustrated.

It is intriguing gossip, and I can't blame them for wanting to know more. But right now, all I can do is hyper focus on the fact that a *paramedic* is here at my work. Zahir's partner was a woman, so it can't be her. I try and convince myself that Zahir might have a boss that needs to get a witness statement from me or something. Is that something fire stations do? Or just police officers?

Oh…god. What if it's not a statement he needs? What if it's taken this long because…what if there were complications for the girl after all and…and those *complications* have only just happened?

No, no, no! She was okay! She woke up! If she's taken a turn for the worst…

Ignoring everyone else, I dash out of the office into the main reception area of our small practice. I'm too panicked to even appreciate that it is indeed Zahir who's standing there.

"Is she okay?" I blurt out without so much as a hello.

Zahir blinks at me. "Oh! Nevaeh? Yes, she's absolutely fine. That's why I'm here." He sheepishly holds up a Ziploc bag with a couple of slightly squashed but very colorful cupcakes inside. "I'm sorry to disturb you at work. I was actually expecting to talk to your dad, but when I mentioned it was about you, they said you were in the building."

Even though he doesn't ask directly, I can here the question in his tone. "Uh, yeah," I explain. "I moved back a few weeks ago."

There's an uncomfortable pause, then he holds up the clear baggie again. "Well, I promised to pass on her mother's number. And these if possible. They want to thank you."

I pull absently at my tie as my heart rate slows. She—Nevaeh—is okay.

That means I now have to deal with the reality of Zahir being here. At my work. He knows where I work.

At my *family's* law firm.

Suddenly, both the fear of what my father might do and the need to protect Zahir from him come back as strong as when I was a teenager. I immediately move closer and place my hand on the small of his back without thinking of what that might mean or how it might look.

"Let's talk somewhere a little more private," I say, steering him into an empty conference room. It's one of the smaller ones where we usually hold our preliminary meetings with clients when we're deciding if we're the right fit for each other, so it's not too big and awkward.

I mean, it's still plenty awkward. But at least it doesn't feel echoey.

"So she's okay?" I repeat.

"Yeah," Zahir says, looking at me like he's surprised that was my first and main concern.

I can't say I blame him. He doesn't know me anymore. He probably wonders if he ever knew me back then. The image of a cutthroat lawyer isn't improbable. Therefore, I don't have any right to be offended that he potentially thinks so little of me as I've given him every reason to. It still stings. But all that really matters is that Nevaeh is all right.

I'd forgotten her name, but I did hear it at the time. I'm glad I can stop thinking of her as 'the girl,' not to mention cease fretting about what happened to her after she left the beach. Apparently, she's making colorful, squashed cupcakes. That's a good sign, right?

"Thank goodness," I say as I move around the room, gripping the back of a chair and avoiding eye contact with him. "I tried calling the hospital, but they wouldn't tell me anything, which makes sense, but I was worried. So...thank you, I guess." I finally look up at him. "For putting my mind at ease."

Carefully, he places the plastic bag down on the table, the cupcakes sagging a little and the frosting smooshing against the transparent side. "You're welcome," he says softly, meeting my gaze.

For a moment, we just stare at each other.

He was always slimmer than me with slightly narrower shoulders and hips. But in the years we've been apart, he's clearly bulked up. I noticed it somewhat at the beach, but he was wearing his uniform, and I was buzzing with the rush of having just pulled Nevaeh from the water. Now, though, he's wearing black jeans and a white V-neck tee that are both clinging to his muscular form like a prayer. He used to wear his dark, curly hair down to his shoulders, but now he has a fade around the back and side with a thick mop at the top that I desperately want to run my fingers through and—

Nope. Stop that right the fuck now.

I clear my throat and look away. "So, uhh..."

"Yes, right." Zahir pulls a scrap of paper from the pocket that's hugging his pert ass. I manage to keep my expression neutral, but apparently my mind is determined to live in the gutter. "This is Mrs. Adams' number—Nevaeh's mom. They really want to thank you for what you did. How you helped." He points at the food bag. "Probably make you some fresh, less mangled cakes."

I laugh at his sweet little joke, probably louder than is appropriate, but I don't care. Just hearing him talk to me again is a relief I didn't know I was waiting on all these years. But the apprehension has always been there, gnawing away, that the memory of this person who once meant the world to me was going to fade completely into oblivion.

"Thank you," I say, taking the piece of paper from him.

Our fingertips brush. Electricity jolts through my heart,

but unsurprisingly, he snatches his hand away then grimaces, no doubt wanting to ignore the moment ever happened.

The shiver down my spine tells me it did. So does my racing pulse and throbbing cock. Christ, it's like I can *taste* him. As if chasing that taste, I lick my lips before taking a breath and trying to make my mouth utter coherent words. It's difficult with my hands and knees trembling with adrenaline. It's a different kind to what I experienced on the beach, but no less overwhelming.

"Zahir," I say, my voice full of reverence for simply being allowed to say his name again. To see him. To be so close if I just reached out, I could…

The conference room door bursts open and my father blusters in. For a man supposed to be taking it easy after major surgery, he certainly does seem to enjoy stomping around the place still.

"Colton, there you are. I need you to—" At the sight of Zahir, the words die in his mouth but not for long. "Oh, my apologies. I didn't realize you had a meeting. I did check your calendar."

Of course he did. The implication that I forgot to enter an appointment is clear. Because in his mind, I'm still a child that he has to run around after to make sure I'm not embarrassing myself or the family name. If this actually *was* a client that he'd undermined me in front of, I'd be mortified. As it is, irritation that's been brewing for a very long time bubbles up in me.

"I don't have a meeting, Dad," I say coolly. His eyes widen at my informality. He made it clear that when I'm in this building, he's not my father, but my boss. However, I get a thrill from my micro triumph, and plow forward before he can interrupt me. "This is my friend, Zahir Delacroix. You remember? From San Clemente Academy?"

His expression smooths out. "I see," he replies, matching my cool tone.

He either has no earthly idea who I'm talking about…or he remember *exactly* how much he hated the two of us running around together all the time. He and Mom never said it out loud, but I was always acutely aware that they saw Zahir as brown, poor and Muslim before anything else. They weren't even aware he was gay, but I know that wouldn't have helped the situation in their eyes one bit.

"Your son saved my patient's life this weekend, Mr. Ross," Zahir says with genuine respect despite the fact that my father never earned it from him. "I was passing on the girl's appreciation."

"A girl, hey?" my father cries, his eyes lighting up. I can tell the inappropriateness that's going to spill from his mouth before it happens, but I can't do anything to stop it. "If she's that grateful, maybe she'll give you her number for a date, hmm?" He winks and chuckles at his own gross humor.

"Yeah, she's eight, Dad," I drawl, dropping all pretense of respect in that moment. I love my parents, I do. But their obsession with me meeting a 'nice girl and settling down' is getting obnoxious. Even if Nevaeh was my age and not a child, why does he think it's okay to crack jokes about a hypothetical woman *owing me a date* because I helped her?

I can tell I've embarrassed him by the way he harrumphs and wrings his hands, puffing out his chest. I'll pay for that later, no doubt. Never mind that he was the one out of line. All he'll see is that I was disrespectful.

"Well, how was I supposed to know?" he grumbles.

"I should go," Zahir says, and suddenly I don't give a shit about my father and his nonsense. I can't let Zahir slip away yet again.

"I'll walk you out," I say, nipping around the table to open the door as Zahir approaches. He slows his walk and narrows his eyes like he wants to tell me where to shove it. But he simply nods and exits the room.

Not wanting my father to undermine me any further, I nod cheerfully at him before following Zahir across the lobby and out into the sunshine. The practice is part of a small but nice parade of stores that is too fancy to call a strip mall. In between the two rows that host an independent coffee shop, a fashion boutique, a hair and beauty salon, and a florist is a burbling fountain and well-maintained shrubbery. I pause to speak, grateful that he does as well.

"Sorry about that," I say with a rueful chuckle. "You probably remember what he's like."

"Yes," Zahir says, his voice flat.

The hope and excitement that was tentatively rumbling in my belly fades away, leaving me disappointed. But really, what did I expect? For us to laugh and joke like the good old days?

That was a lifetime ago.

"So you're back for good, then?" He juts his chin toward the office. "I Googled your dad's company and came here to see if they had a way to get in touch with you for Nevaeh's sake. But then I was told you started working for the practice a few weeks ago."

"Uh, yeah," I say guiltily.

He had to search online because we certainly never came here when we were teenagers. Hell—I remember telling him I would set foot in this place as an employee over my dead body.

Turns out that my dad's *almost* dead body was all it took.

I sigh apologetically. "I would have let you know I was back, but…I wasn't sure if you still lived here."

Sure, that's it, buddy. Not that you were terrified of seeing him and facing the consequences of your actions.

"Still here," he says in that same firm, hollow voice.

"Never left. This is my home. And now I have fulfilled my obligation to my patient, I don't see any reason why we should cross paths again. I hope you'll be very happy in Redwood Bay once more. Although I imagine you'll be spending more of your time in San Clemente."

The implication that's because it's fancier lingers in the air. Because he thinks he was never good enough for me or my family. My grandfather set up business here because it's all he could afford at the time, and we've stayed here for nostalgic purposes. But my parents moved us to San Clemente as soon as they could and absolutely look down on anything else in Redwood Bay, including the people.

So, yeah. I'm sure they still believe that someone like Zahir isn't good enough for me. However, that couldn't be further from the truth, at least as far as I'm concerned.

He turns to leave and my heart somersaults in my chest. "Wait!" I cry.

He pauses, looking at me expectantly.

If I knew what I wanted to say, that would really help. There are probably a thousand—a million things—I should tell him. But instead, I feel my resolve crumble. The disdain in his eyes is clear. I have no right to ask anything of him.

It doesn't mean I can't try, though. I didn't become a brilliant attorney by shying away when the shit hit the fan.

"I am living in Redwood Bay," I say simply. "My dad had a heart attack and surgery. So I moved back to a place close to the office. I'm not going anywhere soon. And I...I'm sorry. For everything."

I wish I could say that I came back for him, but we both know that's not true.

This time, though, I can see myself *staying* for him. Even if just for a little while.

For a second, the words simply hang in the air as we stare at each other. Then he huffs out a sad laugh, shakes his head, and turns to walk away, really doing it this time. I watch him until he vanishes out of sight.

Dizziness washes over me, but I take a breath and rub my chest, letting it pass.

No, that didn't go well. But I have more information than before, and so does he, actually. We both know that the other is living in town, and I can make an educated guess that means he's at the Redwood Bay firehouse, so we both now know where the other works as well. Sure, he basically said he never wants to see me again, but me being the sonovabitch I am, I cling to the hope that we could still *accidentally* run into each other.

I glance at the paper I've got crumpled between my fingers, then smooth it out. We're linked now by this event, this girl. Saving Nevaeh's life together creates a bond, no matter how unwelcome it might be. Perhaps there's still a chance for me to find my way to back to Zahir.

It doesn't matter how long it takes. I'm going to make him see how truly sorry I am. It's not just a word I've thrown at him. I mean it with every breath I take. And he doesn't have to forgive me. I understand how much that would be asking of him. I just need him to believe me.

With my new mission clear in my mind, I spin around and head back inside the office, prepared to face my father. I'll take his ire. Just speaking to Zahir again after all this time makes me feel like I've got a suit of armor on, which is probably ridiculous considering how much he obviously hates me.

Everybody hates me. I'm a lawyer. But I'm not going to rest until Zahir understands that the boy I was before loved him and never should have left him the way I did. After that, I'll let the chips fall where they may.

But I'm not giving up on Zahir Delacroix. Not this time.

CHAPTER 6

Zahir

I FIGURED THAT GOING HOME ALONE TO STEW ON MY interaction with Colt would be a bad idea. That's how I find myself driving the familiar route to my teta's home like I'd originally planned when I'd gotten off work a couple of hours ago. I might be too late for breakfast, but like most grandmothers, I'm sure she'll be delighted to feed me no matter the time of day.

Sure enough, she opens the door of her modest home and her face splits into a dazzling smile. "Habibi!" she cries, throwing her arms around me like she didn't just see me a couple of days ago. "As-salamu alaykum. You should have told me you were coming."

"Wa-'alaykumu salam. If I'd texted, Teta, would you have seen it? Is your phone even on?"

She scoffs and ushers me inside so I don't let all the cool air out. "Why would I turn it on unless I need it?" she says.

Silently, I shake my head and smile. We've had this argument more times than I could ever hope to count, yet she never seems to grasp the concept that someone might need *her*.

Actually, I think she pretends not to understand to preserve her peace and quiet. Just the fact that she lives by herself and not with my parents is a little outrageous, but she's always been madly independent. Her husband—my grandpa—died so young that she had no choice to be anything else, really. My dad worries about her a lot, especially since he and my mom moved farther upstate. I tell him she's fine, but I think she takes a certain amount of glee in stressing the rest of the family out.

I'm her favorite because I'm not so easily rattled. She enjoys a challenge.

"Have you eaten? I'll make tea. Will you stay for lunch?"

"I haven't eaten," I lie, because the cookies and cupcakes seem like they happened hours ago, and I would never miss out on a chance of being fed by Farah Delacroix. "Tea and lunch would be wonderful."

She snorts and wanders back into the kitchen, waving me in the direction of the back yard. "Like I was going to let you leave with an empty stomach."

Her patio is covered by an awning, so even though I'm back outside in the heat, at least it's shady as I sit at the table, looking at the pompoms of deergrass dancing in the warm breeze. The flowers that line her winding flagstone path are all vivid pink, yellow and orange, just like the throw pillows on the sofa I'm resting on. Teta has always despised anything demure or subtle, claiming that life is for living and no one should be ashamed to take up space or mark their presence as they move through this world.

I've always thought it was her who I got my artistic inclinations from, even though she's never shown much interest in painting anything other than the walls of her home. But she's always been my biggest fan, relentlessly encouraging me when I thought I was no good.

How long has it been since I picked up a brush? Too long.

I don't have the time, money, or space to indulge in my passion like I used to. Although Yara and Lili from work took me to a paint and sip class last year where we captured a rather beautiful naked man on paper for a couple of hours.

That was damn good fun, but it's not how I used to express myself back in the day. My thoughts drift to the art studio at San Clemente Academy and how I'd lose myself in there for hours whenever possible. Still life wasn't really my thing. I preferred a slightly surrealist, abstract style if I was working on scenery. But my favorite was when I'd try and express my feelings on the biggest canvases I could find with bold colors and swirling forms. It had all been very cathartic for a teenage boy who felt like he never belonged anywhere.

Expect with Colt.

I cringe to think how the artwork he inspired would look now. Both when I thought we were in love and after he left and broke my heart. There were a lot of paintings during that time, too many to try and recall what even one looked like now. But I have no doubt they were…intense. It's probably best if they have been lost to time.

My grandma kept every single one of my projects when she had the bigger house. I assume she put them in the trash when she moved here like I was always begging her to. She shouldn't be cluttering up her life with my old junk out of a sense of obligation or sentimentality.

But in moments like this, when my mind is in turmoil, my fingers itch to hold a brush so I can pour everything from my heart out onto a canvas. If I were able to grant myself a wish like a djinn, I'd snap my fingers right now and conjure up an enormous white space where I could sweep thick colors as high and as far as my arms could reach.

For some reason, I'm yearning to paint the beach. I try not to think about why that's pretty obvious.

Luckily, my teta interrupts my musings by arriving with a

tea tray. The glasses were a housewarming present from my cousin a couple of years ago, but the silver pot was her mother's, brought all the way from Morocco when my grandma emigrated when she was still a child. I've always loved it as a symbol of our family's strength and endurance.

Also, it has four little legs that when I was a young boy I was convinced would come to life at any moment and the pot would simply wander off.

"What's on your mind, habibi?" my grandma says with a frown as she pours me a glass of the hot, sweet, minty tea. The station has a decent coffee maker. It's one of the things Captain Valentine refuses to be stingy about. But no one makes tea like Teta.

I shrug and reach for a cookie to let my drink cool for a moment. My grandma always cleans out the Girl Scouts every year, and I'm delighted to see she's cracked open the Caramel deLites, finally. Like I said, Yara's cookies and Nevaeh's cupcakes seem like days ago now, so what's one more before lunch?

Or two.

"I just got off shift, that's all," I say with a smile, not wanting to worry or bother her.

But she narrows her eyes at me as she picks up her own tea, as usual not concerned by how hot it must be under her fingers or on her tongue.

"You only just got off now?" she says, checking her watch and grimacing in sympathy. "Was it a tough night? I'm so sorry."

I sigh because I already know I can't lie to her. It's a miracle I've been able to keep recent events to myself for this long. Besides…as far as I know, she's literally the only other person on the planet who knows the truth of what really happened back in high school.

"No, it was an easy shift, actually. Even the earthquake didn't give us much trouble."

She tsks. "That wasn't a quake. That was a baby little tremble."

I laugh, agreeing with her, but still proud that things like that don't faze her. Women of her generation were so often taught they were helpless, especially immigrants with her skin color. Teta knows when to be scared of something really dangerous, and a meager 4.2 on the Richter scale isn't one of those times.

"So, what's got you so sad, hmm?" Of course she's not going to let it go. I pick up another cookie and twirl it between my fingers.

"I had to run an errand after work," I say, which is true. She just sips her tea in silence, though, piercing me with her gaze like I'm under a microscope. I sigh again, already knowing I'm not going to wriggle out of this. "Colton Ross is back in town."

Teta gasps and fires off a series of curses in Arabic and a few in French as well for good measure. "That bad boy!" she finishes off with a scowl. "What's he doing back here? I hope he's *ashamed* of himself."

It's been nice to have Yara defending me, but she met Colt for all of three minutes during our call. Teta had my best friend over for dinner and sleepovers countless times when we were kids. She knew how 'special' he was to me and was there for me when my whole world fell apart. Her outrage warms me and reminds me that I'm justified in having all these complex emotions.

"Well, he's a man now, not a boy," I inform her gently. "And he seems to have moved back here for the time being after his dad had a heart attack."

Teta clutches her chest, but I shake my hands at her,

sending cookie crumbs scattering over the table. I put the thing down on my plate and brush my fingers clean.

"Mr. Ross is okay. I saw him today, in fact."

"Alhamdulillah," she says in relief.

I know she won't let me get away with not telling her the whole story, though, so I carry on. "It appears that Colt has come back to work for his dad or take over the family practice when Mr. Ross retires. So...I guess he's going to be staying for good."

"Why would you go see him?" Teta wails, fidgeting anxiously with her loose-fitting hijab. "After all he put you through! The way he broke your heart into a million pieces."

As simply as I can, I explain what happened on the beach and then Nevaeh's visit to the station this morning. "It was my duty to pass on the information."

She tuts before stuffing a whole Caramel deLite into her mouth. "You're too good for him," she mumbles around the cookie.

"I know," I say heavily. "He did say sorry, though."

I'm still not sure how I feel about that. Nor the way his face lit up when I spoke with him. Nor his blatant concern for Nevaeh's wellbeing.

For years, I've had this image of him in my mind as a callous playboy. The guy who used me to experiment and lose his virginity with before running off to college to be the good little lawyer his daddy always wanted him to be. The phase of his bisexuality he could keep hidden in the closet so whatever unsuspecting woman he eventually married wouldn't be frightened off.

The man I saw on the beach and again at Ross & Associates doesn't exactly match up with the picture I've been painting all these years. Usually, I have no trouble bringing the images in my head to life on canvas, but this is the other way around. It's real life that doesn't align with my imagination.

He's a lawyer, though. A successful one, by the looks of it. Despite my shredded heart, I never caved into the temptation to search for him online and see where he ended up. Wherever it was, it wasn't with me, so why should I care? But it's easy to see that he's flourished in his profession, and I don't really see how you can be a competent corporate lawyer if you don't excel at bending the truth or outright lying.

Which is an elaborate way of convincing myself that the charming man I've seen on these two occasions is an act.

Except…he didn't know I was going to be there either time. He certainly had no clue I'd become a paramedic in town when he risked his own wellbeing to save a stranger's life. That selflessness isn't just at odds with the Colton Ross that's been living rent-free in my brain for the better part of fifteen years. It's…admirable.

Attractive.

I hate that his smile still makes my heart skip a beat. I hate how he's grown from a gorgeous teen into a striking, handsome man. But I hate the most that he really doesn't seem to be the monster I've made him out to be.

Teta is still doing her best on that front, however. I listen with affection as she rants about how he can say he's sorry all he wants, but he still treated me like garbage, and I shouldn't forget that for a moment. She does have a point.

"You're not going to see him again, are you?" she demands, concerned as she slips her hand over mine and grips surprisingly hard for someone of her age.

"I highly doubt it," I assure her.

As I say it, though, my heart pangs in my chest. Logically, I know I never want to run into him again. Today has given me that closure Yara was pushing me toward. Or at least it's given me clarity. I don't know if I can ever truly forget and forgive the way he made me feel worthless by leaving town with little more than a brief, vague note wishing me well before saying goodbye forever. I had childish dreams of *marrying* that man one day.

So, no. I have no intention of going back to his law office or hanging around at the beach. But there is a small, pitiful part of me that looks a lot like my eighteen-year-old self who is mourning Colton Ross all over again. Just knowing he's so physically close but just as far away as ever is kind of cruel.

Nothing has changed, however. His father clearly still regards me with the lowest contempt. After that tasteless joke about getting a girl's phone number, it looks like he's just as determined to see Colt marry a woman as before. That tells me that even if Colt ever came out of the closet as bi, marrying a man is probably never going to be a possibility for him.

Which is fine. I'm not interested. I haven't been for fifteen years. So I'm sure I'll get used to the idea that Colt is around town, and after some time, he'll fade from my mind just like he did before.

I refuse to ever let him have power over me again. That I *can* promise my teta.

CHAPTER 7

Colt

"Mr. Ross! You made it!"

Nevaeh jumps off the climbing frame as I approach the playground, from just high enough that it makes my heart stutter for a second. But she barely stumbles as she hits the woodchip ground and then breaks into a run, throwing her arms around my middle like we're long-lost friends.

"Hey, kiddo," I say patting her shoulder as her mom and brother approach at a more reasonable pace. "You're looking about a million times better than the last time I saw you."

The little girl lets me go and beams up at me, shielding her eyes from the sun. "Thanks to you and Mr. Del. You're my heroes!"

The mention of Zahir makes my heart stutter for a second time in as many minutes, but thankfully the rest of Nevaeh's family reach where we're standing.

"Thank you so much for meeting us here, Mr. Ross," her mom says warmly. "On a Friday afternoon, too. I'm sure you're very busy, but it means the world to Nevaeh."

I shake my head. "Nowhere else I'd rather be," I tell her truthfully. "And please, call me Colt."

"Only if you'll call me Elizabeth," Mrs. Adams says with a chuckle.

"We made you your own rainbow cupcakes, Mr. Ross!" Nevaeh's brother, Dashel, informs me as he tugs on the corner of my open shirt.

"But you already made me some!" I say, over-exaggerating my surprise. These kids are kind of infectious to be around.

Nevaeh wrinkles her nose. "Those got squished. You needed proper ones in a box."

"They insisted," Elizabeth says apologetically, but I shake my head.

"That's so kind of you guys, really."

"Come sit!" Dashel says as Nevaeh drags us to a bench.

"You can sit with my mom here, Mr. Ross," she says seriously. "That way, you'll have the best view of us on the monkey bars."

I laugh as I sit where I'm told. "Yes, that's very important," I tell her with a nod.

Within seconds, I've got a fresh cake in my hand and the children have torn back into the heart of the playground, shrieking in delight as they naturally join in a game with a few other kids around their age.

"You have an amazing family," I tell Elizabeth, feeling glad I texted her earlier in the week and set up this little meeting. Replacing the image of Nevaeh half-drowned on the beach with her gallivanting around the park is doing my soul a lot of good.

Elizabeth sniffs and I glance over, alarmed that she appears to be fighting back tears. "Thank you so much," she whispers, reaching into her purse for a tissue. "They're all I have now. Their daddy was deployed overseas but...like I said, it's just us now. If I'd lost Nevaeh..."

"Hey, hey, it's okay," I promise her as she takes a second to dab her eyes and blow her nose. "I'm so incredibly sorry for your loss. But Nevaeh's fine. Look at her. She's strong, like her mom."

Elizabeth gives me a watery smile before taking a deep breath and regaining some of her composure. "Thank you. We lost my husband a couple of years ago. The pain has eased some. But seeing my baby girl unconscious like that has brought a lot of it back to the surface. I think it has for the kids in a way, too. They might not necessarily understand it, but I think that's why Nevaeh has been so fixated on thanking you and Mr. Delacroix. Our little family has been through so much and, well, not to trauma dump on you, but I think having a male role model has been good for them, even if it's just for a hot minute." She huffs out a little laugh. "She calls you her guardian angel."

Considering how much I've railed against the idea of having kids of my own, her words warm something inside of me.

"Honestly, I'm honored," I tell her with a grin. "I'm not sure I'm much of a role model for anyone. But if baking some sparkly cupcakes gives her a sense of normalcy, I'm happy to eat them."

I illustrate this by peeling back the cupcake casing to take a bite. I like that I can enjoy the small sugar rainbow on top without worrying if anyone's going to think anything of it. Which is ridiculous. Kids should be able to enjoy rainbows whether they are about Pride or just something fun. So should adults. But I've been carrying this shame and fear around with me for a couple of decades and apparently it's not so easy to just shake it off.

Logically, I know only a douchebag would concern himself about being seen with anything that could be misconstrued as 'girly' or 'gay.' But my father's words ring in my ears as clearly as ever. As a corperate lawyer, I have to maintain a tough guy image.

As a human being who is secretly very fucking gay, I'm going to enjoy every single one of these damn cakes.

"Okay," I say as I lick frosting off my lips. "Somehow not being flattened does make this taste better."

We both laugh and watch the kids for a few moments. After a while, Elizabeth speaks again.

"You saved a life, Mr. Ross," she says softly. "My husband would say that makes you a good role model if he were here. Don't downplay that. There are plenty of people who wouldn't have been paying enough attention to see my little girl going under. And others who would have turned away, letting someone else take care of the situation. Because of you, she's still here. She can grow up and be anything she wants. She has options."

I glance at her, the urge to insist that I'm not good. I'm a selfish coward. But this moment isn't about me and my past sins. It's about celebrating Nevaeh Adams and what is hopefully going to be a long life ahead of her.

I hold up my now empty and folded wrapper. "Well, if she wants to grow up and be a chef, I'd say she's off to a good start."

That breaks the somber mood between us as we laugh again. I watch Elizabeth beam with pride as she watches her daughter hold her son's hand, helping him balance at the bottom of a climbing wall.

"So Mr. Delacroix was able to pass some squashed ones on to you?" Elizabeth asks, then rolls her eyes. "Of course he did. Otherwise, how would you have gotten my number and been able to text me?"

"Ah, it's cool," I assure her. "You've got a lot on your mind. I forget what day of the week it is half the time. Today's Thursday, right?"

She laughs loudly, then immediately covers her mouth, like she's not used to making that much noise these days. But she's still grinning when she lowers her hand, which makes me glad.

"Mr. Delacroix said you two went to school together," Elizabeth prompts, selecting a cupcake for herself from the box. "Or rather his partner did. But it felt like you hadn't seen each other in a while?" Then she immediately shakes her head. "Sorry, that's probably personal."

I shrug. It is, but she would have no way to know just how personal or complicated our history really is. Besides, I relish the chance to talk about Zahir to someone. It's been killing me bottling everything up.

"No, it's fine," I assure her, debating whether to indulge in a second cake. "We did go to high school together. We used to be really good friends. But I moved away for college, and we lost touch. Nevaeh brought us back together. So in a way, she's *my* guardian angel, too."

Elizabeth blinks and gives me a warm smile. "Well isn't that just wonderful? So you two are hanging out again?"

"Ah, not exactly," I say with a wince.

I should just shut my mouth. This nice lady has been through enough. She doesn't need to hear my problems as well. But she's looking at me expectantly, like she's got all the time in the world for me, and it's as if I can't help myself. I've never let myself talk to anyone about this, and it suddenly feels like if I don't unburden myself, I might just combust.

"It's been so long now, it feels awkward," I say, grossly simplifying the situation. "And it was my fault we stopped talking. I got too wrapped up in my new life. But since I've moved back into town, I'd like it if we could be friends again. I'm just not sure how to extend that olive branch. I'd do anything to make it right again between us, but I hurt him. I'm not sure if he'd want that or I even deserve to be given a second chance."

I didn't really mean to add that last part, and heat creeps

up my neck as I wonder if I've said too much. I meant to make it seem like we were just friends. Maybe best friends but not…not boyfriends. That feels too dangerous to admit out loud.

But Elizabeth is looking animated, and she reaches out to grip my hand with hers. "We could take the pressure off and organize something more casual. Then you could test the waters and see where you stand."

"We?" I repeat in amusement. From the mischievous sparkle in her eyes, I feel like I've gotten myself a co-conspirator.

As if to prove my point, she grins and nods. "The kids and I were planning on going back to the beach soon—maybe tomorrow even. I don't want Nevaeh to become afraid of it. I was thinking of making a picnic, so why don't I reach out and see if both the paramedics wanted to swing by and assure my baby girl that the water isn't anything to be scared of." She quirks an eyebrow. "And if you just happened to be with us, maybe you could talk to your old friend then?"

For a second, I just stare at her, a dopey smile on my face. "You'd really do that for me?" She nods and I shake my head. "Are you sure *you're* not the lawyer? That's pretty cunning."

She shrugs. "If the last couple of years have taught me anything, it's that you never know when life can take an unexpected turn. If you need help reconnecting with your friend, I'd be delighted to help facilitate that. It's important to seize the day in case tomorrow takes the opportunity away from you."

Her words are somber. However, she's still smiling. I take a breath and puff out my cheeks, feeling torn.

Zahir was damned clear he didn't want to see me again. But…it's not a big town. The chances of us running into each other are high. Maybe if Elizabeth and her family are there as well as his colleague, he might not immediately storm off and give me a chance to properly apologize. That's all I want. To tell him once and for all that I know I was an asshole and never should have treated him the way I did.

Elizabeth squeezes my hand. "He's important to you, isn't he? Even if you haven't seen each other in a long time."

"Yeah," I croak out, embarrassed at how my voice catches with emotion.

I don't know what she might infer from that. Thirty-three years in the closet and I'm inches away from coming out to a near stranger. But if Elizabeth guesses anything, she doesn't say so.

"That's settled, then," she says, waving at her kids who are paused at the top of the slide. "I'll find out when he's free, then we'll plan a picnic."

"This is slightly diabolical," I say with a chuckle. "But, sure. Why not?"

"Life's too short for regrets, Colt," she tells me seriously. "That's 'why not.' Now, do either of you have any dietary restrictions I should know about?"

Her no-nonsense mom style is like a much-needed hug. Very different to my own mother. I'm helpless against Elizabeth and her scheming.

So, okay, this is slightly manipulative. But if I just sit on my ass then nothing will get resolved. It's not like I'm going to beg Zahir to forgive me or even see me again.

I would never dream that he'd want to take me back.

I don't deserve that.

But this guilt is eating away at me now I've seen him again. It was much easier to ignore when he was on the other side of the country. But it's obvious he's still incredibly hurt by what I did. I don't blame him, but I can't sit back and do nothing either. I have to make it right. That's the part of my job I *do* love. Seeing justice served. I have to do right by Zahir, even if he's reluctant to let me.

So, yeah. Maybe we need one more meeting. It's a free beach and he can turn around and leave the second he sees me if he wants to. I hope he'll stay for a minute, though. Just long enough for me to say my piece. I'll rehearse it this time, like a closing argument in court. I'll be quick and concise, and then…

And then perhaps that really will be it. Perhaps we'll spend the next however many years awkwardly avoiding each other in the grocery store. Perhaps we'll actually never cross paths again. But at least I will have done everything in my power to convince Zahir that none of it was his fault. It was all on me. I didn't present my case properly outside of the office. I just need one more chance to get the words out, and then I'll shut up about it.

I'm like an addict jonesing for a final hit before committing to rehab. If I can see Zahir one last time, then perhaps I can find a way to let him go.

For good.

CHAPTER 8

Zahir

"THIS IS SO NICE!" YARA SAYS HAPPILY AS WE PILE OUT OF HER Barbie-pink Honda Civic. I told her I could probably just walk to the beach like usual, but she argued the whole point of a group excursion was to carpool.

Lili and Teddy exit the back seats, and Lili shields her eyes to look out toward the ocean. "It's windy, but hopefully that means most people will be in the water making the most of the waves rather than on the beach."

"I brought sunscreen," Teddy says earnestly, hefting an impressively big bag onto his shoulder. "And plenty of snacks and water."

Lili snorts. "Thanks, Probie. I brought my bikini, a six-pack, and not much else."

I chuckle as Yara locks up the car and we start our decent to Redwood Bay's namesake beach. I'll admit, it *is* nice to have an excuse to get everyone together and make a day of it. That's probably why Captain Valentine approved the meet-up in the first place, even if he couldn't make it himself.

Usually, it's not encouraged for first responders to socialize with people we've tended to. However, the invitation from the Adamses came via Anton, as his daughter, Rebecca, and Nevaeh are good friends at school. Apparently, Mrs. Adams is keen for Nevaeh not to become afraid of getting back into the water after her ordeal, which I wholeheartedly agree with. She invited Yara and I along for a beach picnic so we can help assure her it's perfectly safe, as well as the rest of Rebecca's family. That then turned into a general invite for the entire One-Thirteen, most of whom jumped at the opportunity.

It's sweet that even though we work together, we spend a lot of our free time in each other's company, too. They really are like a second family to me. But outside of events like birthdays, it's unusual to have such an enthusiastic turnout, especially at such short notice.

For Nevaeh's sake, I'm grateful. What better way to prove to her that she has nothing to worry about when it comes to swimming again? So long as she stays closer to the shore and away from the riptides in the future, of course. I don't doubt she'll have a lifelong respect for the water now, though.

"Hey, guys!"

I turn and pause halfway down the path that leads to the sand, smiling at the now familiar sight of Lochlan and his boyfriend, Dario. They wave as they start to follow us, their two dogs eagerly bounding in front of them to greet us before charging on ahead. Queenie is a stocky, slobbery British bulldog who rocks down each step like a little tank. Whereas Rocky is a gangly Dalmatian pup who careens up and down several times at lighting speed, barely managing to stay upright as he tries his best to take everyone's legs out from under them.

"Oh, be careful!" Dario cries at us with a wince while Lochlan laughs apologetically.

"Sorry," he tells us. "My son still doesn't have any manners, but we're working on it."

"It's fine," I assure them as we all begin our climb down once more. "They're just having fun."

My heart warms seeing Lochlan holding hands with his new boyfriend. He took a slightly scenic route recently into discovering his true sexuality. But now he's found his man, he's never seemed happier. I wish them nothing but the best.

And if I feel a minuscule pang of regret in my chest in that moment, that's nobody's business but mine. I can acknowledge to myself if no one else that this whole Colton Ross incident has been tough. Hearing Yara's commentary on it has been even tougher. She's brought to life a couple of home truths that I've done my best to ignore for years.

Coming face to face with Colt made them almost impossible to hide from any longer.

I've never loved so freely or so fiercely like I did with him. I've tried convincing myself that was mostly down to teenage hormones and the throes of the many firsts we shared together. But after all this time, I think I finally have to admit that a part of me has consciously held back ever since, terrified of getting burned the way I did with him.

There were always good excuses to break up with the guys I dated in my twenties and then the ones I refused to even bother getting close to in my thirties. Or at least, that's what I told myself. But deep down, I knew it was because I didn't trust they weren't lying about how they really felt. Because I believed Colt when he told me I was the most important person in the world to him. I believed him when he said we'd be together forever.

I know we were just kids. But his sudden departure left an indelible mark on my soul, a fissure in my heart that has never fully healed...and it's possible it never will.

This pivotal moment in my life felt like a warning that to be loved was to be vulnerable. He'd been the only one I'd trusted during that time in my life. Everyone else at that school—students, parents, teachers—they all treated me like an outsider for my religion, my class, my skin tone, and even if they didn't consciously know it, my sexuality. Colt was the only person I let see my true self.

And it wasn't good enough for him to come out for or to stick around town or to even keep in touch with.

So, yeah. When I look at Lochlan and Dario as they walk hand in hand, I feel proud for them and wish them nothing but the best for their future ahead. But I also see a glimpse of the kind of life I'm not sure I'll ever allow myself to have.

I can't help but morn that a little.

But today isn't about me. I'm quickly reminded of that as we head to the spot where Anton said they'd settled, and our gaggle is met by the squeals of three excitable children. "They're here! They're here!" Rebecca cries, waving her arms as if she's directing a plane to come in for landing.

"Hi, Becca Bean!" Yara yells back, waving back with just as much enthusiasm.

Rebecca, Nevaeh and Dashel all come running over to us, but the dogs meet them first, barking and jumping around with frantically wagging tails. The mood is jovial as we start laying blankets, erecting beach umbrellas for shade, and cracking open drinks and food. Anton is already set up with his daughter, and he's joined by his best friend—also our colleague—Sawyer Nelson, as well as his ex-wife and her new husband.

Meagan had been engrossed in conversation with Elizabeth, Nevaeh's mom, but she jumps up to hug us all as we set up around her. I adore that she's been Anton's number one fan since he had the courage to come out despite his family's objections. Their divorce was swift and friendly, and Anton was even one of her bridesmen when she got married to Brent recently.

Rebecca's stepdad is eager to help everyone pitch their

beach umbrellas so there's good shade coverage for those that want it. Lili stubbornly spreads her towel on the burning sand and flops down on it in her skimpy bikini like a starfish, informing all of us we can only disturb her if it's time to turn over and cook her back. Yara is already passing around homemade sandwiches. Teddy hands out water while Sawyer hands out beer, and the kids frolic with the dogs at the edge of the surf.

It's a pretty picturesque scene.

"How's Nevaeh feeling?" I ask Elizabeth as I pluck a couple of grapes from a bunch to eat.

She nods and sighs happily. "I think today was exactly what she needed. I've also signed her up to some advanced swimming lessons. But just being here and seeing life going on as usual for all these other people has given her confidence. We had a nice talk with one of the lifeguards not on duty when we arrived as well, but honestly, having all you guys show up has made her feel like a celebrity."

"I think she can be an honorary member of the One-Thirteen now," Sawyer chimes in, raising his bottle in a toast. Several other people join him, and Elizabeth beams with pride.

We're probably there for around half an hour when the parents call the kids back to us for a re-application of sunscreen, much to the little ones' annoyance. I chuckle as they grumble and moan while they get coated in cream, especially Rebecca as she's much lighter than the other two. But the process is interrupted when Nevaeh squeals and starts pointing and jumping up and down.

"Look, Mom! Mr. Colt came too! Just like he said he would!"

Despite the heat of the day, my blood runs cold. I whip my head around and see that, yes, Colton Ross is several feet away from us, apparently ready to join the picnic from the looks of the large cooler and beach blanket in his hands. He's wearing a light-blue, short-sleeved, untucked shirt with the top buttons undone over knee-length khaki shorts. His sandals probably cost over three hundred dollars, and I imagine aren't ever meant to get wet, and his fancy watch catches the afternoon sunlight like it's sending out Morse code.

Everything about his outfit screams that he's too good to hang out with the likes of us. However, he's currently frozen in place like a deer in headlights. His eyes are covered by sunglasses, but he definitely seems to be staring at us all in mild horror. His hesitation throws me.

I glance at Yara, but she looks equally dumbfounded and shakes her head vehemently at me. Okay, so she clearly didn't set me up in anyway. I guess he messaged Elizabeth Adams back after I gave him her number and he's here to be a part of Nevaeh's recovery as well?

Which means I can't chew him out. Because that's a really nice thing to do. But my heart is racing, and I send a silent curse out into the universe. Seriously? It's only been a couple of weeks. Do our paths really have to keep crossing like this?

"Hey!" Elizabeth cries before I can look at anyone else. I feel like everyone must be staring at me, but realistically, nobody should know anything's amiss other than Yara, and even she doesn't know the full picture. My eyes are locked on Colt, so I can't tell. "You made it!" Elizabeth continues as she waves him over. "Come join the party."

It's like Colt unfreezes as he laughs and takes a stilted step forward. "Uh, yeah. It's quite the gathering. I'm not intruding, am I?"

"Not at all," Elizabeth says, getting to her feet and brushing sand off her palms before moving to hug him. Then she keeps an arm around his back as she makes introductions. "Everyone, this is Colton Ross, the hero who pulled Nevaeh from the water when she got into trouble."

"Oh, wow, nice to meet you, man," Anton says sincerely as he shakes Colt's hand. "You're definitely welcome here."

Elizabeth nods. "Colt, this is most of the first watch from the One-Thirteen firehouse, including Nevaeh's best friend and the rest of her family. And of course, you know Zahir."

Now everybody's heads swivel my way. I try and remain cool, but it's difficult not to curl my toes against the sand in discomfort. "Um, yes. Hello again."

"You know Del?" Lili pipes up, clearly curious. I'd pray for them all to stop talking, but I know it's never going to happen with this band of troublemakers.

I see Colt falter for a second, but only because I still apparently know him so well. I'm sure to anyone else, his perfect lawyer façade seems natural. "We went to school together," he says cheerfully.

"Did you also go to school with Lochlan?" Teddy yelps, his eyes going wide. "With Cassius Garda?"

A couple of people laugh, and Lili gives him a playful shove. "Give it a rest, Probie."

"Naw, Del went to the fancy San Clemente Academy," Lochlan says, winking at me. "Us lug nuts went to the regular high school."

"Colton and I lost touch," I say to give some explanation to the inquisitive faces around me. But it's as if my gaze is tethered to Colt's, and all other sights and sounds feel like they're coming from underwater.

Yet again, I'm forced to reconcile the image I've held for so long of this man with the evidence in front of me. He clearly didn't know we were all going to be here and is feeling awkward about the position he's put me in. Which means he cares.

About me.

Or maybe he's just weighing up the danger of me outing him after all these years. I'd never dream of doing such a thing, but it was Colton's obsession with staying in the closet that drove us apart in the first place. I wouldn't be surprised if that was his concern right now regardless of what he knows about my integrity.

"You should sit next to Mr. Del, then, Mr. Colt!" Nevaeh announces, grabbing his hand and tugging him toward me, breaking the spell between us. "If I hadn't seen Becca for years, I know we'd have a *lot* to talk about!"

I look up as he stands before me. I don't want to play pretend around him again. All that time spent ignoring each other in the school corridors seemed worth it back then as I knew that behind closed doors, he was completely and utterly mine. But he never was in the end. The idea of sitting in the middle of most of my friends all afternoon making small talk feels like torture.

Before I can open my mouth to protest, however, Colt hands Yara his heavy-looking cooler of supplies and drops his blanket haphazardly, running his now free hand anxiously through his blond hair.

"There's a lot of Champagne and sparkling grape juice in there," he says to Yara with a grin that I can tell is trying to conceal his nerves. "Please feel free to share it around. Zahir, uh, perhaps you might join me for a quick walk?"

My knee-jerk reaction is to say no. The idea of being alone together—even if it's on a crowded beach—seems dangerous. I don't know if I can trust myself to be sensible when my emotions toward him are careening all over the place.

But if I tell him 'no' without giving a good reason, I'll look like an asshole. Well, I won't just look like one. That's what I'll be. And I have no desire to cause a scene when we're here to provide Nevaeh with new, drama-free memories from the beach. Besides, my friends will never leave it alone if I act like a dick.

So that doesn't leave me with many options.

"Sure," I say with a tight smile and rise to my feet, slipping them back into my flip-flops. "Save me some bubbles," I murmur to Yara. I have a feeling after this conversation, I might need a glass of the good stuff to take the edge off.

Best to get whatever's about to happen over and done with.

CHAPTER 9

Colt

THIS HAD ALL SEEMED LIKE A FUN, SILLY, HARMLESS IDEA UNTIL I arrived on the beach and saw over a dozen people gathered around Zahir, most of whom turned out to be his damn team from the firehouse.

Then I just felt like a manipulative chump who was trying to get away with being an asshole. Again.

I'm so relieved he's agreed to give me some time alone, but as we start walking down the shoreline, I'm lost for what I can say. They don't exactly make Hallmark cards that read 'Sorry I was a total dick to you fifteen years ago,' do they?

"I guess you weren't expecting to see me here," Zahir says eventually, breaking through my jumbled thoughts.

Shaking my head, I decide I'm done with all the bullshit. Well, mostly. He doesn't need to know this whole picnic idea was supposed to be a way for us to have one last chance to connect. That feels so pathetic in this moment.

"No," I reply to him. "I mean, yes, I was expecting…no. I mean…" Huffing, I collect my words into a sensible order. "Elizabeth said she was going to invite a few people to help Nevaeh get reacquainted with the beach. I hoped you'd be one of them. In fact, she strongly hinted you would be. And I was planning on trying to get a moment to talk to you. But then I saw all your friends there, and I felt like such a little bitch playing stupid games…"

I sigh and dwindle to a stop, rubbing my forehead and feeling all the fight blow out of me. He looks so gorgeous in a black tank top and denim shorts, his brown skin glistening in the Californian sunshine. He hasn't got sunglasses on, so I take mine off and squint. It's worth it to feel like there's less of a barrier between us.

He folds his arms across his chest, illustrating yet again how much he's bulked up since we were kids. I just want him to take all those muscles and…

Yeah. Pack that in right now, Ross.

"So, what did you want to talk about?" Zahir prompts.

His tone is patient but he's not exactly opening the door to this conversation with welcoming arms. Which is fair. I have no right to expect anything more from him. I'm lucky he's being civil at all.

Taking a breath, I attempt to steady my nerves. The rehearsed speech dances on the tip on my tongue, but it all seems to fucking fake now.

"I'm sorry," I try as a start.

His expression doesn't change. "You said that last time."

That's fair. I nod. "Because it's true. But last time I didn't say *what* I'm sorry for."

He quirks an eyebrow. "I believe 'everything' was your answer to that."

I roll my eyes and cross my own arms over my chest, mirroring him. "'Everything' isn't wrong. But that's not taking full accountability like I should. I…Zahir. You were the single most important person in the entire world to me. I had to leave, but I didn't want to hurt you. I ducked out like a coward because I was a damn kid, and I thought that would spare us both a terrible and painful goodbye. To absolutely nobody's surprise, that was the worst thing I could have done. I've never forgiven myself and…and I guess I just wanted to make sure you knew that."

He shifts his feet in the blinding sand. "You wanted me to know it was awful? Yeah, Colt. I know that already. I lived it."

My heart aches. However, I grit my teeth for a second before forging ahead. "No. I want to make sure you know that you didn't do a fucking thing wrong. You were perfect. I loved…you were my whole world."

I wince. We never actually said we loved each other out loud. It seemed too big, too heavy, too important to put into words and make official. In fact, I always just assumed he loved me back, but maybe that was wishful thinking. If he did, it's clearly long over now. He seems to be ignoring my slip-up, though, so I plow on.

"It's not an excuse for how I treated you, I know that. But my father had my whole life mapped out in stone. There was no deviating from that path. I considered asking you to move to Massachusetts with me a million times, but you were so happy here with your family and…"

He sighs and shakes his head, looking out over the water. "And your parents wanted you married to a socialite to have two children with and living in a house with a white picket fence before you turned thirty-five."

The truth of his statement hurts. It sounds so pathetic when spoken out loud like that, but the expectations from my parents loomed over me like a monolith back when I was a teenager.

"If it's any consolation, all I got was the law degree," I tell him ruefully. I start walking slowly again in the direction we were going before. "No serious girlfriends or proposals or whatever."

"No kids?" He's trying to keep it light, but I can tell behind the joke he's got a hint of concern.

I scoff. "Yeah, I've left a trail of illegitimate babies along the East Coast with all those women I didn't sleep with."

Even though I'm laughing, he's still frowning at me. "But you have been dating women, right?"

I'm not sure what he's getting at. Does he want to make me squirm and suffer? That's fair but…it's also not really the Zahir I remember.

"Here and there," I say warily. "Enough to keep up appearances. But never seriously. I didn't want to hurt any of those girls. They were all really nice. Funny, smart, ambitious—all wife material in theory. I didn't have the heart to lead them or my parents on, only to disappoint everyone in the end. Although I guess I'll have to let Mom and Dad down eventually. I just…I don't know. I'm a coward who runs away from things for as long as I can, apparently."

If anything, the frown on his face has gotten deeper. "Why would you disappoint them? You've done everything they dreamed for you."

The laugh that escapes my throat is on the verge of hysterical. "The law half of it, yeah. But now after Dad's heart attack they want me to take over the family practice much sooner than anticipated so they're going to be obsessing over the wife and babies half of the legacy relentlessly now and I just don't think I can do it."

We've stopped walking again. "Commit to a marriage?" Zahir asks. His words are so sad, like he's losing something new all over. I'm not sure I understand what's happening.

"Marry a woman," I explain, even though I thought that was pretty obvious. "Live even more of a lie than I have been my whole life. I couldn't deceive anyone to that extreme. It would make a mockery out of her life even more than mine. I'm a lot of things, Del, but I'm not that cruel. I promise."

He blinks, his jaw slack as his chest rises and falls. "But...
you're bisexual?"

For a second, his words simply don't register. Stupidly, I
blurt out a little laugh before I can catch myself. But his
horrified look immediately sobers me up again. My mind
races over all the time we spent together, attempting to work
out why he would think that.

Because that's essentially what I told him, wasn't it? What
my parents drilled into me. I treated it like an inevitability
when I was young because the future seemed so far away,
and Zahir was so very much in the present it felt like it was
too distant to matter. But I always thought I'd feel different
when I 'grew up,' and accepted I needed to fit the shape of the
American dream.

He took that to mean I was bisexual. That's what he's
thought, all these years.

Holy fuck...

Does he think he was just a phase? A dalliance? An experiment to satisfy some kind of bi-curiosity?

How...how can I keep discovering that I hurt him even
more than I possibly imagined?

"Zahir," I say, my voice strangled.

I want to reach out and take his hand so badly, but I force
myself to hold back. It would be selfish. He needs space right
now. As much as I'm desperate to comfort him, I'd also be
comforting myself. After causing this terrible mess, my needs
must stay firmly on the back burner.

"I'm gay as absolute fuck," I continue. "I've never even
properly kissed a woman. It's why I broke up with them all
so quickly or managed better long distance. I've been in the
closet this entire time. You're the only real relationship I've
ever had. *That's* why I'm never going to be able to marry a
woman. I'm not sure I can ever come out, either, without it
destroying my parents. It's not just our family's legacy and

reputation at stake. They've made noises about me going into politics, of thrusting me into the public eye. In their eyes, being gay just doesn't fit with that. But committing to spend my life with a woman truly would be a complete and utter sham."

For several moments, we just stare at each other. I can practically see the cogs whirring in his brain. "I thought you left me for..." he utters.

"I just did as I was told," I tell him. "There's never been anyone else, Zahir. Not in any way that mattered. I..."

Whatever I was going to say, I catch myself before I do. This isn't why I wanted to finally have this conversation. The damage I've done to the love we once shared is beyond repair. I'm not here for forgiveness or to beg for a second chance or even to give Zahir my blessing to move on with his life. I don't have the right to do *any* of that. I simply wanted to set the record straight. Or gay, as it turns out. I've done that now.

Without ceremony, I turn on my heels and begin walking back to the group. I'll give Elizabeth and the kids a hug each, but then I'm leaving without looking back. Zahir Delacroix is still the most important person in the whole world to me, and all I've done is cause him pain again and again and *again*.

"Colt, wait," he calls from behind me.

Shaking my head, I don't pause. "I just needed you to know that you didn't do anything wrong and apologize once more for being the biggest asshole this town has ever seen. I won't bother you anymore, I promise. You won't see me again. It was selfish, but I just had to explain myself. And now I've made it worse. Who knows? Maybe I'll grow a backbone and tell my parents I'm a dirty queer. Apparently, that's acceptable in some parts in this day and age. Perhaps they won't disown me or drop dead of shock."

I'm rambling and I know it. But it's better than turning

around and facing Zahir when I've just turned his world upside down. Did he really think I'd left him without a second thought? That I'd settled down with a girl I met in college? Pretending like he never existed?

Like *we* never existed?

It seems so.

Instead, he's lingered like a ghost in the back of my mind without fail for over fifteen years.

Somehow, this misunderstanding makes my betrayal so much worse.

I want to stop and ask him if *he's* happy. I haven't noticed a wedding ring on his finger, but that doesn't mean he isn't with someone special.

The look on his face just now tells me that's not the case. In my gut, I know that in some way, he clung to the memory of us as well.

It kills me that we can never be together, that I can never make him happy. But I'm not so much of a douchebag that I don't admit that he absolutely deserves to be happy. I want that for him. I want the very best of everything for him.

Even though that can't be anything to do with me.

I arrive back at the group before I know it, already opening my mouth to give my excuses. But before I can make an exit, one of the women who isn't Zahir's partner props herself up on her elbows where she was sunbathing, grinning up at me.

"Speak of the devil, and he shall appear!" she cries with a mischievous grin. "Or...devils, I should say."

Zahir stumbles to a halt beside me. "Huh?" I say dumbly.

"Del," Elizabeth calls out as we step into the shade so we can see everyone clearly. "Your team was just informing me that you're an accomplished surfer, just like Colt."

We glance at each other. For a second, my heart pangs knowing that he's kept up our passion after all this time. It feels like something that will tether us together even when I intend to keep my promise to never see him again.

"Uh, yeah," Zahir says with a hint of confusion. "It's great exercise but also kind of like mediation."

I beam at him. "That's exactly it," I say softly.

A little hand grabs mine, and I look down to see Nevaeh swinging between me and Zahir. "Can you teach *me*, then?" she asks earnestly, practically vibrating with excitement. "Mom's got me extra swimming lessons. But I bet if I could surf, I'd never be afraid of the ocean again!"

"Uhhh." I look back up at Zahir before down at Nevaeh again. "You want one of us to teach you?"

"Why not both?" she squeaks innocently. "That way, you can be friends again, like me and Becca. Oh! Can you teach her, too!"

"And me!" Dashel adds, jumping up and down, making the dogs bark.

The moment stretches out. Zahir appears dumbstruck, so I dig deep and pretend like I'm in court. You can't freeze in court. "Oh, I'd love to, sweetie," I tell Nevaeh. "But I'm not qualified—"

A sandy foot kicks my ankle. I whip my head around to see the bikini-clad firefighter smiling fiercely at me. "You know how they charge a fortune for classes on this beach, Mr. Lawyer Man. Help a single mom out, huh?"

"If I supervise, you don't need special qualifications, right?" Elizabeth chimes in hopefully.

"And Del's literally a paramedic," his chirpy partner adds. "What could go wrong?"

This is my fault. I allowed a nice woman with too much on her plate to convince me that this ruse would be worth it to get the chance to talk with Zahir. But it's all blown up in my face. I've made everything worse, and now—*now*—I can't let a little girl down or embarrass Zahir in front of his colleagues, especially not when it's easy to tell they're also his good friends.

I made this mess. So I'm just going to have to suffer the consequences, no matter how painful they might be for me.

But not for Zahir.

"Sure," I say, plucking my best smile out of my ass and acting like everything's just hunky-dory. "I can teach you to surf, and all my *coolest* tricks, too. But maybe one of the other paramedics can help me—?"

"I'll do it," Zahir blurts out, cutting me off. I turn to look at him and our eyes meet. He nods at me before glancing down at Nevaeh. "Colt and I will train you guys to be the best surfers on the entire beach."

"YAY!" Nevaeh screams. Then she pulls us both in for a hug, so my face is suddenly inches away from Zahir's. "This is going to be SO FUN!" she shrieks.

It's certainly going to be something.

CHAPTER 10

Zahir

"Bye! See you tomorrow!" Yara cries through her open car window. Lili waves back at us as she walks down her garden path toward her house. We already dropped Teddy off after our day at the beach, so now it's just me and her left. Yara raises her window again to keep the cool air in, then pulls away from the curb, heading to my place.

There's a very pregnant pause.

"Are you okay?" she eventually asks, her voice quiet and her eyes firmly on the road.

I sigh, not sure how to answer that. "It's complicated," I tell her.

She hums and focuses on the road for a minute. "He looked as shocked to see you as you were him."

"Kind of," I explain. "He said he was hoping I'd be there so we could talk. It was actually all *you* guys that threw him off. He was worried about what you might think."

"Because he's in the closet?"

I watch the world go by through the window. The sun is setting and the palm trees that line the sidewalks wave merrily in the evening breeze. I would never out anyone no matter how they've treated me. But seeing as Yara's already guessed the situation, it seems pointless to deny it. Especially when I could really do with a sympathetic ear right about now.

"He is still very much in the closet," I agree. "But I don't think that's what he was afraid of. I think he was concerned you guys might work out how much of a dick he was to me when we were kids and think he was trying to manipulate me into something now."

"And was he?" she asks.

I shake my head. "I really don't believe he was. He said he just wanted to apologize properly and take responsibility for everything he did. That genuinely meant a lot to me."

I fall silent then, though. Because as nice as it was for him to take ownership of his past mistakes, somehow learning the full truth has left me even more hollowed out than ever.

How can I have gotten it so wrong? Maybe it was easier to think of what we shared as only a bisexual fling to him. A wild summer to let off steam before going off to college and living the rest of his real life. If that was the case, it made sense to me why I'd be so easy to leave behind and forget about. I convinced myself it hurt less because he hadn't done it to purposefully shatter me.

There's never been anyone else, Zahir.

At least I *tried* dating after he left. But it sounds like his relationships have either been isolated, anonymous hook-ups with men or chaste, only-for show, short-term affairs with women.

"He knows how completely and utterly he broke my heart back then," I murmur, not looking at my partner as I speak. For the first time in my life, I feel like I want to actually defend Colt and his actions, not simply explain them. I've always tried to have empathy for his situation, but thinking about the circumstances of his departure always left me feeling bitter and angry more than anything else.

Now?

I'm not so sure.

I saw the moment he slipped his lawyer mask on this afternoon. When it was just the two of us speaking, he was raw and remorseful. After years of assuming that he walked away from Redwood Bay—from me—and never looked back, I can't help but feel like he's regretted the way he treated me and missed me ever since.

Perhaps I did matter to him the way he mattered to me?

Does that make a difference now?

He seemed adamant he was going to remove himself from my life and leave me alone. I thought that's what I wanted and before today, I would have welcomed it. But everything's changed. He didn't ride off into the sunset and get married to a woman. He's been living half a life all this time, denying who he really is to appease his controlling parents.

It's obvious he can see that's kind of crazy. It's not like they have any power over him now. He doesn't live under their roof. He isn't relying on them to pay his college tuition. It's not like he's desperate for an inheritance and doesn't want to be written out of the will.

He just wants them to love him. And he knows that coming out as gay and disappointing them will jeopardize that.

I...I feel sorry for him. After hating and resenting him for so many years, it's dawned on me today that he's the one that's been suffering while I've had my family and friends, free to pursue a fulfilling career of my choosing. His life has been dictated to him since birth.

Yet he was still determined to protect me from his presence earlier on the beach when Nevaeh was asking for surfing lessons. He tried to give me an out. Before I could weigh up the pros and cons, I took that option off the table.

I don't want an out. I want to see him again.

And that scares the absolute shit out of me.

With a jolt, I realize that Yara has stopped the car outside of my place and killed the engine. I turn and look guiltily at her, fully aware that I've been zoned out for the last few minutes. If she spoke to me, I didn't hear it at all. But she gives me a sympathetic smile and squeezes my knee.

"You're right," she says gently. "I can see it's complicated. I guess you have to reevaluate some things, huh?" I nod and rest my hand on top of hers, grateful for her support and understanding. "Just promise me one thing, Del, okay?"

I raise my eyebrows. "What?"

"That you'll look after yourself, first and foremost," she says, her tone completely serious. "You've said this guy can be manipulative."

"That's what I thought," I say, my words trailing off. I was working with so much misinformation. Things I thought were set in stone are crumbling away like sandcastles as the tide comes in. I'm not sure what to believe anymore.

More than that, I'm scared to hope. What I've seen of Colt in the past couple of weeks makes him seem like a good man, who is genuinely ashamed of his past behavior and is trying to do the right thing now in so many ways. I see a brave, caring person who risked his life to save a little girl's. Someone with a mission to finally tell me the truth, even at the expense of his own happiness and dignity.

There's just too much I don't know. Which is why spending more time together in a safe, public environment doesn't seem too crazy to me. Surely with Elizabeth and the kids around, Colt won't try anything underhand with me. Anton also said he, Meagan or Brent would be around to watch Rebecca as well, so I'll be even more insulated from any bullshit Colt might try and pull.

I need time to see which version of Colt is the real one and which is the mask. I need to work out if I can trust him and…

And what? Am I seriously considering letting him back into my life? Being friends? *Dating?* No, that feels like several steps too far, even for my imagination. But the idea that he didn't intentionally screw me over and use me back when we were teenagers is alluring. It would be nice to reflect back on those times and not feel like I'd been the world's biggest fool. If I could trust that what we shared was real and that he's now sincerely remorseful, I think that could give me some peace.

What do I really have to lose? So long as I keep my guard up and protect my heart like Yara's asking me to, what's the worst that could happen? I'll either get my low opinion of Colton Ross confirmed, in which case I'll be the same as I ever was. Or I'll discover that he's perhaps also been a victim in this situation.

It's difficult not to be optimistic for the latter. Instead of dwelling on it too long, I smile at my partner and squeeze her hand. "I promise not to let myself get duped. I'll keep my wits about me when it comes to Colt."

She exhales and nods, then peeks slyly at me. "I mean…I don't blame you for being blindsided by him. That man is *hawt.*"

I drop back my head and laugh. Yara isn't usually one to talk about crushes or be sexual in any way. I guess that's Colt's power, isn't it? He's so ridiculously good-looking that he gets away with so much shit other people wouldn't, and he makes those around him lose their common sense, even if just for a minute.

To think someone like that would hold me up as the standard to which he's been judging everyone in his life ever since is slightly preposterous, but…that's what he said. I don't think anything's changed much since school, though. Everyone wants him, and it's flattering to think it's me he's chosen over anyone else. It turned my head before.

I can't allow that to happen this time. It will hurt too much if he leaves again. In fact, I think it'll break me.

But I have to find out for myself, once and for all. Who is Colton Ross, really? What kind of man has the boy grown into? How does he act when his father isn't looming over him, controlling his every move and judging his every mistake and indiscretion?

The safest thing would probably to walk away from him and never look back. But I run toward danger for a living. It's my calling in life. And I'm tired of holding myself back from that life just because a boy broke my heart and made me feel worthless and replaceable so many years ago.

By spending some more time together, I'm taking charge of my destiny. I can gather more information and make an informed decision on how I feel about the past and how that's going to affect the direction I take in the future. It's like I've been stumbling around in the dark for too long, telling myself truths that might very well turn out to be lies. How can I live an authentic life if it's built on broken foundations?

So, yes. I'm going into this arrangement with open eyes but also an open mind. Maybe at the end of it all, I'll still resent Colt and not have it in me to forgive him.

But he said he didn't want or expect forgiveness.

And I might come out of it seeing why I loved that boy in the first place. It's possible I'll be able to reassure myself that my judgement back in school wasn't completely misplaced.

If I don't give him a second chance, I think I'll regret it

forever. So long as I don't let him have any power over me, I should be able to keep myself safe, right?

Realizing I've drifted into my thoughts again, I shake myself and lean over to hug Yara. "Thank you for your support."

She scoffs. "Hey, any time. That's what I'm here for, partner. Just remember your promise, and we'll be good."

"I will," I assure her.

Finally, I get out of the car and wave her off before heading inside my place. It feels unusually quiet for some reason. Yet again, the urge to paint is overwhelming, but I do the next best thing instead. I find a sketch pad, pencil and eraser, then head out to the back porch to curl up in the armchair as twilight falls around me. My mind wanders as I idly capture snapshots of plants and wildlife, filling the page with little drawings that don't really mean anything, but help soothe my soul, nonetheless.

The world is beautiful, but if I'm being honest, I know I've been hiding myself away from it, too afraid of getting hurt again like I was before. Is that how I want to spend the rest of my days? I doubt it. If I don't change something now, when will I?

It's almost like I put everything on pause when Colt left. Now he's back, I've finally pressed the play button once more. I wish I could fast-forward and see how it all turns out, but that's not how it works. I just have to be patient and trust that I'm doing the right thing. Or at least that I have enough wisdom not to let myself get burned like before.

Either way, this is happening. The two of us are going to give Nevaeh some surfing lessons. Anything beyond that is in fate's hands now. I just pray whatever transpires, I'm strong enough to survive it.

Because what existed between Colt and I when we were

young is still shining brightly. I feel like a moth being drawn to the flame. If I'm not careful, I'll find myself reduced to a pile of blackened ashes. It's up to me if I let those ashes go cold.

Or if I rise from them like a phoenix, reborn.

CHAPTER 11

Colt

"That's it! You got it! Try it once more for me?"

It's the following Sunday, and I feel genuinely thrilled as I watch Nevaeh, Rebecca and Dashel throw themselves back on the sand on their bellies, digging by their hips as they simulate paddling. Then when I give them the signal, they pop up by doing a kind of press-up with their arms before jumping to their feet, like they were jumping on their board in the water.

"Wow, are you sure you guys haven't had lessons before?" Zahir asks. "You're basically pros already!" He jams his hands on his hips and scowls at the kids like he's the big bad wolf, and they all dissolve into giggles. It's too precious, really.

"No, Mr. Del!" Nevaeh shrieks in her dramatic tone I've come to very much enjoy. "This is the very! First! Time! I SWEAR!"

He whistles and shakes his head. "We better warn the Olympic committee, then. Because—wow."

More giggling. More delight. And then these three tiny kids do the exercise another five times, never complaining, only wanting to get better and better so next time we could maybe try it on the water (with us holding both the board and their waists, of course).

The whole time, Anton and Elizabeth cheer and applaud like it's the Super Bowl. I thought that kind of behavior would be annoying, but it's really not. To these kids, their parents' attention means the world and…yeah. I can relate to that.

My parents never came to a single one of my athletic meets. They were not very subtle about their embarrassment when I was in the school play. The only reason they tolerated any kind of extracurricular activities was because they knew it would help with my Harvard application. But in their eyes, competitive sports and the arts were at best a distraction from my studies, and at worst, uncouth.

At the time, I just accepted it. I didn't know any different. But watching these kids thrive is opening my eyes to just how important having a well-rounded childhood is. I think back to my colleagues sneering at their teenagers' hopes and dreams, and it makes me appreciate just how many challenges this generation is facing as they grow up. There's so much pressure to succeed and be the best. But is there enough joy?

There certainly is for these guys today. I was worried when Zahir and I decided to start them on dry land drills for their first lesson that they might whine and get bored. But they've done no such thing. Although now we've finished our session, they're begging us to try just sitting on the kid-sized board they've been sharing in the water.

"Pleeeeease, Colt," Rebecca wheedles, batting her eyelashes at me. "We can't come all the way to the beach and then not get in the ocean!"

That was actually my exact plan. I didn't bring any

swimwear because the idea of getting in any way naked around Zahir seemed like a disaster waiting to happen.

Especially when things are going so well.

Okay, yeah, all we did was text a few times to plan one lesson, then spent most of that lesson talking to the kids and not each other. But the fact that we're doing this at all feels miraculous to me. I'm not sure if it's simply wishful thinking on my part, but I can't help but think there's less tension between us as well. Like we've both released a breath we've been holding.

Or perhaps he's just on his best behavior in front of the kids. Who knows?

Speaking of which, said kids are dancing on their toes with their hands clasped in front of their chests, giving both me and Zahir puppy dog eyes in their quest to get in the water. To be fair, I'm the only one not dressed for it, and that's on me. In fact, I probably look like a dick right now. It was foolish to think I could avoid getting wet. There really is only one thing I can do.

"Okay, you win," I groan. The kids cheer as I slip my sandals off. No sense in ruining them. "But just a paddle, alright? I don't have any other clothes with me."

"We promise!" Nevaeh cries.

"Hey, we can go in with them if you'd like," Zahir's firefighter buddy, Anton, offers. But I shake my head.

"Nah, it's fine," I assure him and Elizabeth. "I promised to teach them. Next time, I'll know better."

I glance at Zahir in his board shorts and T-shirt. He laughs and gives me an easy smile, making me hopeful that he at least doesn't think I'm a tool for not dressing appropriately.

To start with, we start by repeating the drill, this time on the board in a couple of inches of water. As no one was sure how serious the kids were going to be about this hobby, Anton and his ex-wife have currently only invested in one board for them all to share for now. The three of them are being very good with taking turns, though. I'm impressed.

With just my feet in the surf, my chinos feel safe initially. Zahir is holding the top of the board, deeper in the water. When we progress to getting the kids to sit on it and dangle their feet over the sides, I only have to wade up to my knees to keep the thing sturdy.

But then Murphy's law strikes, and I step on a rock so sharp I wonder if it's actually a shard of thick glass.

Or I would have thought that if I hadn't been too busy shrieking like a banshee, snatching up my foot, and toppling into the water.

I'm grateful that everyone gasps instead of immediately laughing at me. I'm also grateful that I put my phone in the breast pocket of my short-sleeved button down. The garment flapped open over my T-shirt as I fell, so my cell only gets a little splashed before I yank it out and hold it up to where it can stay safe.

Once I realize no real damage has been done other than to my pride, then I do laugh. That gives the kids permission to dissolve into fits of giggles again.

"Oops," I say sheepishly.

"You okay?" Zahir asks, wading through the water to me before dropping down and…

And then he's lifting my foot out of the water, inspecting the tender spot.

We're touching skin to skin. He's voluntarily touching me.

My brain bluescreens. It feels like there's an electrical current running between us, super charging my heart. It's only when he looks at me and raises an eyebrow that I remember he asked me a question.

"Oh, yeah, I'm fine," I say with a cough. "I think it was just a rock or seashell. I'm not even bleeding, am I?"

He shakes his head and smiles warmly, rubbing my sole with his thumb. The pressure on the injured area feels good.

"I think you'll live," he assures me with a wink.

For just a second, I get a flash of how comforting he must be to his patients. He sees people at some of the worst moments of their lives and pulls others from terrifying crises. If I was having a really bad day, I know it's Zahir's face I'd want to see.

It's as if we both realize we're looking into each other's eyes at the same time. He glances away, flustered, as I slide my foot from his grip.

"Are you okay, Mr. Colt?" Nevaeh asks in concern by my side. Rebecca and Dashel are hovering behind her. I look around and see that Elizabeth and Anton are wrestling the surfboard back onto the sand. I guess the lesson is probably over for the day.

"Yeah, kiddo," I say ruefully as I haul my ass up, saltwater rushing from my drenched shorts. "I'm fine, just a klutz. You promise not to tell anyone?"

Rather than laugh, she sticks her bottom lip out and slots her hand against mine. "You're not a klutz. You just had an accident. It can happen to anyone."

I look at this small child and wonder if she's been beating herself up for almost drowning. That hadn't occurred to me before, but I guess even tough kids get wobbly sometimes. If she can deal with something so huge as that, I can take inspiration from her and get over my embarrassment today.

"Anyone ever tell you you're pretty wise?" I ask her.

"Dashel tells me I'm a know-it-all," she says with an eye roll.

"You are!" her brother squeaks as we all make our way back onto the sand. I laugh and hear Zahir laugh too.

I like sharing moments like this with him.

Probably too much.

While the parents round up their kids, I sigh and look down at my soaked clothing. I think my only option is going to be to hang out here for a bit and try and get them to dry, otherwise I'm going to ruin my car's upholstery. But I don't have any food or a book, and I'm not sure how much battery my phone has left. So rather than sounding like a relaxing prospect, it feels like I'm going to be bored as fuck.

"Do you want my shorts?"

I blink and look at Zahir. He's holding out a pair to me, presumably the ones he was intending on changing into as he wore his swimwear here. I'm stunned. Not that he's being kind and considerate—that's who he's always been as far as I'm aware. But that he'd voluntarily give me something of his. Doing that means we'd have to coordinate me giving them back. I could probably just bring them to our next surfing lesson with the kids, but still…

"You'd trust me with them?" I blurt out.

He shrugs and looks slightly awkward. "They're just shorts."

We both know they're not, though. He'd be well within his rights to ignore my plight and let me destroy my car seat and still sleep soundly tonight. But this is why even though I know it's unwelcome on his side, my stupid heart pitter-patters every time I'm near him. He's just such a decent human being in a world so often overrun with selfish mean-spiritedness.

I should take them. It's a practical solution that would save me either having to replace my upholstery or languish in boredom for the next few hours. But taking anything from him feels like too much when I've already broken his heart, betrayed his trust, and forced him into living a lie for all that time when we were teens.

So I shake my head and smile sheepishly. "Then you'd be the one stuck in the wet clothes. I'll just ride it out."

"Well, I…"

He pauses and bites his lower lip. I notice that Anton, Elizabeth and the kids have quietly left. Part of me feels bad that they obviously felt like they couldn't interrupt us. But the other part is not only grateful they didn't, but gets a thrill that they picked up that our vibe was an intimate one. Even though I know it's selfish, I'm desperate for any private time I can get with Zahir at all.

"Yeah?" I prompt, not sure what he was going to say.

He studies me for a moment, then appears to come to a decision. "I don't live that far away. It's about a fifteen-minute walk, so I didn't actually drive. Did you…I mean… you could come back with me for a shower and a change of clothes. Unless—"

"That would be awesome," I cry before he can change his mind.

There's no way I'm going to second guess a chance to spend a whole walk together and see his place. I'm probably stepping into dangerous territory, but I can't bring myself to care.

I know I don't deserve Zahir Delacroix. However, if he's going to freely offer me his time and attention, I'm not strong enough to resist.

Zahir's expression is hard to read, but I think he's okay I accepted his offer by the little half smile that tweaks at his lips. "All right, then," he says with a nod. "You got your things?"

My backpack doesn't have much inside it. Mostly just my keys, water, sunscreen and a small towel, but I'll at least be able to brush the sand from my feet with that. I grab the bag and my sandals before nodding back at him. "Lead the way," I say.

In my chest, my heart gallops nervously. He's extended an olive branch to me when he really didn't have to. I absolutely cannot under any circumstances fuck it up.

So of course, that's exactly what I do.

CHAPTER 12

Zahir

This feels like an alternate reality. Or perhaps some kind of surrealist painting.

Colton Ross does not belong in my home.

Yet here he is.

The walk from the beach was mostly quiet but surprisingly not awkward. However, now he's standing in the middle of my living room, and neither of us seem sure what to do. I'm fully aware that the onus is on me to break the tension as this is my place. But my voice is caught in my throat as a debate rages inside me whether or not this was a terrible idea.

Because I know he shouldn't be here. I shouldn't have opened my mouth and extended the invite. But now he is…it feels so right. So natural. Like we've traveled back in time to senior year.

"Uh, do you want something to drink?" I finally offer, remembering my manners. My teta would be ashamed of me for my rudeness. Well, she'll be horrified if she ever finds out I let Colt in my home voluntarily. With any luck, she'll never have to know.

Colt blinks, like he's not sure if I'm talking to him or not. "Oh, um, sure. What have you got?"

"Water, juice, tea, iced tea, coffee," I rattle off. Then, before I can stop myself, "And beer."

Immediately, I know that's setting a certain kind of vibe. But I can't stop the thrill I feel when he grins in surprise. "I'll take a beer."

Nodding, my feet take me into the kitchen without much input from my brain. Which is lucky, because my thoughts are hurtling around my head like a tornado.

This just isn't what I expected. Where's the hotshot asshole lawyer that up and left overnight to move to the other side of the country to start a dazzling career? The man beside me as I pull two bottles from the fridge is almost... shy. Eager. Uncertain.

Humble.

He's that sweet boy I'm sure I was the only one he let see back in school. Everyone else saw the captain of the debate team, a star athlete, a guy that could have been prom king if he hadn't been too cool to run for it.

I'm the one who helped him with his chemistry home-work. Who ran lines with him the single time he was brave enough to be in the school play, even just as a side character. Who held him when he had his one and only meltdown in our final year of school, sobbing in my bedroom, but refusing to tell me why. It's pretty obvious what that was about in retrospect.

And I'm the one who looked into his eyes as we leaned in for that first kiss. Fuck, I haven't allowed myself to think of that moment in so many years. Before it can overwhelm me, I busy myself finding the bottle opener and handing Colt his beer.

"The bathroom is just on the left, there," I say in a some-what stilted fashion. My messed up brain translates those words as I speak them to, 'Here's where I'd like you to get naked in my house.'

Unhelpful.

"There are spare towels in the closet," I continue. "Help yourself to any products you need. I'll pull out some sweats and a T-shirt to get you home. You can give them back when we next see Nevaeh."

There. The implication is clear that we're being friendly, but I'm not inviting him to stay all evening or offering to make him dinner or anything like that.

I'm also trying not to show the near aneurysm I'm having working out if I should offer him any underwear with the sweatpants. Saying that outright seems too personal, but I've realized that either way his junk will be rubbing all over something of mine.

Whatever. That's what laundry detergent is for. I just need to not dwell on it, starting with not mentioning it in the first place.

"All good?" I ask.

"Thanks, man," he says, pausing outside the bathroom. "I really appreciate this. I feel so stupid thinking I could go to the beach and not get messy."

Oh, this is messy, all right. And I don't just mean the sand and saltwater.

"Don't mention it," I say, trying not to look like I'm backing away when I am, in fact, backing away. "I'll just get the, um, your clothes. My clothes. Uh…"

"Thanks," he says again.

He leans on the doorframe, the beer bottle dangling from his thick, strong fingers as he smiles at me. I see that dopey teenager I used to think of as being mine again, and I have to spin onto my heels and head into the bedroom before I do something truly regrettable.

For a few seconds, I just grip the side of my dresser and

take a few deep breaths to center myself. It would be pointless to deny that my body is insanely attracted to Colt, possibly even more than when we were younger. Sure, we were both riddled with hormones back then and made out every second we could. But there's no beating the allure of maturity and wisdom.

And washboard abs and bulging biceps and…

"Yeah, yeah," I grumble quietly to my dick that's twitching in my shorts. "I got the memo. He's *hawt.*"

Rolling my eyes as I mimic Yara's silly pronunciation, I put my beer down and start rummaging for clothes that I think will fit him but also that don't have any sentimental value.

Part of me wants to give him my vintage pattern Honolulu tee. We used to always talk about taking a trip and going surfing somewhere exotic after we graduated, but obviously we never got the chance. I have to be in the right mood to wear that shirt, because for better or worse, it never fails to remind me of our time together.

I decide that's probably not the one to lend him.

Pausing in front of my dresser, my hand drifts upward to gently press my fingers against my lips, chasing the ghost of that first kiss. Senior year had been almost over, and the whole summer seemed to stretch out infinitely before us. I remember how terrified I'd been of losing Colt, but it never felt like a possibility I could tell him how I really felt. I'd been brave enough to come out to him after an obscene amount of rum one night several weeks previously. When he hadn't immediately dumped me as his best friend, that seemed like the greatest possible outcome I could hope for.

Except in my dreams, he was secretly gay, too. I'd had countless fantasies of him leaning in to kiss me like a prince in a fairy tale. But I knew better than to think that could ever be real.

And then one magical night after graduation, when we'd been surfing all day then taken pizzas and a six-pack to a secluded spot on the beach, we'd been lying in the sand next to one another, he'd turned his head to look at me and…

It was as if time stopped. My heart certainly did when he'd gotten just a fraction closer. Then he'd whispered my name like a prayer, then…

I close my eyes in the here and now, a lump rising in my throat and goose bumps shivering across my skin. No fireworks display could ever match the explosion I felt the moment his lips touched mine. Like he'd been waiting longer than I had for just the right opportunity to make his move. He'd seemed so confident, although afterward he confessed he'd been scared shitless that he was about to ruin everything between us.

I'd assured him there hadn't been anything I wanted more in the entire world than to be with him. We'd made love clumsily on that beach in the dark, then spent the next several weeks exploring each other in every single way we could think of. He already had my heart and soul as my best friend for nearly four years. In those short couple of months, I gave him my body unconditionally, and he had worshiped me as I did him.

Then he was gone. Just like that.

I inhale sharply and blink my eyes back open. My pulse is racing and my cock is throbbing, recalling all those beautiful, joyful, sensual firsts we'd shared together.

"Get it together," I tell myself firmly.

I was fully aware that inviting him into my home was always going to make things complicated and stir up old feelings. There's no need to make this fragile détente of ours unstable because I tripped and fell down memory lane.

After a couple of deep breaths, I feel like I'm on solid

ground once more. "You're okay," I mutter to myself. "He's not going to hurt you like that again. He can't."

Not if I don't let him.

If we're going to be civil and exist in the same town, possibly even be friends, I cannot let the past keep dragging me backward. But perhaps now I've had this first serious wobble after letting him into my home, my body won't get so confused by all those memories so easily next time.

He doesn't have that power over me anymore. I refuse to allow it.

This is my life. He only gets to come back into it if I say so.

Before I can tie myself up in knots any further, I pick out plain gray sweats and a faded red tee without any logos on it. They're just basic things I wear around the house or sometimes working out, so they have no sentimental value. There. Nothing to stress over. I throw them over my shoulder, grab my beer, spin around to leave my bedroom—

And crash straight into Colt, who's only wearing a towel slung around his hips.

"Fuck!" we both yelp as I drop my bottle and jump backward. Luckily, I have a thick rug on the tiled floor in here, so at least the glass doesn't smash. But that now means beer is glugging out all over the shag pile.

"Shit, sorry!" Colt cries, diving to snatch it back up. In the process, the towel slips, and he only just catches it with his other hand, not so successfully covering his dick.

Of course I've seen it before all those years ago.

But it goes without saying that this is entirely different circumstance.

It's like I've forgotten how to breathe. He stands there, the towel barely covering his modesty in one hand, a dripping beer bottle in the other. The clothes I picked out for him have fallen off my shoulder onto the floor and might very well have beer on them as well.

I don't care.

We just stare, eyes locked together. Colt is frightened, crushed. He licks his lips then bites the lower one, his gaze dropping in shame. "Zahir," he whispers. "I'm so sorry."

He's said that to me at least a dozen times now. But in that moment…it's like I finally hear him. He's not apologizing for the spilled beer or almost flashing me or not packing swim shorts in the first place. He's saying the same thing he's been telling me since he showed back up in this little town of ours.

He's sorry that I trusted him with my heart, and in return he broke it into a million pieces and abandoned me for fifteen years.

This time, though…I believe him. I can see how leaving devastated him as well. He's been suffering just as much as I have, only in different ways. It doesn't matter that we've been apart for so long. He was my best friend, and I know him better than I've known anyone in my life. He's hurting and I want to make the pain go away. He's diminished by remorse, but I want to see him shine again. There's no one as brilliant as Colton Ross to me.

And he promised that for him, there's never been anyone else but me.

He's still mine.

And I want him.

I'm done hiding from the world, too afraid to live for fear of getting burned. Time to stick my hand in the fire and deal with the consequences, come what may.

Before the logical side of my brain can kick in, I throw cation to the wind and myself at Colt, grabbing either side of his face and crashing my mouth against his.

The towel doesn't last very long after that.

CHAPTER 13

Colt

I PROBABLY SHOULD HAVE STAYED IN THE BATHROOM. BUT I showered as fast as I could, determined not to take up too much of Zahir's time or crowd him in his own home. After I dried off, he still hadn't returned with the clothes, so I went looking for him.

Then all hell broke loose.

I've tried. I've tried so hard. But at the end of the day, I'm not a saint. I'm a mortal human being and when the only man I've ever loved—the man I was convinced I'd never have a hope in hell of getting back together with—launches himself at me and kisses me senseless, all common sense leaves the building.

The shock lasts maybe half a second after his mouth lands firmly on mine. Then I'm kissing him back like the last fifteen years never happened. My tongue remembers his taste like nothing else and my body loves the way his has grown bigger and stronger. Without thinking, I mirror him and grab the sides of his face, kissing him like I'll never need to breathe again.

Of course oxygen does eventually become an issue, and

even though I need it too, my heart drops as he pulls away and gasps for air. It's only as we stare at each other then, chests heaving, do I realize that my damp towel has fallen to the floor in a crumpled heap. At least I somehow placed the bottle on the dresser, and it actually has most of the beer still inside, although I have no memory of doing that.

So I really am standing there stark naked, my half-hard dick very much making its presence known.

Just as I'm about to expire from every regret I've ever had colliding into me all at once, Zahir takes a breath, gaze still locked with mine. In one fluid motion, he grabs the back of his T-shirt and yanks it over his head, flinging it to the ground.

Well, okay, then.

I'm not sure who moves first, but it doesn't seem to matter. We're like magnets hurtling together, his lips and hands finding their way back to where they were before, but this time with the added bonus of his glorious warm skin plastered against mine.

I still need more, though.

The only word repeating in my head is *'Mine! Mine! Mine!'* as I drop my hands and start fumbling with his board shorts. He never changed from his swimwear—I assume because, like me, he was worried about flashing skin in front of each other on the beach. That seems ridiculous now.

The elastic waist makes them easy to get off, and of course he's not wearing anything else underneath. Then he's moving backward toward the bed, taking me with him as he kicks his way free of the shorts around his ankles. Mercifully, he'd already taken his shoes off at the front door, so there's absolutely nothing between us or holding us back as we tumble onto his bed.

Zahir Delacroix is back in my arms. It's like I can hear a chorus of angels singing all around us. Of course in reality, the air is only filled with our heavy breathing and desperate groans. That still sounds like music to me, though.

He might have been the one to drag us horizontal, but now I twist us so he's on top of me, wanting to make sure he knows he's in charge. We never had strict roles back when we were experimenting, but I've topped every guy I've fucked since. I'm pretty sure he's the only one I'll ever feel safe enough to bottom for.

Right now, however, there's no time for anything that involved. The desperation is tangible as he continues his assault on my mouth with his own and grinds our hips together. I cling to his sides like a lifebuoy, digging my fingers into his ribs like I want to mark him with bruises.

Actually, that's exactly what I want to do.

Zahir is *mine*. I'm ready to give him everything.

If it literally hadn't been over a decade since I bottomed, I would have begged him to fuck me into the mattress right there and then. As it is, when he shoves his hand between us and wraps his fingers around both our straining erections, thrusting wildly against me, it feels almost just as good.

Well, not really. But damn it, I'll take every drop of what he'll give me. The fact that we're writhing on his bed, scrunching up his sheets, kissing recklessly as we hump and slide, chasing release as one…it all feels impossible and yet inevitable at the same time. Like ever since I left town, we've still been tethered together, with an invisible force slowly pulling us back to this predestined reunion.

"Colt," he moans against my lips.

Just hearing him say my name like that sends electricity shooting through my body, and my balls tighten in anticipation. Suddenly, it's not enough for me to just lie back and let him do all the work. Yes, I want him to be in charge. But I also have to do something to show how much this means to me, how much I've missed him.

With a grunt, I shove him, using my superior strength the way he always melted for back when we were teens. Rolling him over, I break the kiss as I hastily shimmy down his body, pushing his hips into the bed as I swallow his leaking cock all the way into my throat.

He shouts and bucks, but I hold him steady, sucking hard as if I'm trying to steal the breath from his lungs through his dick. He tastes like the ocean and musk and something my memory recalls as uniquely him. Woodsy and spicy but also unmistakably warm and sunshiny.

"*Yes, yes, yes,*" he hisses, quivering underneath me.

The temptation to finish him off with my mouth while I jerk my aching cock is strong. But there's still a shred of my upstairs brain working, and I remember that I want us to be equals in this. No—I want *him* to be in control. I can achieve that without being passive.

Before he can tip over the edge, I release his length, enjoying how it bounces and flicks spit and precum on my chin and his belly. He moans and grimaces, but I head back up his body, leaving a trail of open-mouthed kisses along his skin until I reach his jaw, pressing my mouth against it and the corner of his lips.

"I want to make you come now, Zahir," I rasp, watching his expression intently for any hint that this isn't okay. I might die if I have to stop. But one word from him, and I will. "I want to come all over you. Can I?"

He takes a ragged breath, but then he nods, his eyes wide as I loom over him. Relief floods through me. This time, it's me that takes both of us in hand, stroking our members, slippery with spit and precum, knowing it's not going to take either of us long now.

He opens his mouth like he wants to say something, but then he just whimpers instead. "Close," he utters, finally.

I nod, the best I can do to say I feel the same. He's so

fucking beautiful all the time, but in this moment, he looks so perfect and *free.* A wave of complicated emotions crashes over me as my orgasm rips through my body. I try to keep my hand moving as I begin to spurt all over him, but I'm shaking from head to toe. That's when he wraps his fingers around mine, finishing himself off together.

With some effort, I manage to keep my eyes open enough to see him start to come. Long ropes shoot across his taut belly, mixing in like paint with the mess I've already made. Except this time, it's him who's the canvas.

I'm dizzy and exhausted, but I still slam my mouth back against his, kissing him fervently until our highs begin to fade. Then the kisses get gentler and slower as I try and savor the moment.

I should have known it couldn't last.

Reality comes crashing over me like a tsunami, hitting me all at once what a selfish ass I'm being. Zahir might have made the first move, but I should have respected him enough to never have let it happen.

Coldness rushes through me and I draw back, nausea churning in my stomach.

"What's wrong?" he asks, immediately on edge.

But how can I explain? 'It's not you, it's me'? Yeah, right. How lame does that sound? Jesus fucking *Christ.* I had one job here and that was to not hurt him again. What do I do? Flash my junk and jump straight into bed with him.

He deserves a million times better than me. Not just for what I did in the past, but because nothing's really changed in the present. I can't give him what he needs.

The respect and dignity of coming out of the damn closet. My family's business is relying on me. All those people's jobs. My dad's generational legacy. I know if my parents weren't such bigots, this wouldn't be an issue, but the bottom line is they haven't changed in all this time and I'm not sure how likely it is they ever will.

I've messed him around enough for one lifetime. I can't gamble with his heart again that anything will improve. It's out of my power just as much as it was as a scared teenager.

"Colt?" he says sharply, and I gulp, my mouth suddenly dry.

"I'm sorry," I rasp. "I shouldn't have…I've made everything worse. Zahir, I…"

Words fail me. All I do is fuck him over. I'm a selfish, morally bankrupt asshole who doesn't deserve to get what he wants, especially when it's only going to hurt the most important person I've ever known. I should never have careened back into his life. Nothing good was ever going to come from it.

"Please forgive me," I manage to say through my thickening esophagus, scrambling off the bed to get my poisonous presence away from him.

I don't actually expect him to forgive me as I stumble through the house, snatching up my damp clothes from the bathroom so I can at least get my shorts back on before I run out the front door. He had no reason to forgive me for what I did fifteen years ago. But this?

This is it. There's no way he won't hate me now and never want to speak to me again. That's what I get, though, for daring to think I could fly this close to the sun. Just like Icarus, my hubris is my undoing, and I have no one to blame but myself.

No matter how much he's going to hate me, I'm certain I'm going to hate myself even more for a long, long time to come.

Possibly forever.

CHAPTER 14

Zahir

'*Please forgive me.*'

Those words have been going around my head nonstop since yesterday, haunting me.

If Colt regretted having sex that fast, it's me who should be begging for forgiveness. I never should have been so stupid as to kiss him. I definitely shouldn't have invited him into my home, or my life for that matter. Yara was right.

And she knows it. At least she's not calling me out on it.

Yet.

The past is the past and I was a naïve fool to think anything could possibly be different this time around simply because we're adults now. I have worked so hard to find peace in my life. Yes, there might be some solitude as well, but I'll take that over the earth-shattering disappointment that's been dragging me down from the moment Colt sprinted out of my home, leaving me covered in both of our cold, drying cum.

The shame was almost unbearable as I eventually dragged myself into the shower to get rid of the evidence. It still is, but at least it's easier to stand it with clothes on.

The crushing blow no doubt felt worse because for just a few minutes, I was flying high in utter bliss, the kind I hadn't felt before, not even as a teenager when we first got together. Back then I didn't know what pain was yet to come. The euphoria of reclaiming our connection was so much sweeter as it was much harder to earn.

Except it was gone in a flash, and the pain is now as excruciating as I feared it would be. The added layer of humiliation isn't helping, either. I should have known better. I let my hope override the truth.

The thing is, though, that in that moment, I absolutely felt that Colt wanted the intimacy as much as I did, if not more. He was desperate, considerate, loving, caring…all the things I remember his younger self being. He was absolutely in it with me until the end.

Then it was as if someone yanked the wool from his eyes and he realized where he was and what he was doing, and everything dissolved in an instant.

But *why?* He asked me to forgive him, but he didn't do anything wrong. Not this time. I was the one who made the first move. I'm guilt stricken worrying that he was naked and vulnerable and I somehow took advantage of him. Did he truly consent to what happened? I pulled back from that initial kiss to take my shirt off. I would hope that was enough opportunity for him to have told me to stop if that was what he wanted.

I keep replaying every second, trying to figure out if there was a point at which I missed a sign or a look he could have given that meant he was unsure. If there was something, I can't for the life of me recall it. That doesn't mean it didn't happen, so anxiety still twists in my guts. However, all I can picture is the way he pushed me around the way I used to love, and how he asked to make me come and to come all over me. He *asked.*

If I try and stay calm and rational about the whole encounter, I genuinely don't think I crossed a line with him. But that doesn't mean something didn't go wrong anyway, because it clearly did.

Colt wanted forgiveness. That means he knew sleeping together was a bad idea as soon as the orgasmic high dissipated. Which means that even if he's into me the way I'm into him…it's not enough.

Nothing's changed, has it? I knew it logically before, but I guess now I've had a practical demonstration. I'm certain the attraction between us is mutual. By leaving my place the second that common sense came crashing back down, though, he's making it clear that he still has no intention of coming out.

Even if he is gay and not bi like I thought for all these years. So if I can't be enough for him to live authentically… will anyone?

I'm angry at him for treating me like this, but if I hadn't made the first move, perhaps he could have resisted temptation. We're both to blame. That just leaves me agonizingly sad for him that he's refusing to stand up to his parents and be the person he wants to be, the person he *should* be. Is his whole life destined to be a pale imitation of happiness and achievements? I see all too frequently how a person can lose everything in an instant, oftentimes without any warning.

When Colton Ross's time on the planet is done, is he going to look back and see nothing but regret?

I know I should be more concerned with my own tattered heart and conflicting feelings. However, my world is rich with family, friends, and a career that I know is my true calling. Sure, I could possibly open myself up more, but maybe now I will. The hurt I've been afraid of all these years has reared its ugly head and I might be drained and devastated today, but I am still standing. I'll recover. Perhaps this will finally allow me to try entering into a relationship with someone new?

After all, the worst thing that can happen…just happened. I let Colt back in and he proved me right. I doubt anyone else can wound me that deeply, so why not be brave and attempt something new?

Not now, though. I will at least give myself time to grieve.

It's finally the point at which to let this thing between us die. I should have done it fifteen years ago.

Yara has let me be quiet the whole return drive. We pull back into the station after a call to a house fire. Luckily, it wasn't too serious, but we did take the family into San Clemente General to be treated for smoke inhalation just as a precaution. The guys got the blaze out before we even left, so I'm not surprised to see the rest of the One-Thirteen back before us. Although by the way they're still sorting the kit out and tending to the rigs, I'd guess they didn't beat us by much.

"Del," Yara says as I kill the engine on our bus.

I know it's childish, but I pretend like I don't hear her and continue out the door, intending to head into the back and do the inventory checks and replacements immediately. It's standard practice anyway, but I'll also do anything to avoid talking about Colt or seeing her pitying looks right now.

She made me promise I'd keep my head, and I lost it the first chance I got. I don't have anyone else to blame for how wretched I'm feeling other than myself.

"Hey, guys," Lieutenant Flores calls out from where he's working on lunch in the kitchen area. "Everything go okay with the family?"

I nod, walking a little farther into the heart of the house to speak to him. The stock take can wait a minute if I'm not being forced to examine how much of a careless idiot I've been.

"The little boy was pretty badly shaken," I tell him. "But once Bell found his favorite stuffy for him, unharmed, he calmed down considerably."

"Lucky most of the damage was around the kitchen," Lochlan Bell chimes in from where he's putting food down for Rocky, whose tail is whirling like a helicopter in anticipation.

I'm distracted from the conversation when I glance over at the dining table and see a couple of non-firefighters hard at work. "Rebecca," I say in surprise but then I grin at her. "Are you following me, young lady? That's two days in a row I've seen you!"

She looks up from her workbook and waves enthusiastically at me. "Hi, Del! I'm not following you, I swear. Mommy dropped me off after school as she and Brent have to do boring grown-up errands. I'm just doing my homework, then Daddy said I can watch TV if nobody else minds."

"Of course we won't mind, Becca Bean," Sawyer tells her from where he's checking oxygen tanks. As Anton's best friend, I know Rebecca sees him as one of her own uncles. I love big, complicated families like that. It really does take a village to raise a child.

"And a good job she's doing of her studies, as well," says the impeccably dressed lady sitting next to Anton's daughter, her voice warm with praise.

Mrs. Sylvia Bloom is the fire house's neighbor who's always popping in to see us, often with baked goods or a casserole. Sure enough, I can see Lieutenant Flores putting a couple of pre-cooked lasagnas into the oven as we speak. As a wealthy widower, she's made it her business to fuss over us whenever she feels like, which tends to be most of the time.

Especially if she sniffs even a hint of drama.

"Miss Quick was telling me in between working on her book report that you and your friend Mr. Ross are teaching her and her friends to surf," Mrs. Bloom says, arching her eyebrow like that's the most fascinating gossip she's ever heard. "Isn't that right, Margot?"

The pristinely groomed shih tzu dog, Miss Margot Fonteyn, raises her head from where she was napping on one of the chairs to give a little 'woof,' presumably at hearing her name mentioned. The hair has been pulled out of her eyes by a sparkling rose gold bow that perfectly matches Mrs. Bloom's nails and the purse that's sitting on the table by Rebecca's homework.

That's definitely not an accident.

"Rebecca says that you and Mr. Ross went to school together and that he's recently back in town?" she says.

It might not be worded like a question, but I can hear one anyway. So much for avoiding talking about Colt. Her piercing stare tells me she's smelled blood in the water and she's not going to relent until I've spilled all my secrets.

Suddenly, I'm so very tired. I sigh and slump into one of the unoccupied chairs opposite Mrs. Bloom. Even though they don't have much in common, she reminds me of my grandma in this moment. Obviously, I haven't told Teta what happened yesterday because she'd be unfairly upset with Colt when it's really all my fault. But the overwhelming urge to get some grandmotherly advice overtakes my pride.

Aware that not only Yara but the rest of our team are nearby, I lean my elbows on the table and rub my chest as I speak quietly to Mrs. Bloom. "We were...best friends...at school. But no one knew."

"That you were 'best friends'?" she asks. Her air quotes are obvious even if she doesn't move her fingers. I don't know if I'm relieved she cracked my code or not. Trying to discuss my predicament with people and not out Colt is hard.

I nod. "Yeah. *Best* friends. Then he left for college, and we literally didn't speak again until he arrived back in Redwood Bay a couple of weeks ago."

"He rescued my friend Nevaeh from the ocean!" Rebecca cries, kicking her feet under the table, oblivious to the subtext of the adult's conversation around her.

That's when Yara drops down beside me and loops her arm with mine and rests her head on my shoulder. "I don't think he deserved to be your 'best friend,'" she grumbles. "Now or then."

Rebecca frowns. "But Colt is nice," she says in confusion. "He wasn't mean to you after our surfing lesson yesterday, was he, Del? Daddy said we had to go home as it was past dinner time. I'm sorry we didn't say goodbye, but you guys looked busy."

I sigh and offer her what I hope is a placating smile. "We were busy, so don't be sorry. Daddy was right, and that was polite of you. Do you remember Colt's clothes got all wet?" She nods. "Well, I suggested he could come back to my place and get changed."

"Uh-oh," Yara says under her breath, hugging me tighter. I try not to let any emotion show on my face, but my throat does thicken somewhat. 'Uh-oh' is certainly the right sentiment.

"What did I do right?" Anton asks, sauntering over with Sawyer. They're sharing a bag of pretzels Sawyer's holding, and as Anton reaches for a handful, their fingers brush. I wonder if anyone else spots the way Sawyer's eyes widen, just for a second. It's probably nothing more than him being mad at his best friend stealing his snacks, but still…I wonder.

"You were right that Del and Colt were busy when we left the beach yesterday, Daddy," Rebecca says helpfully. Her tone is innocent, but I feel several pairs of eyes swiveling my way as the grown-ups read more into her words than I'd like them to.

"Busy, huh?" Teddy asks, swinging a chair around and sitting backward on it.

"Can it, Probie," Lili says, coming up behind our youngest member and massaging his shoulders. "You have to earn your right to give anyone a hard time around here." She arches an eyebrow at me. "So…busy, huh?"

"Guys," Lieutenant Flores says in a warning tone from the kitchen. "Maybe Zahir doesn't want to be grilled by half a dozen people at once about him and his friend."

I shake my head, my spirits too low to really care anymore. "I don't think we're even friends after yesterday," I say, trying and failing to keep the bitterness out of my voice.

Yara stiffens beside me. "I'll unalive him," she growls.

Rebecca giggles. "I know that means you want to murder him," she says precociously. "But you don't *really* mean murder, because that's a crime."

Yara winks at her. "You got me kid."

"Why do you want to unalive your best friend?" Lochlan asks, coming in late to the conversation. Then he glances at his own meddling best friend, Lili, who gives him a devilish smirk back. "Never mind, dumb question."

"No one is unaliving anyone," I say heavily. "It was my fault. I made a mistake. I'm simply sad about it, but I'll recover."

"Or you could apologize," Mrs. Bloom says, looking at me like she's the principal and I'm a naughty schoolboy.

I squirm in my seat. "I don't think he wants me to do that. I think the friendship is over…again."

She scoffs. "It doesn't matter. If you are in the wrong, it is your responsibility to make amends. Otherwise, your karma will be out of balance, and it will catch up to you in other ways."

Her ominous words hang in the air for a moment before Yara huffs and tugs on my arm so I look at her. "Is whatever happened actually your fault or are you just letting him get away with more bull-poop again?"

"I…it's complicated," I admit. "But I do think that I was… unfair to him when he came over to my place. Made some assumptions I shouldn't have and confused him about where our…friendship stands."

Rebecca's narrowing her eyes at me like she's trying to break the enigma code, but everyone else seems to be following what I'm saying.

"Are you saying you, um, did a crossword together?" Yara asks, waggling her eyebrows like I can't decipher her meaning.

"What's a crossword?" Rebecca asks.

"A game people used to play before they had cellphones," Anton tells her before also narrowing his eyes at me. "Are you worried the crossword spoiled your friendship?"

I shake my head. "I know it did. But I don't think that matters. Being friends is probably a bad idea after everything that's happened."

"How does Colt feel about the crossword?" the lieutenant asks from where he's making a large salad in the kitchen. Clearly, my disastrous love life is so interesting, even being several feet away isn't stopping him from getting involved in the conversation.

"He left right after we finished…the crossword…so I don't know," I admit.

"I know you guys aren't really talking about crosswords," Rebecca mutters as she doodles flowers on her book report.

"How was he when he left?" Yara asks.

'Please forgive me.'

"I think he regretted doing the crossword," I say, tracing my finger along a line in the table's woodgrain.

"You think or you know?" Mrs. Bloom demands. "Because it sounds to me that a lot of emotions are involved and you're making assumptions. You know what they say about people who assume."

"No?" Rebecca pipes up, interested.

"I'll tell you later," Anton says quickly.

She rolls her eyes. "No you won't. I'll just Google it."

Before Anton can get into it with his daughter any further, Mrs. Bloom reaches forward and wraps her hand around mine. I don't think she's ever touched me like that until this moment, and I blink in surprise as she gives me a rueful smile.

"My darling. Life is long. It sounds like you and this friend of yours have enough regrets. Take my advice and speak to him now that you're both thinking rationally. Make absolutely sure of where you both stand. Not just on crosswords, but the whole damn puzzle book."

"You said a bad word," Rebecca whispers in an accusing tone.

Mrs. Bloom winks at her. "When you get to my age, sweetie, no one can stop you from using all the bad words you like."

Rebecca's jaw drops at this revelation and Anton looks like he's going to have a panic attack. But I'm distracted by Lochlan coming around and wrapping his thick, freckled arms around me from behind.

"Don't give up on your buddy," he says sincerely. "It might all be a big misunderstanding."

I think I understand what's happened between Colt and I all too clearly. There's probably no misunderstanding. But I smile and sink into the comfort of his and Yara's combined embrace anyway. Before I know it, Sawyer's joined in as well.

"Don't let one crossword mess you up before you've got all the facts," he says, oddly serious for once. "You're pretty much the most considerate guy I've ever met. I bet there's more to it than you think. I doubt it's all your fault, if any."

That's kind of him to say. I disagree, but I don't tell him that. The fact that my friends believe in me means so much. No matter what happens with Colt, they're reminding me in this moment that I'm not alone.

Soon, everyone has added themselves to the cuddle pile, except for Mrs. Bloom who obviously has too much dignity for anything like that, and Lieutenant Flores as the timer went off and he's busy checking on the lasagnas. The smell of hot food also appears to draw Captain Valentine and our driver Gene out from the captain's office.

"Everything okay down there?" the captain asks as they begin walking down the steps toward us.

"We're just giving Del moral support, Cap," Lili calls out to him before placing a noisy kiss on the top of my head.

"Thank you, everyone," I say sincerely, which seems to be the cue for them all to let me go. I smile and hope they don't notice the wetness lingering on my lashes. "I appreciate you listening to my problem."

Lochlan scoffs. "That's what the One-Thirteen are for, dude!"

"No problem too big or too small!" Sawyer cries.

"Speaking of big problems," Lili says as she turns and tickles Teddy's sides through his T-shirt. "Shouldn't you be using all those muscles of yours to help Rico dish up lunch, Probie?"

"Get off me!" Teddy shrieks, making the rest of us laugh and Rocky start barking. Miss Margot Fonteyn looks at us all like we're riff-raff, and she's probably right.

But Mrs. Bloom is smiling warmly, and she makes a point to catch my eye in the ruckus. I nod at her in appreciation, and she returns the gesture. "Remember," she says quietly so no one but me seems to hear. "Life is long. Too long to spend it unhappy."

I'm not sure if any good will come of it, but considering

the tangled history Colt and I share, maybe I owe it to both of us not to give up without one last conversation to clarify where we stand.

A spark of hope tries to ignite in my heart, but I'm quick to extinguish it. It's unlikely that this will do anything other than give us the closure we obviously both need. However, right now, that feels like it would be better than nothing.

People are rearranging themselves around the table in preparation for lunch, but I excuse myself. "I'm just going to make a call," I tell them, already wandering out the front of the station into the sunshine for a bit of privacy. I ignore the wolf whistles that follow me. I've wasted enough time on Colton Ross.

This has to be done now, then maybe I can get on with the rest of my life.

CHAPTER 15

Colt

"So what can we do for you today, Mrs. Brown?" my father asks in his cheerful booming voice that he's perfected over the years when dealing with clients. It has a way of assuring people that they are Very Important without being too overbearing.

To my ears, it sounds fake as fuck, but I don't let anything show on my face. I just keep a carefully neutral almost-smile there that hopefully says I'm extremely dedicated to the business on hand today.

The elderly lady across the table from us scowls and fiddles with her locket pendant. It rests over her tweed dress and matching, long-sleeved jacket, the rings on her knobbly fingers the same high karat gold as the necklace.

"I wish to cut some of my grandchildren from my will," she says in a voice that reminds me of nails on a chalkboard. I'm impressed I manage not to wince.

"I see," my father says practically. If he has any moral judgement on her intentions, he certainly doesn't show it, of course.

When he's in his natural element like this, it's hard for me to see the man who was on death's door only a few months ago. I know it makes sense to preempt any future health issues, but as I look at him now, I can't really imagine him ever not living for the thrill of all this. Of getting the best possible deal for his clients regardless of who's 'right' or 'wrong.' He doesn't see it like that. He just sees winning and losing.

And he never loses.

Before I can judge this woman too harshly, I remind myself that she could have a perfectly valid reason for protecting her assets once she's slipped from this mortal coil. She nods and gives a little 'humph!' noise in response to my father's comment.

"Yes, indeed. My son's children are the problem, you see. I know what my dear late husband told you previously—how he wanted everything divided equally. But he wasn't in his right mind, as I'm sure you know. The business of dying made him a little soft, god rest his soul. But I'm here to set things straight and do what's right."

I looked at the case notes before we sat down to this meeting. According to his doctor, Mr. Brown was in good health aside from his heart failing him. He was certainly of sound mind. But if he also made his wife the executor of their estate, there isn't much we can do about it.

"That's very responsible of you, Mrs. Brown," my father tells her solemnly, already taking notes in his looping hand-writing that's illegible to almost anyone but him.

I make out the words 'Fleece her' underlined amid a few other choice phrases. My stomach churns.

"Please, go on," he prompts. "We must make sure your wishes are clearly stated and iron clad."

She smiles primly at him, but it doesn't reach her eyes. "Like I said, it's Donnie's kids that are the problem, Grace and Luke." She wrinkles her nose. "I'd like to limit what

Donnie gets for doing such a poor job of continuing the family name as well. My daughter changed hers when she got married, naturally, so his two children were supposed to live the Brown legacy and pass it onto their own children."

Next to me, Preston subtly nudges my elbow with his. He's still looking at our client, but in his own notes he's scribbled down 'Because Brown is such an unusual surname.'

I think I do very well not to laugh out loud at that, but Mrs. Brown's next words certainly sober me up quick enough.

"Grace is divorced, you see," she's saying with a grimace like she's just sucked on a lemon. "For no good reason I can tell other than I'm sure her husband got sick to the stomach of her. Tattoos, funny-colored hair, more interested in cats than finding another husband. Then she tells me outright that she has no intention of having children even if she can manage to bag herself another fella! And then Luke hardly needs any explanation. He's determined to live his life as a flaming faggot."

Unfortunately, I'd chosen that moment to take a sip of water...which I then choke on and spray all over the table. Preston slaps my back as I clear the rest of the droplets from my airway, while my father simply shoves a box of tissues my way to clean up the mess before addressing Mrs. Brown.

"How awful," he says sincerely.

"It's selfish, is what it is," Mrs. Brown huffs. "If he wants to be a pervert and dress like a woman, that's his business, I suppose. But he insists on flaunting it for all the world to see! And he's got the AIDS, so why should I leave him any of his grandfather's hard-earned money? He'll be dead soon anyway, I'm sure."

"Actually," I say indignantly even though I'm still spluttering slightly. "HIV is extremely manageable these days with a regular life expectancy and—"

"That sounds extremely taxing, Mrs. Brown," my father cuts over me as if I hadn't been saying anything at all. "Honestly, this young generation just doesn't have any respect as far as I can tell. Such behavior should absolutely remain behind closed doors if these people can't keep their fetishes in check."

I swallow, my heart sinking. It's not like this is new information to me, but it's still horrendous hearing my own father saying such hurtful things so brazenly. I don't know if Luke is actually a trans woman or a drag queen, genderfluid or simply gay and fem. Either way, I'm ashamed I don't defend this stranger more fiercely. He doesn't deserve to be spoken about with such little respect, and nor does his sister for that matter. Neither of them deserve to be denied the inheritance their grandfather earmarked for them.

Mrs. Brown sniffs. "If they aren't going to be decent and continue the Brown name, I'm going to cut them from the Brown estate. Actions have consequences!"

"That they do," my father agrees sagely.

I bite my lip and dig my fingernails into my palm rather than say anything I'll regret. Again. But if this woman is reflective of the Brown family as a whole, perhaps Grace and Luke are quite sensible not to continue the generational trauma.

That's the moment my phone chooses to vibrate in my pocket. I slip it out and look at the screen...and my heart almost stops.

It's a video call from Zahir. I was absolutely positive that after yesterday, I'd never hear from him again as long as I lived. Hope and dread swoop equally through my chest.

"Is that an emergency?" Preston asks. He raises his eyebrows at me, and I get the hint.

"Yes, it *is* an emergency," I say solemnly before turning to our client. I'll deal with my father later, who will surely want details of this so-called emergency. Right now, I have to answer the call before Zahir gives up. "I'm so sorry, Mrs. Brown. I need to leave you in the excellent hands of my colleagues for a few minutes."

She waves me off, not even looking at me and already asking my father if there's a surefire way to stop anyone else in her family giving Grace and Luke part of their inheritance after she's gone.

I walk as fast as I can to the door, then practically sprint through the office until I'm outside in the courtyard where I can get some relative privacy. "Hello!" I cry, convinced he's going to be gone before I can connect us.

But there he is, also outside on my small screen. He's just across town, under the same beaming sunshine as I am, and suddenly it doesn't feel like he's so far away, after all.

I can't imagine why he wants to talk to me after the way I treated him yesterday. I'm so ashamed of what I put him through, and I've been a wreck myself ever since. However, I'm too weak to ignore the chance to speak to him now, even if he's planning on screaming at me for being the worst human being on the planet.

His expression is hard to read as he realizes I've picked up. "Colt," he says, his voice thick with emotion. "I…"

We just stare at each other and I can feel my resolve crumbling as my heart breaks all over again.

"I'm so sorry," I tell him for the hundredth time. You'd think those words would be meaningless to him by now, but he raises his eyebrows hopefully, like he doesn't completely hate my guts.

"I'm sorry, too," he says. Now that blindsides me.

"Huh?" I blurt out before looking around and moving to an even more secluded, shadier area. As it's a Monday, the salon is closed, so I park myself in front of that. "Why the hell would you be sorry?" I'm genuinely so confused.

He squeezes his eyes shut for a second before looking back at me. "I know you don't want a relationship. That you can't...live that life." He means come out. I appreciate his discretion as much as I hate it. "I made the first move and should never have put you in that position. I just hope you didn't feel..." He gulps and looks so distressed I can't stand it. "I hope you didn't feel forced into anything."

For a moment, I don't understand what he's saying. Then realization dawns on me as well as horror. "What the fuck?" I cry, then hastily look around to check no one heard me before continuing at a more reasonable volume. "You didn't force me to do a damn thing. You didn't take advantage of me or assault me or anything like that, so get that line of thinking out of your head right now."

He looks a little stunned, but I'm sure it's nothing compared to the fury I'm feeling toward myself, so I push ahead before he can continue beating himself up for no good reason. *Holy crap.* How I keep finding new and exciting ways to fuck him over, I don't know.

"What we did was incredible, okay?" I tell him fiercely. "I loved every second of it, but that's exactly why I had to leave. I knew it was shitty to run, but it would have been even shittier to stay and mess with your expectations any further. You deserve a million times better than me, Zahir. I treated you so horrendously I don't even have the words. And I can't offer you anything different now. I'm..." The truth of my words hit me as they fall out of my mouth, twisting the knife even more through my heart. "I'm stuck in this hollow life and as much as I'd give anything to be with you, I will never, ever drag you back into the closet again. You deserve to be free."

The moment stretches out as he stares at me. "You'd give anything to be with me?" he utters in disbelief. I don't blame him, because it's obviously bullshit.

I roll my eyes. "Other than disappoint my bigoted parents and blow up my career, yeah," I say sardonically. But he's already shaking his head in exasperation.

"Colt, stop. We're adults now, not teenagers. If we really wanted to see each other, we wouldn't have to throw a parade. I'd just ask that I could maybe tell my friends. But your parents could remain oblivious and I don't see how it would stop you from being an amazing lawyer."

"How do you know I'm an amazing lawyer?" I quip back so I don't have to deal with any of the real feelings bombarding me right now.

He tuts. "Because I know *you*, asshole," he growls. "Of course you're amazing at it."

I swallow, not sure what to say. Not sure what I'm allowed to want or have. "You deserve so much more than to be anybody's secret," I rasp.

He looks away for a second before addressing the screen again. "So you're telling me that's why you abandoned me yesterday? Because you think you know what's best for me?"

"Uh…I was trying to protect you," I defend myself weakly.

He narrows his eyes. "Well, just so you know, that's bull-shit and I'm still mad at you for making me feel worthless."

"Again," I mutter.

But he wags a finger at me. "Colt, life is long."

"I thought it was short," I counter with a frown.

He huffs. "It can be both. The point is, I'm tired of dancing around this thing between us when it's clear we both still feel the same. You keep saying I deserve someone better, but I don't *want* anyone else, not until we've given us a real shot. If you keep cutting things off prematurely because you're afraid of what *might* happen, we're never going to find out what *actually* happens."

Words fail me. He doesn't want anyone else? He's still

willing to give me another chance, even though I can't be everything he needs?

"Unless you don't want that," he says, his enthusiasm deflating slightly.

"Zahir, fuck," I hiss. Shaking my head. "I want that more than anything. I want *you.* I told you there's never been anyone else, not in any way that mattered. I don't know if I can be enough for you but...holy shit, if you're seriously willing to let me try, I'll give you everything I possibly can."

He presses his lips together, his eyes shining. My heart is thumping in my ribcage.

"Have dinner with me," he blurts out. "I want to just sit and *talk.* I want to get to know you again and find out some of what I missed when we were apart. Just spend some time together. Does that...how does that sound?"

I exhale, feeling a little dizzy. "Would you be my first houseguest?" I ask, nerves flaring like I'm asking him to prom. Of course we didn't get to do that either, but if he's really asking to give our relationship some kind of chance...

I could cry with relief and happiness.

"I'll cook for you—for us," I continue. "No interruptions. Just peace and the whole night to get reacquainted."

He probably knows I'm asking for us to avoid going out in public for various reasons. No, I don't want my parents or any of my colleagues to see us and complicate this delicate thing we're nurturing. However, it's more important to me that we're not bothered by waiters or under the pressure of closing time. I want to talk until the sun comes up if possible.

And yes, the fact that my bedroom would be twenty feet away is also a consideration. I'm still a sneaky bastard, after all.

"I'd love that," he says, sounding like he means it. "Okay, I'll let you get back to work. I need to eat some lunch before we get another call. But I'll text you my availability, alright?"

"It's a date," I say softly.

"Yes, it is," he says firmly.

We close the call, and I stand outside hugging my phone to my chest for another minute until I really have to go back inside to face Mrs. Brown and my father.

Is this real? Zahir seriously still wants to give this a chance? He's willing to risk trusting me after I fucked up so many times?

Who knows where this might lead. All I know is that our story isn't over yet, and that's enough for me.

CHAPTER 16

Zahir

Despite the rest of the One-Thirteen hounding me relentlessly after my call with Colt, I kept the details of the conversation to myself. However, it was difficult to hide the ridiculous grin that kept creeping onto my face throughout the rest of our shift.

It's true what I've been telling myself all along in that nothing has really changed. But I can't stop myself from feeling like *everything* has changed. We've turned a corner in a way we never got the opportunity to after high school.

I'm not naïve. The deal with his parents, the family business, and his career are huge obstacles that could very well tear us apart just like they did before. The difference is that when we were teenagers, I never questioned Colt's feelings for me. I simply knew he felt the same way about me as I did him. Then I spent the next fifteen years thinking it had all been nothing but an experimental summer fling for him that meant nothing.

Now I know better.

If what drove him out of my door the other night really was fueled by his conviction that he's fundamentally not good enough for me because of his past actions...that means he cares. A *lot.* And while I've thought of him as a liar all this time, I'm now sure that's not the case. He might have neglected to say certain facts out loud and allowed me to believe in things that weren't going to happen. But he's never actually been deceitful to me as far as I'm aware.

Yara will possibly kill me, but I can't help myself from starting to trust him again. If he says he wants to be with me, then that's all that really matters. I'm willing to address those other road bumps when we hit them. For now, it's enough to give him a shot and spend some time together. If our feelings, attraction, and emotions can give us a strong enough foundation, maybe we can overcome the other outside forces or at least find working compromises?

So here we are, ready to try again. Starting by spending Friday evening at his place. Alone. We aren't running into each other by accident or one seeking the other out to pass information along or even agreeing to meet with a third party. This is just going to be us two, on purpose, by choice.

The deliberateness of it puts the option of commitment on the table. Obviously, nothing is guaranteed. But the fact that we're no longer dancing around the subject is as much a relief as it is terrifying.

I've had plenty of first dates, most of which never really went anywhere. I was usually a little nervous purely because I'm not a fan of awkward silences, but I hardly ever put much pressure on them to go well. Deep down, I think I was probably sabotaging them from the onset. I was so afraid of getting my heart broken again that I didn't want to even open myself up to the possibility it could lead to anything serious.

As I walk up to Colt's apartment complex, I'm feeling a whole host of varying emotions. It's not a first date because we've known each other since we were fourteen. He was my best friend and my first love. A decade and a half might have passed since we parted ways, but even the short time we've spent together over the last few weeks has caught us up considerably on our adult lives. We've even already had sex.

But there is a bubbling anticipation as I press the buzzer on the outer door and nerves of a different kind. On the one hand, it's Colt. I've never clicked with anyone in my life like I have with him. It should be easy and casual. On the other hand, this fresh new start between us feels delicate and vulnerable and so fucking important. Those countless dates with other guys had very little riding on them.

This has everything.

Once inside, I jog up a couple of flights of stairs, but hesitate outside his door, taking one last moment to really consider the implications of what we're doing. I've gone over and over it and I'm sure the pros outweigh the cons, but this is such a big step that I'd be remiss if I didn't pause and breathe for an extra second or two.

When all my thoughts settle, one stands out above the rest.

I want this. I want to spend time with Colt. That's all that really matters.

Lifting my fist ready to knock, I feel a burst of nerves like butterflies in my stomach. Before I can hesitate further or even make my presence known, the door opens suddenly inward. Colt stands over the threshold as my hand hovers midair, and we blink at each other.

"You came," he says breathlessly.

"Of course," I reply, finally lowering my arm sheepishly. Okay, so perhaps we're both a little nervous and there might be some awkwardness, after all.

But that means we both care, right?

Colt seems to come to his senses and steps back with a small chuckle. "Come in, come in."

Once I'm in the short, narrow entrance hall, I slip my shoes off. There are doors to my left and right as well as a little more hallway on the right, too. That way seems to be the bathroom and maybe the bedroom, so I'm not surprised when he indicates I should go left.

My bare feet slap lightly on the tiles, and a ceiling fan turns lazily overhead. To my right, large windows show palm trees rustling outside in a comforting way.

The space inside is noticeably sparse. Colt hasn't been back in Redwood Bay for long and I imagine he's not certain what he's doing long-term, so I assume he's renting. Still, the lack of personality is jarring.

I look back at Colt and he's staring at me. My face heats like I've been caught doing something bad. But he rubs the back of his neck and sighs.

"It's pretty depressing, isn't it?"

I shrug. "It just needs a little TLC."

He shakes his head and moves to the open kitchen area, pouring us a glass of water each. "I'd love to tell you that my place back in New York was much better, but I barely even had any house plants. There was a series of large black and white photos of the city that I liked. My colleagues got them for me one year after I closed a huge case. But they're so generic, they wouldn't look out of place in a hotel room. I haven't even unpacked them." He hands me a glass. "I haven't unpacked a lot, actually. Half of my stuff is still in a storage locker in town."

I sip my water and think about what he's telling me. "Did you feel like you couldn't show who you really are?"

He scoffs and leans against the counter. "Damn. We're, like, two minutes in and the heavy shit is already creeping out. Yeah, that's probably it. I've been carefully projecting this neutral, masculine image for so long, it's like I don't even remember what sparks joy for me anymore. I didn't want to risk anyone seeing the 'real' me. Still don't, I guess."

I hate that so much. "What would you do with this place if you could? If there wasn't anyone who'd judge you for it or if no one set foot in here aside from you?"

"I'd hang your art," he says quietly and without hesitation. I blink, not certain if I heard him right. But he looks into my eyes and offers me a small smile. "I didn't see anything when were at your place. Do you have some hanging elsewhere?"

Ouch. I swallow and glance away. "I don't, no," I say with a sad chuckle. "That side of my life was something I mostly shared with you and my teta. After school finished, I didn't get much time to paint what with all my training, and I no longer had the free studio space to work in. So I just sort of let it go."

He nibbles his lower lip. We're both propped against the breakfast bar, glasses of water cradled protectively in our hands, as if they're acting like shields. It's unsurprising that we'd both be feeling a little defensive after jumping into such a raw conversation right away. But I'm glad we're being authentic rather than skimming the surface with small talk. I'm so exhausted of hiding who I am for fear or being judged or rejected, and it sounds like he is, too. Maybe even more so.

"Painting makes me think of you," I say softly. "It was as if you were the one I was trying to bare my soul for, so I had to get my feelings out onto the canvas for you to see."

"And that's why you don't have any up on your walls now," he guesses correctly. "Please tell me you didn't throw them away."

I shrug. "No idea. My teta had them all in her bigger house, but I assume when she moved, she sold them or gave them to Goodwill or whatever. I never asked. It's okay," I assure him. "I've spent a lot of time dwelling on the past. I try my best now to focus on the present and look to the future."

He nods and licks his lips. "I get that. The past is done. There's nothing we can do to change it. But we can control what happens in the here and now. Would you still paint, though? Can you create new pieces?"

"Do you still want to see into my soul?" I say with a laugh, intending it as a joke to lighten the mood. But Colt's expression is completely serious and sincere.

"Yes," he says, his gaze unwavering from mine.

Slowly, he places his glass down, then steps closer to me, taking my water from my fingers and placing it next to his before cradling my hands in his.

"I've missed you so much, Zee."

My breath catches. No one calls me that but him. I haven't heard it in fifteen years. My heart races, like that one tender nickname has unlocked a door, pulling me back into the past like a time traveler.

"I've missed you, too," I admit, my eyes burning so I have to close them. I haven't admitted that to myself in a very long time. I haven't admitted it to anyone else ever.

He rubs his thumbs across my knuckles in a soothing manner. "I'd really like to kiss you, if I may?"

Not trusting myself to speak, I manage a stilted nod. The only thing that could stop me going for this right now would be the fear of losing this all again. But I can't lose anything if I don't even try to hold onto it. I'll deal with the future when it comes.

This moment, I'm focusing on the present and nothing else.

Our last kiss was frantic and messy. This one is sweet and tentative. His lips ghost over mine, barely skimming before coming back for a little more each time. I whimper as I lean in, chasing his touch. I slip my hands out of his so I can slide them over his hips, tugging so our stomachs bounce against each other.

"I was going to cook us dinner," Colt mumbles against my mouth. "I got expensive wine."

"Later," I promise him. I want all that, I really do. No man has cooked for me in years, and I want to keep talking like this, earnestly with our hearts on our sleeves.

But I need something else first.

"Take me to bed," I utter, starting to shuffle us in that direction. "Please, Colt."

He grins. "If that's what you want?" He's paused the kiss now and is walking backward toward his bedroom, our hands interlinked again.

"More than anything," I say. "We don't have to do much. I just…will you hold me?"

His expression softens and he squeezes my fingers as he leads the way. "I'll hold you, Zahir. And if you want to keep our clothes on, we absolutely can. But just know that a clothing-free option is available as well. Also—orgasms."

I groan, fighting my knee-jerk reaction to take things slow. What does slow even mean when we have so many years of history between us?

"Orgasms sound good," I admit.

A wicked glint sparkles in his eyes. "They do, don't they?"

His bedroom has about as much personality as the rest of the apartment, but I'm not really paying much attention to the décor if I'm being honest. He's kissing me again and now we've reached our destination, I pull my hands from his and slip them under his T-shirt, feeling his hot skin against my fingertips.

"Zee," he murmurs into my mouth, and my entire body shivers.

I don't see any point in wasting more time than we already have, so I keep pushing my hands up, lifting his shirt over his head. Still kissing my mouth and trying to maneuver us toward the bed, he mimics me, exposing my torso.

He's grinning as we tackle our belts and zippers next, and I laugh along with him. Last time was so intense and probably clouded by both of us hesitating, unsure if we should be doing what we did. Now we're both in this together, on purpose, and I can feel myself having fun like I did that whole magical summer after graduation.

"You're my sunshine," I mumble between kisses.

"You're my ocean," he replies automatically, and my heart melts that he remembers our silly little saying. Of course he does. What we had wasn't a meaningless fling like I thought. I've been so harsh on him for so many years.

I'm very relieved that I got it so wrong.

We were naked last time as well, but that was all a bit of a blur and over far too quickly. This time, he pauses to sit on the edge of the bed, his hands resting on my waist as he breathes heavily and lets his eyes graze over my features. I rest my hands on his shoulders and do the same, drinking in all of his golden skin and taut muscles. Despite many years on the East Coast, he still smells like sunshine to me, hence the nickname. I wonder if I still smell like the ocean to him.

My cock is half-hard, but when he leans in, it's to kiss my stomach rather than give me any relief. But then he's sucking and nipping at my hipbone, and his fingers are digging into the flesh of my ass, and I have a feeling he's trying to mark me.

Mark me as his.

I groan and card my fingers through his soft, thick hair, giving him space to do whatever he wants. Having lost so much time between us, now it feels like it's standing still.

Eventually, he shifts back on the bed, drawing me down with him so we're lying side by side once more, kissing mouths and caressing fingers over sides, backs, and arms. When he slips his middle finger against the tip of my crack, he pauses and leans away slightly to look into my eyes.

"Yes," I say before he can even ask me anything. I know what he wants, and it's the same thing as me.

I have to feel him inside me again or I might just burst into flames.

He only tears his eyes off me to reach into his nightstand and pull out lube and condoms. Part of me wants to tell him we don't need the rubbers. We never used them before as neither of us had fooled around with anyone else previously. Obviously, a lifetime has passed since then, and we've both had a lot of sex with strangers. I know I didn't have any issues at my last medical examination, but now doesn't feel like the moment to stop and ask Colt about it.

And actually, considering all the harrowing emotions we've put ourselves through, I can appreciate taking this part slow. By giving ourselves a little extra protection physically, it somehow makes me feel better psychologically as well. Like I might be jumping off the cliff, but I do still have a parachute on.

For now, he leaves the condom box and instead squeezes a little lube onto his fingers. I'd kind of forgotten how much he insisted on taking care of me before. Of both of us. His love language is definitely about actions, which is why up and leaving was the only way he could break things off, I suppose.

No, no more of that. The past needs to stay in the past. We're living for the present.

It's not difficult to be in the here and now when he rolls me onto my back, spreading my legs so he can kneel between them. He props himself up with one hand, hovering over me and brushing our noses together. With his other hand, he runs a slippery finger up and down my crack.

"You still like it like this?" he asks.

I'll like it anyway with you, I think. But I simply nod to answer his question. I want to be face to face for this time. I like being on my back with him crowding me. In that way, this is actually similar to last time. But as he kisses my mouth and begins to finger my tight hole, I know in my bones I don't have to worry about him bolting off on this occasion.

He promised to cook me dinner. He's not going to fuck and run.

And this doesn't feel like fucking as he gradually stretches me out and kisses me tenderly. It feels like making love.

I wonder if that's what it really is.

When he eventually suits up and begins to ease his way in, I'm sweating, trembling and panting, alternatively clinging to his shoulders and the bed sheets to keep me grounded. "Shh, it's okay, I've got you," he soothes, although he's not exactly keeping his cool, either. He's red-faced and dripping as he grits his teeth and pushes deeper inside me, grunting like an animal.

He's perfect. I don't want Colton Ross, hotshot lawyer who always has his shit together. I want my Colt, hesitations and fuckups galore. I want the mess and the uncertainty because as long as we stay earnest and curious, I truly believe we could share something more authentic than we've ever experienced before.

I wrap my legs around his waist and kiss him hard as he bottoms out. He nestles himself as far as he can inside me before giving an experimental roll of his hips that makes me moan wantonly into his mouth.

"I'm done waiting," I growl and tug his hair, making him laugh and give me a dazzling smile. "Fuck me, Colt. *Please.*"

"Okay, baby," he murmurs before nipping at my earlobe and thrusting suddenly.

I cry out and cling to him, blinking as I gasp for air. *Baby?* He never called me that when we were teenagers. But that one word now has short-circuited my brain and it's all I can do to cling to him as we begin to writhe.

I've never been anyone's baby before. Yeah, I'm sure guys have said it during sex at some point, but I don't remember a single one of them. They weren't Colt.

As much as I'm trying to be sensible about not jumping into commitment after our complicated history...I really, *really* want to be his baby.

Thankfully, I'm soon too lost in the physical sensation to let my thoughts distract me any longer. He angles my hips and starts nailing my prostate like he never forgot the exact spot even after all the distance between us. We kiss and grunt and hold on to one another like a life raft in a storm.

I can tell he's getting close by the way he's scrunching his nose, which I love because it means that I've remembered his little quirks, too. "Touch me," I beg him. I'm perfectly capable of jerking off my own dick, of course. But we both love it more when he's steering the ship.

His fingers feel like they only wrap around my length for mere seconds before I'm arching my back, gnashing my teeth with my eyes screwed shut as I start blasting ropes of cum all over my belly.

"Oh, fuck, Zee," Colt gasps as he rams even harder into me. "Yes, baby, like that. Fuck, fuck, *fuck...*"

Even through the condom, I feel when his cock starts throbbing and spurting inside me. I hold him against me as we both ride out the shockwaves, vibrating together as the incredible high dissipates.

Regardless of everything I've been feeling and telling myself since we set up this date, as soon as I catch my breath, the worry kicks in and my gaze snaps to Colt.

Who kisses my mouth. Sweetly.

"I'm not going anywhere, I promise," he tells me as he begins to soften inside me.

"This is your place," I whisper.

He chuckles and nuzzles our noses together. "I'm not

kicking you out, either. In fact, I'm going to invite you to shower with me, then I'm going to cook us dinner, and if it's not too bold…please stay the night, Zahir."

My heart skips a beat. Does he really mean that? "I don't have a toothbrush," I blurt out stupidly.

But he just laughs gently again and rests our foreheads together. "I bought a spare today just in case," he tells me.

Out of everything so far this evening, that's possibly what makes my insides flip the most. He was always planning on asking me to stay. He *wants* me to stay.

He wants this. He wants us.

"In that case, I'll stay, then," I tease him. "But dinner better be good."

"If not, there's expensive wine!" he cries before smothering kisses all over my face as I laugh. Finally, he captures my mouth, moving with care and attention. I can feel his heart beating against my chest.

The mess between us is getting cold and his cock must be overly sensitive still inside me. But we don't move to the shower just yet. I think he wants to hold onto this moment as much as I do.

Which is silly, because the way this evening is going suggests it's just the first of many. But I guess we know there's still a shadow on uncertainty looming over us, trying to cloud our sunshine and perfect waves.

We'll deal with the rain when it falls. For now, summer has finally returned.

CHAPTER 17

Colt

I THINK ZAHIR THOUGHT I WAS JOKING WHEN I SUGGESTED WE go surfing together. It's been over a week since our first date where we decided we were going to give this thing between us another try. He's been very patient with me, always agreeing to meet at my place or his. But I meant what I said.

He doesn't deserve to be anybody's secret.

While going a restaurant might be a step too far right now as I navigate how much I want to tiptoe out of the closet, I genuinely don't see any issue with two friends hitting the waves together. So long as I can control myself and not hump him on the damn sand, it should be fine.

Although with how much sex we've had in just under ten days, that might even be asking too much.

Having a date out in the open really isn't, though. I don't just want this to be about fucking and staying in our own private bubble like we did when we were at school. No, I don't feel I can fly my Pride flag any time soon. That doesn't mean we can't go out. We just have to be a little mindful.

My main concern is that Zahir knows I'm not ashamed of him. The realization that he thought I'd dumped him without a second thought or that he'd just been some kind of experiment to me has kept me awake more than a couple of nights. The situation might be complicated, but my feelings for him aren't.

I loved him then and I think I'm falling even more in love with him now.

I'm not sure if he feels the same, and since I'm the one causing the issue, I can't expect him to or put any pressure on him for an answer.

But I can hope.

As it's getting late into Sunday afternoon when we arrive, the beach isn't as crazy as it sometimes gets. I prefer to get here at the crack of dawn and get some time in before work. However, *someone* has been keeping me up at night lately, so now is the best option for both our schedules over the next few days.

Besides, the whole point of this little excursion is for me to show him off a bit. There has to be a few people around for me to do that.

This time, I absolutely wore appropriate attire to get in the water. Having been naked many, many times now, getting changed in front of Zahir isn't an issue anymore, funnily enough.

We don't talk much as we head into the surf, falling into sync like we used to do back in the day when it felt like we lived on this stretch of beach. His presence is so strong and steady beside me, though. As if we've been tethered by that invisible sting all this time, but it's getting brighter and more resilient now.

If one of us pulls away this time, will it break? Or will it snap us back together closer than ever before?

For a while, we ride the waves side by side, and I lose track of when and where we are. This could be today or fifteen years ago. Wanting to appreciate the moment for a minute, I signal to Zahir that I'm going to sit out the next few. He asks if I'm all right and I tell him truthfully that I'm fine.

I just need to watch him in his element right now.

It's wild how he comes alive in different ways. Out on the water, when he's painting, and now I've even seen him when he's at work. He always brings such passion to everything he does, not to mention his compassion, skill, gravitas…

How could anyone not love him?

I'm fully aware he has plenty of people around him that know how special he is. And although it's worked in my favor, I can't believe he never had a serious boyfriend in all this time. But I suppose who I'm really thinking of is my parents.

How can they not see how incredible this man is?

They were always very unsubtle with their disdain for my choice in a best friend when we were at school. My mother used to 'joke' that of all the nice boys in my class, I had to pick Zahir. She didn't like anything about him because all she saw was his skin color, his family's average income, and their religion. But what her and my father hated the most was his softness, I know. They've always been so desperate for me to be what they see as the height of masculinity, an alpha male that other men would admire and follow.

It's crazy to me how they can't see those qualities in Zahir. I think it's obvious that he's far more of a leader than I could ever be. Sure, I put on a good show in the courtroom where I know my stuff. But that's all it is. A *show.* Zahir is never fake. When he speaks, others listen, because it's always from the heart.

Every now and again, my mother makes one of her other 'jokes' that someday I'm going to go into politics and that's why she's so obsessed with my image and me being this inspiring figure head. I'm pretty sure she's manifesting me to become the district attorney by forty then use that as a natural segue into running for governor.

I can't imagine anything worse, so I keep telling myself it's just a joke. But my father's insistence I take over as managing partner from him at the firm is absolutely not a joke, and despite his excellent recovery so far from his heart attack, that timeline seems to still be very much on the fast track.

The Colt that my parents envision isn't the Colt that's currently sitting on a surfboard watching his man masterfully thunder down the tunnel of water as it crashes onto the shore of Redwood Bay. It isn't the Colt that makes chocolate chip pancakes in the morning for that same man, either. It's certainly not the one that baulks at most of his shallow, petty clients these days and can't think of anything more horrifying than being in the public eye.

I'm terrified they won't love that Colt. That they *can't* love him, because he's a betrayal of the Colt they've carefully created. Do I have it in me to take the risk of disappointing them so much it might very well tear our family apart?

I think back to Mrs. Brown and her disinherited grandchildren. How crushed will my parents be if I don't pop out half a dozen kids with a nice girl they've approved? Will they be content for my cousins to continue the Ross name? Not just the name, but the gene line. Somehow, I doubt it.

The thing is, that's *never* going to happen. I'm never going to deceive some poor woman into marrying me, let alone have sex with her enough to produce even one baby. So what are my alternatives? Be lonely? Or be with someone like Zahir?

No, not someone *like* him. Just him.

I almost feel sorry for my father. He thought calling me back home would kickstart the next phase of my life earlier than expected. And I'm sure that my mom firmly believed that if I was close by, she could start meddling in my social life more effectively. But all it's done is thrust me back into Zahir's arms, someone they never have and I'm sure never will approve of, and made me question every single aspect of my life from my career right down to how the hell I am—or am not—decorating my apartment.

The truth is, I'm not sure what's going on with anything or anyone other than Zahir. So long as we can keep seeing each other like we have been this week, I'll be a happy man. Of course, there's no guarantee about how long we can keep this up, either, but I'm choosing not to fret over that today.

Today, I'm going to paddle my board over to my lover and join him on a few more waves before the sun dips too low.

The way he beams when he realizes I'm back beside him makes my heart loop-de-loop like a coaster at the Critter Canyon amusement park they're refurbishing after the incident last year. When it reopens, I want to take Zahir there and get on every single ride, but especially the tunnel of love. That's why those things were created in the first place. So the kids could have a couple of minutes to canoodle without creating a damn scandal. Society is so much more evolved nowadays. Why is it just my parents who are stuck in the dark ages?

When we head back to the shore, I can practically feel Zahir's contentment vibrating off him. There's something so liberating about surfing. It's just you and the water rushing around you. I wish everyone could find a way to feel like that. They'd probably be a lot less stressed.

Speaking of stress levels, mine spike when someone calls out my name just as we're walking back onto land. I know the whole point of this was to not hide the fact that I'm spending time with Zahir. Yet at the same time I didn't expect anyone to actually recognize me out here. What if they challenge me about the nature of our relationship?

Chill, Ross. This is the beach, not open court.

When I turn around, I feel foolish, as there was never anything to worry about. Of all the familiar faces I'd genuinely be pleased to see wandering along the shoreline, Preston Windward is near the top of the list. The only ones above him would probably be Elizabeth and her kids.

My colleague waves casually, coming across as effortlessly cool in that alpha male way my parents definitely want me to exude. Preston, however, is not a douchebag. I'm not sure how he manages it.

He's not alone, I realize. In my defense, it was hard to spot the dog was with him initially due to the way they're racing up and down, leaping as they dig holes in the sand and bite at the water rushing back and forth by their paws.

"Jack, come here," Preston calls with a laugh. The brown and cream dog is medium sized with a solid build that makes me just a little nervous as I haven't been around animals much in my life. But Jack lollops along with his tongue hanging out, and I soon realize that he's just a big, dopy baby.

"Hey, man," I say as Preston approaches with his dog, who has not only come when called, but now sits obediently by Preston's feet, wagging his long tail. "How's it going? Who's this?"

"Yeah, I'm good, I'm good," my colleague says brightly, grinning down at the dog who looks adoringly back up at him. "This is Jack Sparrow. He's a boxer, so he's got a lot of energy that needs running off daily. I only adopted him a couple of months before you arrived, but he's already come on so much."

"He's a rescue?" Zahir asks appreciatively.

Preston nods. "From right here in Redwood Bay. My mom always drilled into me 'adopt, don't shop.' She's got about a dozen fur babies back home on the farm at any given point in time."

"I have some friends who would agree wholeheartedly with you," Zahir says warmly.

Preston's nodding, but then he looks between us, a smile creeping on his face. "Oh, this is your emergency, isn't it, Ross?" His tone is conspiratorial rather than scandalized, however, which I'm relieved by.

I laugh and glance at Zahir. "Sorry, guys. Where are my manners? Zahir, this is one of the other senior partners at Ross & Associates, Preston Windward. Preston, this is my friend Zahir Delacroix. We went to school together. Preston was the one who helped me get out of a meeting to take your videocall when we, well, you know."

Zahir looks at me warmly. "I do know." Then he holds his hand out to Preston, and they shake firmly. "Thank you."

"Any time," Preston says, sounding like he means it.

And just like that, someone I consider a friend more or less knows about me and Zahir. And the world hasn't ended. My father hasn't erupted from under the sand to scream about how I'm a 'flaming faggot' bringing disgrace on our name by flaunting my perversions out in the open.

It feels so damn good.

"Do you surf here much?" Preston asks, subtly changing the conversation.

I nod. "And run. If I can come here before I get into the office, I'm a much more pleasant human being."

"I feel that," Preston scoffs, both managing to agree with me and insult me at the same time. This is why I like him. "You ever fancy some company for a 5K, let me know. I suck at hauling my ass out of bed, so am always on the lookout for a good accountability buddy." He winks at me then turns to Zahir. "If that's cool with you? We could do it together if running's your thing, too? Jack is a great motivator, I promise."

My chest swells that Preston would not only want to include my friend who he only just met, but also be considerate in case he'd misread the vibe.

"That sounds fun," Zahir replies sincerely. "I work shifts, but the pattern is regular, so I could probably tag along from time to time."

"Zahir's a paramedic," I tell Preston, my heart bursting with pride.

Preston nods and claps Zahir on the shoulder. "Wow, that's a real goddamned calling. How did someone who's basically an angel end up with a devil like Colt here?"

"I'm so an angel," I say with a pout.

"Oh, he's a devil all right," Zahir quips to Preston like they're in cahoots. But then all color drains from his face. "On t-the waves, I mean. Uh—"

I touch his elbow, feeling oddly calm. "It's okay, baby," I say, deliberately using the new nickname that I'm fully aware makes him melt into a puddle. I don't want to hide in front of Preston, but I do glance at him to make sure that we're still cool. If we're not, we're not. I'll be sad, and he could make my life hell at the office if he felt like it. But I don't want Zahir shrinking away like he did just now.

Preston snorts. "I have no doubt this asshole fucks like he fights in closing arguments. Fast and dirty. Good job you're a trained medic, huh?" He adds a wink.

There's a tense moment where I don't think Zahir or I can believe this interaction just happened. Then I burst out laughing, decades of relief bubbling their way out all at once.

"Douchebag," I snipe, taking back what I thought about him earlier, if only in jest. I whack his arm, which makes Jack bark and start dancing around us.

Finally, Zahir laughs as well, clearly relieved and probably a little shocked.

"Anyway, I better keep going with this monster," Preston says fondly, giving some subtle signal to Jack, who instantly races off again, picking squabbles with the surf. "It was great to meet you, Zahir. I'm serious about that running thing, Ross. Let's make it happen."

"See you tomorrow, *douchebag*," I tell him fondly and, without thinking on my part, we share half a hug with a backslap. That's certainly never happened before, but it felt right in the moment. He goes along with it and doesn't seem to think it was strange.

Perhaps we are genuinely friends now, not just work acquaintances?

Zahir and I watch him wander off as the sun slips a little farther behind the trees. Then I turn to face Zahir, and he raises his eyebrows at me.

"So…that happened," he prompts. I nod and hum. "How do you feel about it?"

I take a deep breath and huff it out again before lifting my hand between us, wiggling my fingers in an invitation. "Really fucking good," I inform him with a grin.

He looks from my face to my hand, then slowly reaches out to accept it.

There we go. We're two men holding hands out in the open. It's pretty clear to anyone who might see us what that probably means. But at least right now, I don't care. I feel invincible.

"Was that the first time you came out to anyone?" Zahir asks, sounding a little awestruck.

I shrug. "Did I really come out?"

Zahir chuckles and squeezes my hand. "Maybe not technically with all the words. Maybe you're still in the closet, but you just opened the door and waved your feather boa at him."

That makes me properly laugh, and we separate so we can pick up our boards from the sand and start making our way back to his place. "I don't think I'm ever going to be a feather boa gay, but I'll defend anyone who is pro bono."

"Oh, give it time," he says. The light may be fading, but his smile is luminescent. "Wait until we go to your first Pride parade."

For a split second, the idea feels me with fear, simply because that's how I've felt my whole life. Being gay hasn't been something I could celebrate. It was something I hid in shame.

But not anymore. At least, not all the time. Not most of the time, in fact.

That's not even what dismisses the fear as soon as it's surfaced, though. What scares it away is the fact that Zahir said 'when' not 'if.'

When we go to my first Pride. Like it's an inevitable thing.

Like he's seeing a future for us the way I'm trying to.

The details are hazy, but the hope is strong. Perhaps that's all we need?

CHAPTER 18

Zahir

COLT CAME OUT TO SOMEONE.

He really did it.

I thought going out in public together was a big enough step, but he just…did that.

I'm still wrestling with the guilt of putting my foot in it. I honestly don't know what came over me to jeopardize his privacy like that. Not once when we were teenagers did I ever come close to doing something in that way.

When I talked with him about it afterward, though, he suggested that subconsciously I sensed not only was his friend Preston someone safe, but he himself was ready to take that next step. He said if he'd really wanted to, he could have run with him being a devil in a non-sexual context, so in the end it was still his decision to confirm our relationship and therefore his not-straight status. I'm still not comfortable with what I did, but Colt says it's all good, so I have to trust him and move on.

And I do trust him, something I thought would never happen again after he left. But he's worked hard, and he's earned it, which is a relief because carrying around all that resentment and bitterness for so long was bringing me down.

There's a lightness in my step now. The guys at work have made comments and are constantly speculating on mine and Colt's relationship status, but I've left it to their imaginations so far. Like with Preston, if Colt has something he wants to share with them, he'll do so when the time is right.

Even just the thought of introducing them all formally makes my head spin. The idea that I could be with Colt and not have to guard it like a state secret is liberating.

There's a sensible part of me that knows we're not out of the woods yet and we've still got a long road ahead of us. But no relationship starts off with absolute certainty. In fact, there's no guarantee how long anyone has with their loved ones, whether that's because people change or realize they've made a mistake about their compatibility or because fate intervenes and pulls them apart whether they like it or not. I see every shift how fickle life can be.

It feels good to finally be taking charge of my own destiny after so long lingering in the background of my own story.

Not just with regards to Colt, either. For the first time in I don't even know how long, I've dug out my little portable paint palette. It only has eight colors, but the other side has space to slot in some cardstock and there's a loop on the spine to hold a small brush with a lid, and the whole thing folds in half so it can neatly slip in my pocket. My teta got it for me years ago as a birthday present, but I never even considered using it.

Until now.

I've set myself up on a bench in the redwood forest the town was named after. Considering these mighty trees aren't native to southern California, I feel blessed that so much effort was put in several decades ago to man-make and maintain this ecological spectacle. Obviously, they aren't as tall as the ones you find up north, but they're still vastly different to chaparral shrubland and palm trees in the rest of the region. There's something uniquely calming about being surrounded by these giants.

The air is cooler and slightly more moist up here, and the shade offers respite from the beaming sunshine. The forest dampens any sound, too, so it's a great place to come and unwind. I breathe in deeply.

As I capture simple scenes with my brush, my thoughts drift freely. Naturally, Colt is at the forefront of my mind. I try not to dwell on our more intimate moments because I don't want to embarrass myself in public. However, it's tricky not to. We might not be hormone-riddled teenagers anymore, but we're still having sex every chance we get. I think without saying it, we're both trying to make up for the years we lost.

It's not just that, though. It's the way he sneaks out of bed to make me coffee in the morning. It's the silly memes he sends me every day. It's the way he spends more time looking at me when we watch movies together than at the screen.

It's the way he's making me believe in a future together.

Of course, my grandma has noticed my change in demeanor, but she suspiciously hasn't asked any questions about it. She just comments every now and again saying how well I look or how cheerful I am. The fact that she hasn't asked if I've met someone tells me that she knows it's Colt that's having this effect on me. But I'm too nervous to ask her outright if she's okay with it.

Because she probably isn't.

To her, he's still the bad boy who broke my young and fragile heart. I'm sure she's convinced he'll do it again. Part of me is aware she could have a point. Just because he doesn't want to, doesn't mean it's not going to happen. He's hardwired to please his parents. There's nothing about me that's pleasing to them, I know. Even if I was a woman, I'd be a poor social match for their son in more ways than one.

The fact that I am a man is the most glaring objection, but I can't help but think they'd have less of a problem if grand-kids were still a possibility. I'm not sure what Colt thinks about becoming a parent. That feels like a Big Conversation that we're not ready to have just yet. But I love kids and have I've considered adoption a lot over the years. Surrogacy could also be an option. However, there are so many kids out there in the world already in desperate need of loving homes, I can see myself being drawn in that direction.

Who knows if that's a path I'm destined to take? Insha'Allah. If he wills it, then maybe one day. But for now, it's enough to content myself with the present, which I'm easily drawn back into as a little face suddenly pops up in my line of sight, as if summoned by my latest thoughts.

"Whatcha doin'?" the small boy asks, pointing at my pocket palette.

I smile at his innocent curiosity. "I'm painting a picture," I tell him, turning it around to show him my woodland scene. The child's jaw drops open.

"You did that?" he squeaks in disbelief.

I nod, then glance around, wondering who he's with as he can't be all the way up here by himself. He's got to only be four or five years old. Sure enough, there's a man sprinting toward us down the path with two brown terriers on leashes scampering excitedly beside him.

"Noah, what are you doing?" he cries in a panic. I smile and give him a wave in what I hope to be a reassuring manner.

"He was just asking about my picture," I tell the man I assume to be this boy's father, also showing him what I've been up to. "Did he slip away from you?"

The man stops in front of me and puffs as the dogs lick the boy, making him giggle. "Yeah," says the dad. "I swear he's going to be a running back when he's big enough to hold a ball." The man ruffles his son's hair. "Or maybe he'll be a chef and just run after his kids like he makes his folks do. Who knows."

I like this guy's attitude. "I guess that's the fun with having children. It's a surprise how they turn out."

"Every day is a surprise," the man agrees. "You have any yourself?"

I smile, reflecting on my musings just now. "Not yet, but maybe one day."

"Well, it's never a dull moment," he says with a laugh. "Come on, Noah. Let's leave the nice man to his painting. It's awesome, by the way."

I glance down at the scene I've been capturing. It looks quite basic to my eyes, but I smile and accept the compliment the way it was intended. "Thank you."

I watch the four of them walking away, the dad explaining to his son about why it's important to stay near him and stranger danger, which is totally fair. He had no idea if I was bad news or not.

The encounter still leaves me feeling warm and hopeful. I'm not convinced I believe in signs, per se. But having a small child pop up just as I was contemplating parenthood certainly feels like the universe might be giving me a little nudge.

It's wild to think that just a few short weeks ago I was furious at Colt's reappearance in my life and now I'm seriously considering a future together that could involve building a family. I'm not sure if that's what he wants or if he'd even consider it, but in that moment, something becomes clear to me.

If he's going to commit to us, that will probably involve

some drastic upheaval in his life. Will he really consider that seriously if he's not certain how I feel? I've been so terrified of being vulnerable and wearing my heart on my sleeve, but how can I expect him to risk such big sacrifices if I don't put my cards on the table and make sure he knows I'm all in? By protecting myself, I could be giving him doubt that will just lead to us unravelling again.

I can't ask him to be brave if I'm not willing to do the same.

Looking down at my little painting, an idea strikes me. If his love language is action, then maybe that's how I need to communicate with him. I could tell him I love him. Those words are long overdue to be spoken out loud anyway.

Or I could show him.

I make sure the palette is dry enough before closing it, standing up, and stretching. If I'm going to paint him something, it's going to be the beach, and it's going to be on bigger sized paper with more than eight colors. The beach has always been our special place, but it's also where destiny brought us back to each other a few weeks ago. I'm going to bare my soul to him exactly the way I used to do, but for the first time, I'm going to paint specifically for him as a gift that I want him to hang on his wall. It's up to him if he takes it down when his parents visit. That's his journey to go on. But I want a way to show him that I'm not just committed to him, but that he's bringing out the best in me.

We're never going to move forward if he's constantly reliving how he hurt and betrayed me in the past.

The idea of exposing my belly like this scares me. I'm not going to let that stop me, though. Yara and my teta will probably warn me that I'm taking a huge gamble or even making a big mistake. But I know Colt is the one for me. If I let him slip through my fingers because I'm too afraid of getting hurt again, not only will I *definitely* get hurt again, but I'll also never forgive myself.

I don't want Colt to look back on his life with remorse, and I don't want that for me, either. So it's with purpose that I walk back down the path to where I parked my car, ready to swap redwoods and dirt for palm trees and sand.

When Colt first reappeared in town, my fear came from allowing him to have power over my heart again. But the power is all mine. I'm going to make it clear how I feel and where I stand. What he does after that is up to him.

Life is too short or too long. Whichever way you look at it, I don't want to waste any more time, especially when it comes to Colton Ross.

CHAPTER 19

Colt

As I step out of my car at the storage facility, I'm buzzing from head to toe. Like, my whole body is vibrating with glee.

When Zahir came over to my place last night, he brought a present with him. A series of three small paintings he'd done on the beach of people surfing that he specifically wanted me to put up in my apartment. I could tell that he was nervous about this request, but as soon as I managed to swallow the lump in my throat, I'd sprung up to find the adhesive picture frame strips I'd already bought to hang up my photographs from New York.

As I'm only renting right now, I can't go banging holes in the walls. But I'm seriously over the lack of personality in that place, so you bet those paintings were on display in a matter of minutes. Zahir pointed out sticking them down like that would make them harder to take down if I had any company over. I assured him that if I have company, I'll tell them my *boyfriend* painted those pieces *for* me.

After his brain unfroze from me using the B-word, we had sex for about six hours, and he called me *his* boyfriend every chance he got. Twenty-four hours later, I'm still giddy with excitement, which led me to come here.

If he's all in on this relationship, then so am I. That means I'm staying in Redwood Bay and I need to start acting like it. I'm not sure if I'm going to keep all the bland stuff I currently have in my storage locker. However, I'm freshly motivated to sort it all out and get rid of anything that I previously purchased in an attempt to hide who I really am.

Then I'm going to replace those things in colors and styles that say something about my true self. I refuse to keep passing over furnishings that might be considered even a little bit gay.

I'm a little bit gay. I'm a *lot* gay. It's ridiculous that in the twenty-first century I've felt like I had to conceal that for so long. If my parents turn their noses up at anything in my home, then they don't get to visit. It's that simple. I'm done trying to be their perfect alpha male.

The only other time I've been here was to drop everything off, so I remind myself of my unit number then follow the arrows that lead me in the right direction. I pass a couple of people milling around at their own locker spaces and nod in hello, but mostly, it's as quiet as I would expect for a Thursday evening.

Until I turn a corner and suddenly come face to face with someone it takes me a second to place. Her eyebrows shoot up in immediate recognition, though.

"Colton Ross?"

The older woman is barely above five foot and has a scarf draped loosely over her head and around her shoulders. It's that context that eventually makes me clock who I'm standing in front of.

"Farah?" I splutter. "I mean—Mrs. Delacroix! I mean—as-salamu alaykum." I touch my hands together and bow ever so slightly, hoping I haven't completely mangled my pronunciation.

"Wa-'alaykumu salam," Zahir's grandma replies, tilting her head and looking me up and down. "You look well. It's been a long time."

I shift guiltily on my feet. Of course she was going to bring up the fact that I left town and ghosted her grandson the first chance she got. I don't blame her. Zahir wasn't the only one I neglected to say goodbye to. Farah was always so kind, making sure I felt welcome every single time I went to her house—which was a lot, probably more than Zahir's parent's place—and never let me leave unfed. She was warmer to me than my own parents or extended family ever were.

"You look well, too," I say, trying not to let my awkwardness get the better of me. But all I can think of is that I want to say I'm sorry, but I don't know if that will be opening a can of worms.

Farah doesn't look flustered like I feel. She's studying me with narrowed eyes, her hands resting on the top of her purse that she has slung around her body. Other than a few more lines and grayer hair, she looks just the way I remember her. I'm glad she was there for Zahir when I couldn't be.

When I chose not to be.

"So you're back in Zahir's life," she says eventually, cutting to the chase.

"Um, yes, ma'am," I say. I'm not sure what to do with my hands, so I shove them in my pockets. "I know what happened before…after we left school…honestly, it was unforgivable." I exhale and decide that if we're not dancing around the issue, I'm just going to go all in. "Zahir and I have talked a lot and I've apologized many times. I didn't think he should be allowed to forgive me, but you know what he's like."

Her face softens a little as a smile tweaks at the corner of her mouth. "I do know what he's like. As stubborn as he is kind."

It's my turn to laugh as I nod. "That's very true. Mrs. Delacroix...I take full responsibility for the great harm I caused your grandson in the past. I was extremely unfair to him. It's not an excuse, but I was just a kid myself and I didn't know how to handle the situation better. But I do now."

"Oh?" she says, raising her eyebrows.

I glance around, but nobody else seems to be in the area. It feels strange to be standing in an alley of fluorescent green garage doors, sparse concrete underfoot as the evening sun beams down overhead. I wish we were in her back yard—she always had such colorful flowers—drinking sweet mint tea like the old days. But this is where we ran into each other, so this is where it's going down, I guess.

"I know actions speak louder than words," I continue explaining, "so I intend to keep proving this to Zahir and to you as well if necessary. But he's everything to me. I...I love him. I want to build a life with him. He makes me a better person by bringing out the real me. I've spent most of my life pretending to be something I'm not, but I think that's over now. Because of him. He's amazing and I want to treat him the way he deserves, for as long as he'll let me."

We just stare at each other for a moment, then this formidable but tiny woman sighs and rests her hand on my arm. "Ahh, Colt," she says, shaking her head. "You were both just babies, weren't you? I won't lie. I cursed your name...a *lot*." There's a flash in her eyes that lets me know how true that must have been. "Only because I hated seeing my darling boy so sad. But now?" She sighs again, and this time she gives me a wry smile and wags a finger at me. "Now, he's happy all the time. He's light and dreamy, like when he was a small boy. Did you know he started painting again?"

My heart wants to burst I'm so full of love and pride for my man. "That's actually why I'm here, Mrs. Delacroix. He made me a triptych for my new apartment. The thing is… well, I'm not very good at decorating. I've been afraid to express myself and then Zahir admitted he wasn't painting anymore. I told him if I could display anything it would be some of his art. So he created the three pictures for me to hang up and…it's like we're both coming back to who we were, you know? But with the benefit of maturity and wisdom we didn't have before."

She rests her hand on her chest and blinks at me a few times. "That's wonderful to hear, truly."

I nod and chuckle, feeling slightly lightheaded from the relief of finally talking to someone about this. "I have a bunch of stuff here that I haven't put in the apartment yet. Seeing Zahir's new paintings up, it made me feel inspired to settle in properly. But then I ran into you, and it feels a bit like fate is intervening."

She hums and pats my arm again. "You might say that. Are you in a rush?"

"Not particularly, ma'am."

"Excellent, follow me."

She takes me farther into the storage site, apparently confident in knowing the way we're headed. She waves around her key like a conductor's baton before we finally stop in front of one of the units.

"Let me help you with that," I say, but she waves me off.

"I've got it, don't you worry." She grins as the lock pops open, then she shoves up the roller door with a flourish.

It's clear she's got some of her own furniture here. I remember Zahir saying she'd downsized a few years ago. But

I can tell right away that most of the space is being used for one thing only.

Zahir's art.

I gasp as I step inside, marveling at all the canvases from large to small. "He thought you'd given these away," I say, turning around absently to try and look at them all, but many of them are stacked together against the walls, so it's going to take a while. My heart leaps as I spot a couple I recognize.

Farah blows a raspberry. "He never asked, I noticed. But no, of course not. As if I could get rid of his best work? It's all here, safe and sound, waiting for the day I knew he would want it again."

There's a lump in my throat and my eyes are a little damp as I move from painting to painting, overwhelmed with joy. Seeing these creations preserved suddenly makes me feel like the last shadows of guilt are finally leaving my heart. I hated that he stopped painting, but I just accepted that the hours he'd poured into these pieces had been wasted and they were gone forever, taking parts of his soul with him. I feel like I'm looking at his hopes and dreams, his innocence and aspirations, pure moments from the time we spent together, before I had to go and spoil it all.

"This is amazing," I say, reaching out to carefully touch the edge of a particularly large one that I remember he got an A for in our senior year. His teacher had even talked about organizing a little exhibition for him with this as the centerpiece, but he hadn't been interested. He'd insisted that he painted for himself and for me and that was it. He didn't want strangers judging his work or trying to interpret the bold patterns and swirling shapes.

I tilt my head and gently lean the canvases in front of it away so I can see the rest of the work better. Like all his best stuff, it's pretty abstract and surreal. But I swear now with fresh eyes it looks to me like the two of us in the throws of passion on our beloved stretch of shoreline.

Perhaps that's just me projecting my subconscious thoughts and it's actually just a boat or a seagull or something. I guess that's the beauty of art—it's in the eye of the beholder. If I want to see a sweet and tender scene of us making love, then quite frankly, that's what it is. To me, anyway.

"Thank you for showing me this," I say thickly, turning to look at Farah. She's watching me with her hands clasped in front of her chest.

"No, thank you, Colt," she says, stepping closer. "You said your actions would speak louder than words, and I can see it's as clear as day how much you treasure my habibi. I'm glad you came back to us."

I swallow around the lump and look at all the gorgeous pieces. "I think this is where I belong, Mrs. Delacroix. In Redwood Bay. With Zahir. We've both been hiding ourselves away for long enough now. His soul is too beautiful not to be sharing it with the world. He's already brightened up my life so much in just a few weeks. If I need to kick his ass to express himself again, I will." I wince. "Uh, sorry for cussing."

She chuckles and pats my back as she moves to inspect a couple of paintings herself. "I just wish I could offer him this area to paint. But they have strict rules about flammable products and having the correct ventilation."

She sighs and runs her thumb over a particularly thick swoosh of purple oil paint, hardened over time.

Something sparks within me and I step back, my gaze sweeping over the contents in the room.

"Mrs. Delacroix," I say, the giddiness I was feeling before returning twice as strong. "I reckon I'm overdue for a big romantic gesture. What do you think?"

"Oh, that sounds fun," she says with a cackle.
I couldn't agree more.

CHAPTER 20

Zahir

"ARE YOU EVER GOING TO TELL ME WHERE WE'RE GOING?" I grumble, even though there's no bite in my words. I can tell Colt knows this by how he grins at me.

"Are you ever going to understand the concept of a *surprise*? Be chill. We're basically there now."

He pulls his car into an industrial complex I'm not sure I've been to before, which is unusual considering how work has pulled me all over town throughout the years.

It looks like one of those areas that used to be factories and warehouses but got shut down during one of the recessions in the eighties or nineties. It appears the space in is the process of being split up and sold off to be repurposed. As we drive down the central road, I see an accounting firm, a T-shirt printing business, a nail salon, and a pet grooming parlor.

I wonder if he's brought me here to tell me he's setting up his own practice to put some distance between him and his father. That's probably selfish of me, but he seems so excited, I feel like this has to be something kind of big for it to make him so jubilant. It's a shame that I think getting out from under his parents' control would make him happy, but I don't think there's any point in sugarcoating it, especially if I'm just thinking it to myself.

In any case, I'm not going to say anything one way or the other until I know where our destination is. We could be going to an escape room or laser tag or one of those places that you get into giant inflatable balls and run around. I have no idea what's on the other side of this complex. There could be open fields or forestland or a damn quarry for all I know.

It strikes me that I don't get many surprises in my life, and I'm nervous. Colt leaving me like he did at a formative age left me feeling insecure about a lot of things. It seemed at the time like he was the only person in the world who really knew me. So no wonder I've spent most of my life avoiding situations that would make me anxious. The station therapist we all check in with regularly was pleased when I pieced that together on my own a couple of years ago.

Knowing this about myself hasn't stopped me from rejecting change and being resistant to the unpredictable. My job has enough surprises every day, but my training and experience makes me feel prepared for that. In my everyday life though…yeah, no wonder I never wanted to go speed dating when Yara tried to set me up or join in with Sawyer and Anton's spontaneous plans. In my defense, sometimes those plans have later involved bailing Sawyer out of jail, so I stand by my reluctance there.

Right now, I don't want that old baggage clouding an experience that Colt is clearly enthusiastic about. He's been playfully secretive about something for the last couple of weeks, and I assume this is the culmination of that effort. I don't want my apprehension to make me come across as ungrateful.

Because what have I been reminding myself of over these past several weeks? That I trust Colt. He's given me his heart again and I have to let him have mine if this relationship is ever going to have a chance at growing into something bigger and long-term.

So yes, I trust him. I know he's not tricking me right now. Wherever we're going and whatever we're doing, he thinks it's something I'll enjoy. Even if he's missed the mark, it'll be the thought that counts.

It's taken me a hot minute to get used to the idea that Colt thinks about me as much as I think about him. I'm having to re-write all my old assumptions in my head. They've been there a decade and a half, so switching off the knee-jerk reactions is going to take time. But Colt cares about me a lot. I know this from all the big and little things he does for me.

So while I might not be able to completely sweep away my nerves, I can at least keep a lid on them. I'll soon know what's going on, then hopefully I can relax.

Finally, Colt swings into one of the parking lots and kills the engine. He turns and looks at me, practically vibrating. "Ready?"

"Ready if you are," I tell him sincerely.

He unbuckles and hops out the car, running around to open my door before I get the chance. Once he's locked his car, he grabs my hand and tugs me toward the front door of the rather gray building we're apparently going inside.

As he punches in a security code he double-checks on his phone, I see a sign that reads 'Monarch Studios.' For a brief moment as I follow him inside, I wonder if it's a photography studio and he wants to prove his commitment by doing a couple's photoshoot. Then I wonder if it's a recording studio and he wants me to sing.

Then I realize how ridiculous both those ideas are and

shake my head as we go up a flight of stairs. Maybe it's a dance studio and he wants us to learn something together. That might actually be quite romantic, but surely he'd have told me to wear comfortable clothes if that was the case, and he didn't.

I'm so preoccupied by my thoughts that I almost bump into him when he stops. He's holding up a key and for the first time since he picked me up, he looks a little nervous. "Um, this is for you. It's yours. But if you don't like it, we can change it up or get rid of it or..." He huffs and shakes his head. "Sorry. I steamrollered into this and now I'm scared it was a terrible idea."

My heart melts and I step closer to gently kiss his lips. "I'm sure whatever it is, it will be wonderful because it's from you."

He lets out a tiny, relieved whimper and nudges his nose against mine. "Okay," he says breathlessly. "I suppose I should just open the door and let you see, huh?"

"Sure," I tell him, rubbing the side of his arm to give him some reassurance. His nerves tell me he's put a lot of thought into whatever's waiting on the other side of the door. The fact that he cares so much is all that really matters to me.

With a final nod, he jams the key in the door, unlocks it, and swings it inside, gesturing for me to go in first.

What strikes me first are the enormous windows that stretch from the high ceiling down to the wooden work benches opposite me, letting in so much natural light. The floor is laminated, and the white walls have an industrial, slightly distressed finish to them that matches the silver lamps and exposed piping overhead where a fan is spinning, keeping the room cool.

I absorb all this in a second or two. After that, my brain latches on to what's in the room...what it's being used for.

My art.

At least a dozen of my paintings have been hung up, with more propped up on the floor against the walls and some standing in easels. I recognize my old stand from my teta's conservatory when I used to work at her place, but the others look new. Maybe not brand new, but hardly used and certainly unfamiliar to me.

"How did you…? Where…?" I try and ask faintly, looking back at Colt.

He lets the door close behind him and moves to stand in front of me, pressing the key into my hand. "Your grandma kept all your important pieces," he explains. "In a storage locker in town. The same place all my stuff used to be."

I blink at him. "You're telling me you did this with my teta?"

He nods bashfully. "We ran into each other and a plan just sort of formed. Well, more of a scheme, maybe. A mission. Where do you think all the potted plants came from?"

I was so stunned that I didn't even notice. But now he's pointed them out, there are at least half a dozen pots spotted around the place, from large leafy ones on the floor to pretty, colorful flowers on the windowsill. They make the place feel almost like a conservatory. I don't know what its purpose was when this place was a factory, but this room is the most perfect, incredible art studio I could imagine. Even the view from the window overlooks one of the few patches of grass I saw in the area.

"You have a sink over there, see," Colt says, continuing to give a tour from where we're standing in the middle of the room. "I'm not sure I'd recommend drinking the water, but it's good enough for cleaning brushes." He chuckles, then directs my attention to some new looking drawers. "We stocked some things up in there, like paints, pencils, a couple of different thicknesses of papers, but we figured you'd probably want to pick your own stuff, so there's plenty of space for that. And the brushes are all in those jars on that table there. Farah said that was the best way to store them. I, um, even installed Bluetooth speakers that you can connect your phone to if you want to listen to music or podcasts while you work."

He blushes, perhaps because saying it out loud is making him realize just how enormous this gesture of his is. Of all the things I was expecting, they don't even come close to the reality I'm looking around at now.

"Colt, I…" my voice is too weak to finish the sentence. "This can't all be mine? It's too much. I…"

He squeezes my hands tighter so I can feel the key pressing into my skin. "I paid five years rent upfront," he says softly, as if that isn't a breathtaking bombshell to drop. "If it's not right or whatever, I have permission to sublet it. But I'd love nothing more than for it to be yours, so if there are things you want to change, we can do that. The landlady said you can even paint murals on the walls if you feel like it. She'd just probably have to cover them up if she needed to look for another tenant."

This is so overwhelming. I can't stop staring at it all. Colt didn't just orchestrate this for me. He conspired with my grandma to do it. It makes me feel seen and important in a way I've never experienced before.

"The sofa?" I ask, because that's apparently the level of vocabulary I'm capable of right now.

He juts his chin at the soft-looking ocean-blue couch. "In case you need a break. Or in case I want to come hang here with you while you work."

I raise my eyebrows at him. "Really?"

He lets go of my hands to hug me, tucking my forehead against his neck. "Yeah, baby. I love watching you create magic. And I love being surrounded by your pieces. You, um, might notice there are a couple missing."

He sounds guilty, and I glance around at all the canvases. I can't see some of the ones that are propped up on the floor, but honestly, it's been so long since I saw my old work that I'm not familiar with them anymore. "Did they get damaged?"

Colt laughs, but not unkindly. "No. Your grandma kept a couple to hang in her place, and I took a big one for mine. We agreed that if you wanted them back, of course you can do whatever you want with them. But seeing as you thought they'd been given away years ago, we thought you'd be okay if they lived with us instead."

He's right. I don't need everything here. I've forgotten painting half this stuff. But the idea they liked something so much they wanted to hold onto it stirs pride within me. What's the point of creating beauty if it's not going to be appreciated, after all?

I think in the midst of my sadness, I forgot that. These pieces are so tied into mine and Colt's relationship, I always felt I had to hide them when we were at school, like we hid ourselves.

But we're not doing that anymore.

"Which ones did you guys keep?" I ask, genuinely curious.

"Farah has a couple that you did of her old garden," Colt tells me, and that immediately makes me happy.

"That's why I painted them," I say with a small laugh. "I knew one day she'd move out of the big house, and she wouldn't be able to take all the stunning landscaping work she'd done with her. I'm surprised she didn't claim them before."

"I don't think she felt she was allowed to," he says gently to me, and he probably has a point.

"And you?"

He looks slyly at me. "There was that huge one you got an A on, right before we graduated. It's mostly black and white lines with splashes of blue and yellow."

Of course that's the one he picked. "You know that was me capturing us making love on the beach, right?"

He bites his lower lip and grins, color rising on his cheeks. "I had a feeling."

I'm kissing him before I even realize it. But I guess it's okay, because he's kissing me right back. "That one's yours, anyway," I mumble against his lips. "It was always yours. Colt, this place is incredible. I love it. I...it's the most thoughtful thing anyone's ever done for me."

"Phew," he says with a nervous laugh. I pull back to look at him properly and he keeps talking. "I wasn't sure if I was going to be opening a can of worms. You started painting again—you gave me that triptych—so I hoped it was something that you were enjoying again. But I was worried it could equally set off a trauma reaction or something."

Bless his heart. I kiss his cheek. "Nothing but gratitude and happiness here, I promise."

He touches my hair then cradles my jaw. "I want you to be free, Zahir. The way you've made me feel free. I want you to bear your soul for the world to see. It's too beautiful to keep hidden away."

"So are you," I say earnestly, feeling overcome by his words. "I...Colt. Will you let me paint you?"

"Like one of your French girls?" he quips. I can see the vulnerability in his eyes.

But, yes, that's exactly what I want.

"Not for the world to see," I assure him. "Not if that's something you don't want. But for me. I'd like you to be my first subject in this beautiful sanctuary. Please."

He swallows, his eyes shimmering in the light streaming from the windows. "I'd be honored," he whispers.

Without speaking, I gently steer him toward the sofa until we're standing beside it. Then I make short work of divesting him of his clothes before easing him down on the couch. When he's lying down, I drape one hand above his head and place the other on his stomach, then move his legs so one is hooked over the sofa arm and the other is resting on the floor.

"Comfy?" I ask. He nods, looking up at me reverently. "You look so beautiful," I murmur.

His body is already a work of art. But there's a history there, too. A scar I remember him getting from climbing out his bedroom window one time to see me. Another I don't know anything about. Tan lines from surfing with me recently. Muscles he's built up over the years to become the strong man he is today.

I've positioned him like this to display his cock prominently. He's not entirely soft, but still mostly relaxed, which is what I wanted. After so long in the closet, I was concerned this might be too much for him. But he looks completely at ease. In fact, he seems a little punch drunk as he smiles up at me.

"You make me feel beautiful, baby," he says. "You're my ocean."

I bend down and kiss his lips. "You're my sunshine," I mumble against them.

Before I can get carried away, I move back and look for what supplies are close at hand. Perfect. There's a new pack of charcoal pencils on the table, and it takes me no time to find the right kind of paper in the drawers to put on one of the easels. Once I'm set up, I meet Colt's gaze and begin unbuttoning my shirt.

The only sounds in the air are the overhead fan and both our heavy breaths. I don't know if either of us even blinks until I'm as naked as he is, and I'm glad this studio is on the second floor where no one can peer through the windows at us.

This moment is just between me and my man.

I move to the easel and start sketching, capturing Colt's prone form quickly in bold strokes. Then I move on to filling in a few details like his gorgeous eyes, nose and lips, several strands of his soft hair, and his budded nipples.

Until there's just one thing I haven't drawn.

I lick my lips, meeting his gaze. I'm pretty sure he's been quietly watching me during the few minutes I've been working. "Touch yourself," I instruct him, my voice hoarse.

He doesn't even hesitate or look away. He just lowers the hand from his stomach to wrap around his cock, swiping his thumb over his tip, making it shine with pre-cum.

"Like this, baby?"

My heart is hammering, and my own cock is thickening. "Yeah," I grunt, flicking the charcoal over the page, immediately bringing to life his hardening length and the way he's pleasuring himself. It's raw and fluid and beautiful.

This is Colton Ross. He might not be able to come out to everyone, but this is me helping him come out to himself and the universe. He's stunning and I won't let him hide away any longer.

As soon as I'm happy I've got what I need, I move away from the easel. I plan on adding a lot of shading and more details later. But right now, I desperately need to feel Colt under me.

He just watches as I approach, naturally dropping his hand and giving me space to straddle him. His cock is rock hard and leaking now, and for a second, I revel in rubbing myself against him as I capture his mouth for a filthy kiss.

But I've still got the charcoal in my hand. I did that on purpose. So before we can get too carried away, I lean back and study Colt's chest as it rises up and down, looking at the perspiration beading on his skin. My palms are already mucky, but I rub even more black dust over them. Then I press one against the side of his neck and the other over his heart, kissing him again as I do.

After I've left handprints on both those spots, I take the stick of charcoal and start outlining under his pecs, around his dusky pink nipples, and along his cum gutters.

"I told you that you were a work of art," I say, smudging the lines with my fingers. We're still pressed together, and I can feel his cock throbbing against mine.

"Sign me," Colt says, completely seriously. It's silly, but in that moment, it feels so sexy as I use the blunted pencil, pressing down hard as I scribble my signature over his hip.

That seems to do something to him. Something feral. The second I'm finished, he knocks the charcoal from my hand, then grabs the back of my neck to crash our mouths together in a fierce kiss. With his other hand, he circles both our leaking members and starts jerking us off, hard. I moan and rut against him, and it's clear neither of us are going to last long.

Sure enough, within minutes he starts spurting sticky white cum all over his chest, and I follow shortly after. I'm a trembling, sweaty mess, but I still have enough strength to prop myself up and swirl my fingers through the gunk, mixing it with the charcoal and painting him even more.

"Beautiful," I utter.

He threads his fingers through my hair and caresses my scalp. "Only because you make me beautiful."

I shake my head. "I just let it out. It was always there, Colton Ross. My sunshine."

I want to tell him I love him, but the moment is so raw and vulnerable, I can't bring myself to take that final step just yet.

Soon, though.

For now, I just drink in the sculpture of a man between my legs, grateful to the millions of moments that brought us here to this one. I'm glad I captured it on canvas. Is it possible that we'll be able to look back together at that sketch in years to come?

I hope so.

CHAPTER 21

Colt

WHEN MY FATHER ASKED ME TO MEET HIM FOR LUNCH ON Friday afternoon, I naïvely assumed it was to meet a new client. To be fair, I've been drifting through work like a zombie lately, so it's not that much of a surprise that I didn't analyze the circumstances more thoroughly.

Either way, when I rock up at the fancy sushi place a few minutes earlier than I thought the meeting was supposed to start, I'm confused when I see my mom wave at me from across the room. The space is relatively big and crowded, leaving the impression that she angled herself specifically so she had a clear line of sight so she could watch the front entrance.

That certainly seems like something my mom would do.

My first thought is that the lighting is artfully low, and the restaurant only has windows at the very front of the building in order to maintain the intimate atmosphere. So perhaps it's just another lady who looks like my mom in the moody setting.

But why would that woman wave at me? I figure it must be my mom, after all, and this has to be a coincidence. *Then* I quickly realize that my father is sitting next to her, so it can't be.

What the hell is going on?

I pass a server as he lights someone's salmon dish on fire right in front of him. The food in general smells amazing and I like the tranquil music playing quietly through the room. If my stomach hadn't suddenly tied itself in knots, I'd have said this place has my kind of vibe.

Carefully, I weave through the tables and head around the circular bar with a huge artificial Sakura tree standing in the center of it. There are additional fake cherry blossom branches threaded through the wooden beams above my head, and lampshades hanging between them that look like paper lanterns.

Breaking up the floor space are several medium sized fish tanks, illuminated blue, each with only one or two koi carp swimming happily through all the aquatic plants. To my right are a series of colorful open parasol tops displayed flat on the wall. To my left is a small waterfall collecting into a stream that then cuts through the corner of the restaurant I'm heading to. Judging by the fact I have to use stepping stones to cross a Zen garden, then cross a little semicircular bridge over the stream to get to where my parents are seated, I'm assuming this is a VIP area.

Of course it is.

I round another fish tank, this one with two baby koi in that can only be a couple of inches long each, which reveals the other side of the table. Or rather, it reveals the third person sitting opposite my parents. Their head turns to reveal a stunningly beautiful blond woman, whose perfect smile lights up when she sees me.

Fuck.

I've been ambushed.

Unable to help myself, I slow as I take the last few steps.

But my mom has already jumped to her feet, her arms outstretched as she greets me by clasping either side of my face.

"There he is! I was starting to worry."

"I'm early," I point out. She just scoffs and squeezes my shoulder—the closest I'll ever get to a hug from her.

"Never mind about all that," she gushes. "There's someone I'd like you to meet! Colt, this is Portia Bamford. Portia, this is my son, Colton Ross."

She grips my elbow surprisingly hard for a woman of her age as she steers me to my seat. It's clear there's no getting out of this easily. So for the time being, I plaster on a smile as the young lady in question rises to her feet and holds out her hand. The fact she clearly wants to shake rather than expecting me to kiss her fingers like a lot of the women my parents have introduced me to immediately earns her a brownie point in my books.

"It's nice to meet you, Colt," she says with a twinkle in her eyes. "I hope we're not pulling you away from anything important. Our moms got talking during book club, and apparently decided we had to become acquainted without delay."

Her tone is playful, which tells me she also appreciates that this is a little ridiculous. But it also suggests that she has no idea that I've been lulled here under false pretenses. For her sake, I decide not to chew my parents out in front of her.

There is going to be a damn conversation, though. This is stepping over the line. I understand they both want me to be happy, but getting impatient and arranging a blind date *with them* is like something out of a history book. You'd think I was a freaking prince who needs to be married off to secure the safety of the kingdom.

"You haven't pulled me away from anything," I assure her as I carefully sit down, minding my left hip. Draping my napkin over my lap gives me something to do as I hide my wince. "I've cleared my afternoon for this."

That's at least true. As I was expecting to be wining and dining a client, I had no intention of heading back to the office afterward.

Speaking of wine, I lean over and pick up the ice-cold bottle of white from the bucket to pour myself a glass. There's no way I'm subjecting myself to this ordeal while sober.

Portia frowns and glances at my lap. "Are you all right?"

I blink midway through returning the wine bottle. "Uh, yeah, sure. Why?"

"The way you winced, I thought you might be injured," she says with a practical sort of concern. "Would you be more comfortable in one of the booths with the sofa seating?"

I'm torn between being slightly horrified she noticed that, and enamored with her blunt but caring suggestion. Now I'm closer to her, I can see in the low lighting that her long hair is more strawberry blonde than platinum. She has high cheekbones and full lips, and although her blouse is done up respectably, I can still tell she has a magnificent rack.

To be fair to my mom, if I was in any way attracted to women, I'm sure Portia would actually be a winner.

"Oh, thanks, but—" I begin, but of course my father talks over me.

"Nonsense. This is the best table in the house, that's why I booked it."

I try not to be hurt that he cares more about appearances than my wellbeing. That's nothing new, after all. It still stings a little, though.

"I just pulled a muscle," I tell Portia.

"Doing what?" my mom asks, immediately getting into my business.

I take a sip of wine and try to rein in my sarcasm as I reply, "Surfing." They don't need to know that the pain was inflicted entirely on purpose and is nothing to be concerned about.

"You're too old to still be indulging in such a childish pursuit," my father grumbles.

Portia, however, seems to dial up the brilliance on her smile as she directs it at me and picks up her own half-finished glass of wine. "I never got the hang of surfing, but I love snorkeling, and I play volleyball competitively."

"Oh, that's cool," I say sincerely. "What team?"

"Portia is a policy advisor for Mayor Hernández," my mom interrupts, blatantly yanking the conversation in a direction she prefers. "But she's got her eye on the governor's office. Isn't that right, Portia?"

"That would certainly make my mom very happy," Portia replies with a smile that doesn't reach her eyes.

"You know, Colt is thinking about getting into politics."

"No, I'm not," I blurt with a laugh before I can stop myself. My parents' glares follow swiftly after, so I do my best to laugh some more, like we're all in on the same joke. "I've only just moved back into town and I'm still finding my feet in our family's law practice," I explain convivially to Portia. "Maybe one day I'll think about moving on from that. But for right now, I owe it to the company to stay put for the time being."

"Oh, you two work together?" Portia asks, giving my father an approving smile that appears to mollify him a little.

Oh. She's good.

"We do indeed," I say, looking around for a menu as there doesn't seem to be any around. "Should we order some food before we get too distracted?"

"We already ordered a selection for the table," my father says dismissively. His attention is on Portia and I'm not keen on the gleam in his eyes, and he smiles back at her. "We all know Colt is destined for more than family law. It's only natural that he'll be moving on soon enough. Therefore, it made sense to introduce you two. There's no harm in thinking about the future, is there, Colt?"

My irritation is starting to become anger. In that moment, it dawns on me that there might never come a point where my parents stop meddling in my life. They're just going to keep doing their best to mold me however they want with little to no regard as to what *I* might want.

Enough. I'm done being manipulated. The ache in my hip makes me feel like Zahir is almost here with me, helping me stand strong as I finally do something I should have done many years ago.

Grow a spine.

"I'm confused," I say, my tone cheerful despite the simmering rage in my chest. "Is this a date or a job interview?"

My parents still as Portia raises an eyebrow and looks between us. Then my mom laughs, clearly flustered. "There's no need to be vulgar, darling. We're all here to have a nice meal and to get to know our guest a little better."

"That's funny," I say with a chuckle. "Because I was under the impression that this was a meeting with a *new client*, Dad. I guess someone at the office got their wires crossed, huh?"

My father scoffs and sips his wine, not meeting my eyes. "Why are you younger generations so obsessed with labeling everything? Can't lunch just be lunch?"

Something reckless is brewing within me and for the first time in my life, I'm not inclined to stop it. "I'm pretty sure it's you guys who are obsessed with labels."

"And what's that's supposed to mean?" my mom snips, struggling to hold on to her pretense of civility.

I shrug. "Status. Wealth. Race. Religion. Gender. Sexuality. Who a person's family is and where they come from. Those things all add up to how much power you think someone has and therefore how much value they are to you."

"Good afternoon, ladies and gentlemen!" the server I didn't see appear announces to the table. "I have your selection of entrees here."

"Just put them down anywhere," grunts my father impatiently.

"Thank you," I say immediately, refusing to let him get away with taking his bullshit out on the staff. It's not his guy's fault we're having a long overdue family breakdown at his place of work.

It's not Portia's, either. However, she seems to be taking the turn in conversation reasonably well. "Could we get another bottle of the sauvignon blanc?" she asks pleasantly as the server puts the last of our plates down from his large silver tray.

"Of course, ma'am," the guy says, looking relieved to have a reason to make a swift escape.

"I think we should just move on from this little misunderstanding," my mom says, her voice forcefully cheerful.

"I'd love to," I say as Portia surreptitiously tops mine and her glasses up. "We can start with me making something very clear. I'm not interested in going into politics one tiny bit. I'm also not looking for a girlfriend right now. I'm so sorry, Portia, for any confusion my parents might have caused."

She gives me a one-armed shrug and a smile. "The food here is excellent, the wine's even better, and I'm enjoying your company. No need to apologize."

"Colton, you're being so rude," my mom says tearfully, wringing her napkin in her hands. "You've only just met Portia. You can't know if you two aren't compatible. And it's not like you're making an effort to date anyone else!"

I lean forward, that recklessness brimming dangerously

close to the surface. "How do you know I'm not already dating someone?"

"Because you'd tell me," she manages to shriek while still keeping her voice down. Of course she still cares what strangers might think of her over her only child's feelings.

"Would I?" I ask, genuinely curious. "When you set the bar so astronomically high? Who is ever going to pass your criteria?"

"Portia!" my mom cries, flinging a hand her way. My not-date pauses with an avocado hosomaki roll pinched expertly between her chopsticks.

"Lucky me," she says brightly before popping the sushi into her mouth.

"Calm down," my father says, his voice low. For a second, I'm a child again, fully aware of how much trouble I'm about to be in.

Then I snap back to reality and remember that I'm a grown ass man and other than his disapproval, there isn't a damn thing I need to be afraid of. Neither my mother nor my father can do anything to hurt me other than say mean things.

And they've been doing that my whole life.

"Or what?" I ask him, taking another sip of wine. Portia's right. It is very good. "You'll fire me? You'll disinherit me? I hate to break it to you, but I left New York filthy rich, and I've barely made a dent in those savings in the time I've been in Redwood Bay. And truth be told, if I have to sit through one more petty divorce mediation, I'm going to quit anyway."

"This!" my mom hisses, her eyes blazing. "This is why I wanted to introduce you to a nice young lady! I thought someone elegant, ambitious, and sophisticated might set you back on track. It's like I don't even know you since moving back home."

I laugh hollowly. "I hate to break it to you, Mom, but *this* is the real me. The guy I've been hiding my whole life to try and please you guys. The other Colt is the one that never existed. And I can't *do it* anymore. I'm so sorry, I really am."

My voice catches, but I do my best to swallow the lump in my throat.

"All I wanted was to make you both proud. To earn your love. But you kept twisting me into your perfect son until I was going to break. Well, it turns out that this is the moment, in this very nice Japanese restaurant, in front of a perfectly lovely young woman who has nothing to do with our fucked-up family history, beside a tank of baby koi. You've broken me. I'm done. I'm out."

"Your sauvignon blanc, ma'am?" the server asks hesitantly. Damn, this guy isn't just as silent as a ninja. He really knows how to pick his moments.

"Perfect timing," Portia says, taking it off him. He doesn't run, but he certainly walks away as quickly as possible.

"I don't know what you're talking about, Colton," my mom says in a fluster, rearranging the little pots of ginger and wasabi in front of her. "Of course we love you. We just want what's best for you. Sometimes you're too much of a daydreamer and you need some help with that. I think it's very uncouth of you to disrespect your father and I like this when we're in public."

"You're the ones who set this whole thing up," I scoff over the rim of my glass.

"What do you mean that you're done and you're out?" my father asks, his voice remaining low, like he thinks he can still scare me. Sucks for him. In the space of about fifteen minutes, it's become abundantly clear that I've got nothing at all to lose. "The plan has always been for you to inherit Ross & Associates. I know you're not talking about walking away from your responsibilities."

"Aren't I?" I ask in amusement.

He puffs up like a bullfrog. "Colton Archibald Ross! After everything we've done for you—"

"Oh, you mean after everything you bullied me into?" I interrupt. "Christ, I've been such a fool. Such a *coward*. To think that I chose your approval over Zahir."

The second I let the name past my lips, I know I've made a mistake. All color drains from my mother's face, while my father's does the opposite and goes beet red.

"Your father *told* me he's been bothering you at work!" my mom cries, tears in her eyes again. "I *knew* there had to be a reason for all these changes recently. That boy was always a terrible influence on you!"

"That *boy* is now a fully grown man and a paramedic," I inform her, fully aware I'm only antagonizing her and not caring one jot. "He spends his days saving people's *lives*. Not that I expect that to meet any of your criteria."

My mom doesn't even seem to hear me. "He almost ruined your chances at school and he's trying to do it again now! Why can't you see that dating someone like Portia would do you so much good?"

The lady in question raises a long, French-manicured finger. "Just a quick aside. 'Someone like Portia' is in fact just Portia, and she's not here to fix anybody's son." She glances at me with a sly smile. "Although once this one's finished with his epiphany, he can give me a call."

"He's not normally like this," my mom says desperately, reaching out like she wants to grab Portia's arm, but stops herself at the last second.

Wise chose, I reckon.

"You are right," I concede. "I normally behave myself and toe the line. Unfortunately, I'm done with that old Colt, so I doubt you'll be seeing him again."

"That's right, you're 'out,'" my father sneers. "Are you

going to quit law and become some kind of hippie? Out of where?"

"The closet," I say before I can stop myself.

Everyone goes very still.

Well…if I was ever going to come out, this isn't even close to how I planned on doing it. But there's no putting the genie back in the bottle now. And quite frankly, I don't want to.

"W-what?" my mom stammers.

"Fuck yeah, dude," Portia murmurs appreciatively, dipping some nagiri in her soy sauce.

"You're not…you can't be…" My mom looks from left to right, as if expecting the paparazzi to be lurking within earshot. *"Gay?"*

I shrug, wondering if I feel so calm because I'm on my second glass of wine or if it's because I truly do not care anymore. It's so funny how years and years of crushing anxiety have all just been washed away like footprints in the sand. They say the truth will set you free, and that's exactly how I'm feeling right now.

"I can be and I am," I tell her with a grin. "Gay, that is. In case there was any confusion."

My father looks like he's clenching his jaw so hard it's going to snap. "This is pathetic. If you think you can embarrass the family name like that—"

"I'm sorry," Portia interrupts again with her manicured finger raised. "Just to clarify that what you're saying is if your son was gay, that would be a scandal in your eyes?" There's no humor in her voice anymore as she licks her lips and fixes my father with a piercing stare.

He splutters and glances at my mom. It's rare that I see him lose his cool, and under the circumstances, I'm not ashamed to admit that I enjoy it a little. "Well, I mean, of course not. It's just…it's not who he is! This is obviously some kind of attempt at rebellion! That's what I meant about embarrassing us."

"Oh, good," Portia drawls. "Because for a second there, I thought you were a couple of homophobic bigots that have been making their son's life miserable his whole life."

"Colt," my mom whimpers as tears fall down her face. "I just want you to be happy. Successful. It's so much harder for those people. Why would you choose that?"

I laugh and rub my head. "To quote the one and only Lady Gaga, I was born this way, Mom. I'm not choosing to be gay. But I am sure as hell choosing to stop being ashamed and living a lie. This isn't a phase nor am I experimenting. I'm attracted to men and only men, so you're going have to come to terms with a very different-looking future from the one you've been crafting for me. The only people who could make my life difficult would be the kind with attitudes like yours. So the ball's in your court now. *You* have to choose whether or not my sexuality is a dealbreaker for you."

I take a breath and try not to let my sadness rob me of the right words in this important moment.

"This is me. The real Colt. And he *is* a bit of a daydreamer. He's gay, he loves surfing, and he's not sure he wants to be a lawyer anymore. He's one thousand percent never going to be a politician or marry a woman. If this Colt is someone you're interested in getting to know, you can give me a call."

I'm surprised how calm I am as I place my napkin back on the table and stand up, offering my hand out to my left.

"Portia, it was genuinely a pleasure meeting you. If you ever want to grab a cone on the beach, you can also give me a call. If not, good luck with getting to the governor's office."

She shrugs and grins at me as she gives me one firm shake before releasing my hand. "Eh. I like the mayor." She looks pointedly at my parents. "We've worked really hard on protecting trans people's access to healthcare in the city. I'd hate to see anyone try and undo that if I left."

I snort and wiggle my hand next to my ear with my thumb and pinkie out, making a 'call me' motion. She winks, and I take that as my cue to leave.

I'm not sure if it's the overwhelming relief flooding through me, or the couple of glasses of wine on an empty stomach. But I feel a little unstable as I move past the tank with the baby koi and start heading across the path through the Zen garden.

Then my phone vibrates in my jacket.

So do several other people's phones around me. Even more phones ping with a message notification.

Frowning, I pull mine out of my pocket to see an alert filling up my screen.

That's when I realize it's not my legs that are shaky underneath me.

It's the ground.

"EARTHQUAKE!" someone near me screams as the glassware hanging above the bar starts vibrating. Within seconds, it's crashing to the floor. The lights begin flickering and the walls groan. The artificial two-story high cherry blossom tree starts to tilt.

People shove chairs back as they abandon their tables and try to run. I stagger as the ground rumbles, flailing my arms as I spin around. "NO!" I roar, flinging myself at my terrified looking mom. In the same moment, Portia grabs my father's hand, pulling him to his feet.

But that's when the lights go out entirely as the ceiling falls on top of our heads.

CHAPTER 22

Zahir

I'VE BARELY PUT MY STUFF AWAY IN MY LOCKER AT THE START of shift before Captain Valentine is calling us all onto the concourse for a briefing. "Any idea what this is about?" Anton asks Lieutenant Flores. He manages to multitask and also drag Sawyer away from his phone, where he's no doubt texting whoever he went out on his last date with.

"Get your asses through this door, and you'll find out," the lieutenant says, already halfway past the threshold.

"Probie! Whatcha do now?" Lili yells at our youngest member.

Teddy rolls his eyes. "We literally just got here, Kwon. If anyone's fucked up already, it's your hungover ass."

She peers above her sunglasses and sips the coffee she obviously picked up on the way in. "Bite me," she says, flashing him a grin.

"Knowing where she's been, I wouldn't recommend it," Lochlan crows, narrowly avoiding getting smacked over the head by her.

"You only out-drink me because you're a beast, Beast," she growls.

I laugh and shake my head, catching Yara's eye as we head out onto the main concourse. "Any ideas?"

"Gene's off for a couple of shifts," she reminds me. "Perhaps it's something to do with that?"

Ahh, yeah that makes sense. I've been so wrapped up in my own personal life, I forgot that it's Passover, so our driver is going to be spending some time with his extended family.

Sure enough, as we reach the common area, Captain Valentine is standing beside a man I haven't seen before. He's probably in his mid-thirties, well built, and standing with his feet waist-length apart and his hands clasped behind his back. I'd guess he's South-East Asian from his facial features and the thick black hair that curls behind his ears. As we approach, he nods at us with a professional smile and confidence in his eyes.

My gut instinct is to like him, but there's definitely something beneath the surface that I'm not sure about. Then again, I'm not one to talk about putting walls up and keeping those around me at arm's length.

"Good morning, One-Thirteen," the captain says clearly as we crowd in front of him and the new guy. "As you might be aware, Driver Engineer Haskell is taking some well-earned vacation time. To cover his shifts, we've been lent Firefighter Drayton Hendrix. He'll be driving the truck in Gene's absence as well as giving us hands-on assistance. I know you'll make him feel welcome."

"Hey, there," Lieutenant Flores says as soon as the captain steps back. He shakes with Hendrix and gestures toward the dining table. "We usually start the day with breakfast together."

"Unless we get a call," Lili quips, causing several people to roll their eyes at how obvious that statement is.

Hendrix looks surprised. "Oh, at the One-Two-Two we ignore calls if we're eating," he says in an Australian accent.

The groups pauses for a fraction and a couple of people narrow their eyes at him. "Oh, man," he says with a laugh. "Don't tell me you guys are that easy?"

I join in with the collective relief at realizing he's just joking. For a second, I was worried we had a slacker on our hands.

"Oh, you're gonna fit right in," Lili says with a clap on his shoulder.

Shaking my head, I smile. "Are pancakes okay?"

"You were on breakfast duty last shift," Yara points out with a frown. "I've got it."

"Can we still get pancakes, though?" Sawyer asks hopefully.

Yara hums as she heads into the kitchen. "So long as you promise to have *some* fruit with them, sure."

"I'll make eggs," Teddy cries, always eager to please.

I might be barred from cooking this morning, but that doesn't mean I can't still be hospitable. "Hendrix, was it? You want coffee?"

He nods and follows me to the machine. "Most people call me Dray," he says, looking around our station before smiling at me again. It's difficult coming into a place where everyone else not only knows each other but are a tight-knit group. I like his vibe and feel like he's doing a good job not being overwhelmed.

"Zahir Delacroix," I introduce myself and we shake. "Lead paramedic. Most people call me Del. So you're usually with the One-Two-Two?"

They're based in San Clemente, but on the outskirts, so they often pitch in to help us with bigger blazes or like when we had that disaster at Critter Canyon Park just before Christmas.

Dray shrugs as I pour us a mug each. "I'm usually where the wind blows me. Putting down roots isn't really my style, so I'm like a substitute teacher, filling in when and where I can. But the One-Two-Two have had one of their guys out with a broken leg for a while, so I've been jumping in with them the most over the past couple of months." He waggles his eyebrows at me. "Now you lucky bastards get me for a couple of days."

"I'm sure we are lucky. Cream?"

"Yeah, and two sugars. So…what's the deal with everyone here? Are you a good person to get the skinny from?"

"The skinny?" I say in amusement as I pass him his mug.

"Yeah, you know? The goss? I find the best way to fit into a place is to understand the social politics as quickly as I can. Is anyone dating? Or have beef with each other?"

I laugh and shake my head. "You might find it a little stomach-churning how well we get on here. Of course there are disagreements from time to time, but as clichéd as it sounds, we're like a family most of the time."

"Depends what your experience of family is," Dray says with a quirked eyebrow.

Ah. That's fair. I think of all Colt's been through with his parents. Sometimes I do forget that when I say family, I mean people who will always be there for you and never let you down.

For others, family is something you escape from and never look back. Considering his accent and how far he is away from where he grew up, I wonder if that's more Dray's definition of the word. We share a knowing, sympathetic look, and I think I get my answer.

"Well," I say, "Captain Julian Valentine has been here for several years, but our longest running member is actually Gene Haskell, the guy you're covering for. He's happily married to a lovely lady. They have five children together and even more extended family who he's spending Passover with."

"Five kids?" Dray whistles. "You know, I did hear this house had a reputation for being rainbow central. Isn't that the case?"

I chuckle as I look over the team. "You mean do we attract a lot of the LGBT community? Yes, that's true, especially here on the first watch. We like to tease Gene that he's our token straight. You see the redheaded golden retriever of a man over there?" Dray nods. "That's Lochlan Bell. Some people like to call him Beast. He was convinced he was straight until he met his now-boyfriend before Thanksgiving last year. It was actually very sweet watching him work it out in real time, even if it did take him forever."

Dray sips his coffee and considers Lochlan for a moment as he and Lili lay the table for us all to eat. "So it's not just gay guys? You're cool with people being bi?"

I blink, thrown by such a question. "Yes, of course," I say. Logically, I know that biphobia and bi erasure exist in many forms in all kinds of spaces, but not at the One-Thirteen. "You see Lili—the woman helping Lochlan lay the table?"

"She seems to be sabotaging him more than helping," Dray says with a snort.

He has a point, and I smile with him. "Well, she's a very loud and proud bisexual, so even if she was the only one, she wouldn't put up with any nonsense. But Sawyer there is equally vocal about being pansexual...mostly regarding how many men, women, and everyone in between he sleeps with."

"Heartbreaker?" Dray asks.

I tilt my head back and forth. "More of a playboy. He's always upfront that he's not looking for anything more than a night, so I'd hope everyone he hooks up with has their eyes open going in. Commitment doesn't seem to be on his radar."

"Not getting tied down is important to some people," Dray comments.

Trying not to be obvious, I glance at him. He's staring at

Sawyer and Anton playing foosball, so I get a chance to study him. Clearly, he's a bit of a nomad, which suggests to me he's running away from something. Or maybe that's just how he finds his peace. Who am I to judge?

I'd also bet money that he's bi himself, and wonder if he requested to try out the One-Thirteen specifically. We do have a reputation for attracting queer personnel and I'm proud of that. Perhaps he's looking to settle down a bit more than he's letting on. If so, I'd like the One-Thirteen to be an option for him.

"Sawyer Nelson is all about living life to the fullest," I say wryly. "I'm sure I don't have to tell you that doing this job can have that affect on some people. So he dates a lot. He's also the most likely out of everyone here to wear killer heels, leather pants, and eyeliner sharp enough to draw blood."

Dray raises his eyebrows at me. "Really?"

"Well, that's Lili's style as well, but I think Sawyer enjoys challenging people's expectations more."

I'm not usually one to talk about people on their behalf, but everyone in this station is very open about who they are and the journey they're on. Sensing that Dray might need to know just how welcome he'll be here, I keep going.

"That's Sawyer's best friend with him, Anton. He got married and had a daughter before accepting who he really is and coming out as gay. His wife and her new husband couldn't be more supportive, and they all co-parent together. It's really beautiful to see."

"And his birth family?" Dray asks, correctly guessing there was a reason why Anton denied his sexuality for so long. My heart pangs as I think of Colt's similar situation, but I'm definitely not going to talk about that today.

Sadly, I shake my head. "They're very religious. Unless he fixes his 'lifestyle choices,' they've said they don't want anything to do with him."

"What about the little girl?"

I grimace. "They tried to sue for custody, claiming she wasn't safe with either of her sinful parents. It got thrown out of court, but sometimes they still try and see her, no doubt to attempt to brainwash her." Before the mood can turn too bleak, I smile brightly. "It's a good thing the One-Thirteen are family to her instead. In fact, I've been helping to teach her to surf recently."

Dray's face lights up at that. "You surf?"

"Since I was a child," I say with a nod. "It's been nice to have an excuse to do it more often again recently. You?"

He nods and grins. "My board is the only thing I own that's too big to fit in my van. So I've got it strapped to the roof and use it every chance I get."

Oh, wow. Is he really that much of a nomad? I don't want to pry too much, but that sounds like he's got one of those tiny mobile homes. I'd be interested to see how he manages that. It must be an exciting life. I just hope it's not too lonely.

Dray nudges my shoulder with his own to get my attention again. "And what about you? Are you out loud and proud like the others?"

It looks like breakfast is being dished up, so I decide to summarize the rest of the team as quickly as I can. "Proud," I agree, "but maybe not quite as loud. The captain and lieutenant are the same. And then Teddy's our probie and Yara's my partner on the bus. They're both a little undecided, I think." I meet Dray's eyes. "That's one thing about us. We're boisterous, but we'll never push anyone if they're not ready for it."

"Except the Beast man over there?" he asks playfully.

I shake my head and chuckle. "Trust me, if Lili hadn't used a battering ram to force Lochlan to reconsider his feelings for Dario, they'd both still be pining miserably for each other."

"Oh, so you're *that* kind of a family," Dray says as we make our way to the dining table.

"What kind of family?" Teddy asks, a hint of apprehension in his voice. Everyone takes a seat as he and Yara dish up.

"Meddling," Dray explains with a grin.

That gets several laughs from around the room. "Oh, you bet, new guy," Lili tells him wickedly. "Give us a couple of hours. We'll be *all* up in your business."

"You are welcome to try," Dray replies.

Lochlan waves his hand in front of his throat in a 'kill it' motion. "Don't challenge her, my dude. It'll become her life's mission."

That doesn't appear to deter Dray. "Bring it," he says playfully with a wink.

The morning passes suspiciously quietly after that. We make it through breakfast uninterrupted before Yara and I are called out to treat a suspected heart attack that just turns out to be heartburn. So after giving the guy some antacids, we're back within the hour to rejoin the rest of the squad.

Everyone knows better than to say it out loud, but I start to worry that it's going to be one of those long, boring shifts that feel like they last forever. Of course, it's good if no one in Redwood Bay has an emergency, and I always appreciate getting some decent sleep when at work overnight. But if we spend twenty-four hours on edge without getting to expel that energy anywhere, I find the unused adrenaline leaves me unpleasantly restless for days afterward.

Luckily…we're not left in limbo for long.

Some time after one o'clock, the station's gray cat, Smokey, comes shooting across the open concourse, looking like she's running for her life. Lochlan's Dalmatian, Rocky, is chasing her, so initially it doesn't seem like such an unusual sight.

"Rocky, be nice!" Lochlan yells from where he's watching some kind of science fiction TV show with Teddy. I shake my head and tsk as I go to resume loading the dishwasher with our plates from lunch.

Then everybody's phones start pinging all at the same time.

"I take it that's not normal?" Dray asks as we all start pulling them from our pockets.

"No," I reply to him. But I barely get a chance to glance at my screen before the tones start sounding. It's not the typical call alert. It's…

"EARTHQUAKE!" Lieutenant Flores bellows. "Take cover!"

He doesn't need to tell us twice. As the ground begins to rumble and more alarms and sirens fill the air, the entire One-Thirteen throws itself on the ground against the interior wall, waiting for the moment to pass. Our administrator, Nancy, hurriedly joins us, climbing awkwardly on the floor in her pencil skirt. Lochlan clings to Rocky. I assume Smokey, like most cats, would rather fend for herself. I hope she's okay, wherever she's hiding.

This isn't exactly unheard of in these parts. I think of my teta scoffing at the meagre 4.2 a few weeks ago. But it doesn't matter how many I experience, every time the very earth starts to tremble beneath my feet, it's an extremely humbling reminder of how much we're at the mercy of Mother Nature. There's no telling how strong the tremors will be or how substantial the damage. I mutter a prayer under my breath, hoping for mercy.

It's definitely more intense than the previous one. I reach out and grab the hand of whoever happens to be taking shelter beside me. It's Anton, and he squeezes my fingers as we share a look. Before the fear can truly take hold, though, calmness descends, and everything stills as if nothing even happened.

I exhale.

"Is it over?" Teddy asks.

We all look to Captain Valentine, who shifts forward and peers out from under the truck. "I guess we'll know if the bells start chiming.

As if on cue, the alarm blares, and dispatch comes over the speaker. "Station One-Thirteen. Jiyū Sushi Bar. Structural collapse. Medical assistance required. Possible search and rescue."

Before the announcement even finishes, we're all scrambling from under the rigs and rushing to get into our turnouts. Once Nancy is upright, she pulls Rocky away from the vehicles by his collar to keep him safe. Looking quickly around, it doesn't seem like there's been any damage to the station. I guess we'll get an idea of the event's magnitude as we drive through town.

I'm just hopping into the ambulance as a rapid click-clacking out front makes me pause. "My goodness!" Mrs. Bloom cries as she skitters to a halt with Miss Margot Fonteyn trotting beside her like a nimbus cloud on a leash. "Is everyone okay?"

"All good here, Mrs. Bloom," the captain calls out to her from the side of the truck. Dray is already behind the wheel, ready to go. "Are you okay?"

"Of course, of course," she says, waving us off like we're starting a drag race. "Go on, get going! Nancy and I will take care of the animals and make sure nothing's fallen down or cracked in half."

"You're the best, Mrs. B!" Sawyer yells, giving the engine's horn a toot.

After that, we don't waste any time hitting the road, sirens blaring.

Nowhere in this town takes more than fifteen minutes to get to, so we arrive at the restaurant in closer to five. On the way, we see plenty of damage, but all things considered it's quite minimal. Mostly toppled telephone lines, some broken windows, and a shit ton of roofing tiles that have shaken loose.

The sushi bar is somewhat out on its own, however, and there are more cracks and potholes as we approach, signaling that this area got it worse. The engine and truck get there first and park as close as they can to better use the equipment on the damaged structure, but I stop the ambulance right behind them.

There are probably other buildings that felt it as bad as this one, and I hope my teta and Colt are okay. Selfishly, I also think of my art studio. I would never normally even consider myself in a situation like this, but Colt put such an incredible amount of care and attention into it, I'd mourn it if it was destroyed after only getting to enjoy it for a couple of weeks.

But that would be nothing compared to any loss of human life, so I'm immediately focused on the scene in front of me again. The restaurant seems to have suffered a partial collapse toward the back left, just like dispatch told us. I've never been here before, so the sight of an enormous blossom tree poking its branches out through where the ceiling used to be throws me for a second. Then I realize it must be artificial with a steel core to be tougher than the wood and tiles of the roof.

The walking wounded have filled the parking lot, and thankfully most of them just seem to be covered in dust with a few scrapes. Teddy is already hauling out a pallet of bottled water from the bed of the truck to hand out. I see someone who looks to have a compound thigh fracture and some others cradling broken arms and head wounds. The fact that all these people have made it out of the structure bodes well for them, though.

We need to establish if there's anyone still trapped inside who needs us more.

"Thank heavens you're here," and older man says, rushing up to the One-Thirteen.

"Are you in charge?" Captain Valentine asks, letting the rest of the team continue with their assessment and triage. Yara and I are already treating the compound fracture guy. He doesn't appear to have any other immediate issues, which I'm grateful for.

"Yes," I hear the man speaking to the captain say. "I'm the manager. We got as many people out as we could, but I didn't think it was safe for anyone to go back in until you got here."

"You did the right thing," the captain assures him, but the manager still sounds distressed.

"We had eighty-nine covers in for lunch," he continues, "as well six in the kitchen and twelve wait staff. Including myself, that's a hundred and eight people, but I've only counted ninety-five out here. A couple could have left without me noticing, but—"

Captain Valentine clasps his shoulder. "Thank you, sir. That's incredibly helpful. My team will check the rubble now. Del! You're with Flores and Foster. Hendrix, you wanna give them a hand to clear the building?"

"I've got this," Yara tells me, referring to the broken femur, and I don't doubt it.

"Yes, sir!" Dray cries, joining up with Teddy and I as we follow Lieutenant Flores through what's left of the front door.

This was probably a really nice place twenty minutes ago, but even though the quake really shook it hard, I hope they can patch it back together easily enough. The most substantial damage is in the back left corner where the giant fake tree has fallen. A considerable amount of the ceiling has come down around it, blocking off that part of the restaurant and exposing the kitchen.

"Fire department, call out!" the lieutenant yells as we fan across the space. Teddy quickly finds a woozy waitress under a flipped over table and helps her to her feet. She doesn't appear to be gravely injured, so I leave him to escort her to safety. That's one out of a potential thirteen, at least. "Anyone here?" Lieutenant Flores tries again.

The building is creaking and there's a pump spluttering noisily from what I guess was a water feature before the blossom tree threw itself on the ground, so it's difficult to hear anything. And as I move through the space, I see that there's more damage than I first appreciated. The floor has cracked substantially where the tectonic shift sent shock-waves right underneath where we're standing.

The lieutenant shakes his head. "I don't think we're getting through this debris easily from this side. I want to see if we can gain access from out the back. Let's do a final sweep and then—"

Luckily, we're already moving toward the front again when the explosion rips through the kitchen. I dive forward and cover my helmet as a new wave of crap rains down on us. After a few seconds, it seems to settle down again.

"Everyone okay?" I call out.

"Yeah," Dray groans from somewhere to my left.

I push myself up and look around. The heat already alerted me, so I'm not surprised to see that whatever went boom has now started a blaze around the most destroyed area. Gas from the ovens mixing with cooking oil, most likely.

"I'm good," Lieutenant Flores says, already on his feet and waving us out as he activates his radio. "We need a hose in here," he tells the guys outside. "I'm heading out back with

Hendrix and Delacroix. We think there maybe people trapped under the rubble."

"Got it, Lieutenant," Captain Valentine says as we're already running through the doors and around the building. "I'll have Foster join you again."

"We might need more hands once the fire's out," the lieutenant warns.

"Copy that."

We're almost at the blazing kitchen when I stumble to a halt, my heart dropping to my boots before my brain can even realize what it's processing.

"Del, what's wrong?" Teddy cries as he runs up behind me.

The lieutenant and Dray pause to spin and look at me. Their eyes dart to the building, but that's not what's stopped me in my tracks.

I'm looking at the other half of the parking lot.

"That's Colt's car," I manage to croak.

"Your friend Colt from the beach?" Teddy asks, swiveling his head as if he might see him.

"My boyfriend Colt," I correct, not thinking what I'm saying, mouth dry, limbs trembling, vision going blurry. "That's definitely his car…"

And if he wasn't outside with the rest of the restaurant's patrons…

Does that mean he's still inside?

Or underneath?

Is he even still alive?

CHAPTER 23
Colt

MY EARS ARE STILL RINGING AS I GRADUALLY PEEL MY EYELIDS open. What the fuck just happened?

I cough and press my fingertips to my head. They come away red and sticky. I can feel something stinging on my scalp, but seeing as I can wiggle all my extremities, I chose to believe that means it's not that bad. I'm sure Zahir said something once about head wounds bleeding worse than they look.

My heart pangs. I'm confused and in pain, but the one thing I know for sure is he's the only person I want to see right now.

That isn't going to happen, though. So I take a breath and focus on the ground where I'm lying. It's dark but I can still see that there's crap everywhere and dust settling all around me.

Earthquake.

Oh, yeah. That's what happened.

"Colt?" my mother's voice rings out.

"Yeah, I'm here," I say back, blinking and trying to look through the gloom. "Dad? Portia?"

"What the fuck was that?" my father grumbles in outrage.

Portia moans. "Still here. I think."

I start flexing my muscles and twisting my limbs, pretty certain that apart from being banged up, I don't have anything terrible to worry about. "Anyone injured?"

"My arm hurts," my mom says, making my heart contract. I know we were just fighting, but I'm never not going to care about her, no matter what. She sounds so scared.

"I'm fine but I'm stuck," my father says with a huff. "Get over here and help me out."

"I'm okay," Portia replies to me. "Are *you* okay?"

"Debatable," I tell her with a laugh that quickly becomes a moan. "I'm going to be black and blue tomorrow…"

As I manage to finally sit up, my words trail off as I see something twitching on the wet floor in front of me. Something small and colorful.

It's one of the baby koi carp. It's suffocating.

Suddenly, I'm up on my feet, spinning around, looking for anything that I can use to help. The empty wine bucket is lying on its side under the table we were sitting at mere moments ago. I grab it and look at the fish tank. The top has been smashed off. There're bits of wall and fake cherry blossom petals in the water, and it's leaking fast through the broken glass. The other koi is swimming around in the few inches of water left, clearly agitated.

"Colton!" my father barks. "Stop fucking around and help me!"

I ignore him.

Only wobbling a little on my feet, I leap over to the tank, scooping up that fish and what water I can in the wine bucket. By some stroke of luck, the fake tree branches appear to have stopped a lot of the dust from settling on the water, hopefully making it more hospitable for the fish.

After getting as much into the bucket as I can without

risking hurting the little thing, I turn around and approach the flapping one on the floor. I don't know if I'm going to hurt it. But if I leave it there, it's definitely going to die. So being as careful as I can, I slip my fingers around its orange and silver body. It has a noticeably round, plump body, which I think makes it easier to quickly pluck off the floor and dunk into the bucket.

I stare for a second as the most recently rescued fish stills. Just as I've convinced myself that by grabbing it, I did more harm than good, it jerks like a dog shaking itself after swimming in a lake. Then the two koi start flitting about in their new mini metal home.

"Jesus Christ," I say weakly. "You scared me for a second there, fishy."

"COLT!" my father practically screams. "Stop ignoring me and—"

"You said you weren't injured, just stuck," I interrupt him calmly. "That fish was dying. It's okay now."

"Fish?" he splutters. Now I'm on my feet I can see that he is indeed pinned down by what I would guess is a metal beam from the ceiling. But as he said himself, he doesn't look particularly wounded. "We were just eating fucking fish! What the fuck are you—"

"Language, Fredrick, please," my mom sobs. Portia is with her, feeling the arm she's favoring.

"Speak for yourself, Mr. Ross," Portia says, not looking up from my mom. "I was eating the avocado and tofu." She offers me a weak smile. "Thanks for rescuing the Nemos. I think your mom might have fractured something, but hopefully it's not too serious."

I exhale, looking down at my bucket of fish, then back up at the rubble cave we seem to be trapped in, the fake Sakura tree looming over us, gently raining petals every now and again, then at Portia's somehow still immaculate strawberry blond hair. The laugh escapes my throat before I can stop it.

"I almost wish I wasn't gay," I tell her, bordering on becoming hysterical. I'm not sure if I'm grateful for or regretting that wine in my empty stomach right now. "This would be one hell of a first date story to tell our kids someday."

"How can you joke about that in a time like this?" my mom says, sobbing harder.

I shrug, putting down the wine bucket and moving closer to inspect her myself. Not that I don't trust Portia. She seems like the kind of person who requalifies her first aid training more often than is strictly necessary. But because despite how awful she's been today, she's still my mom, and I love her.

"It seems like the perfect time to joke," I tell her as I run my hands over the rest of her body, brushing away grit and glass. "Everything about this situation is completely absurd."

However, I quickly realize she's sobbing in earnest. So much so that I begin to worry she's not telling us about some rebar she's secretly impaled with.

Like I said, I love my mom. But I have no doubt that she'd be the character in a zombie movie who wouldn't tell anyone she'd been bitten.

"Stop upsetting your mother!" my father snaps, clearly still needing to feel he's in charge even though he's only slightly better off than a moth displayed on a pinboard right now.

Upon further inspection, however, I'm even more sure that there aren't any other obvious injuries. "Mom, tell me where it hurts."

She takes a raggedy breath. "You'll never have children!" she wails.

I glance at Portia in confusion, then look down at my

balls, honestly wondering if she's noticed some damage I haven't.

"Mrs. Ross," Portia says patiently. "Just because Colt is gay doesn't mean he won't be a father. A lot of couples adopt, and there's always surrogacy."

Holy shit. The earth shifted under us and the goddamned building collapsed around our heads, and this is what she's tying herself up in knots about?

"It's not the same!" my mom continues to bemoan, shaking and fidgeting and probably making her injured arm worse than it already is. "You'll never know the joy of coming together to create a life! How could you do this to me? You'll never love them the same way if it's not your flesh and blood!"

"The way you love me?" I snap in disgust, my short fuse replacing the dark humor of the situation in a flash. "What the hell, Mom? I thought I was crazy for being so afraid of coming out to you for so long. But I was completely right. All you care about is what other people will think and having more of your bloodline to mold in your perfect image."

I shake my head, picking up my new fish friends, and standing up so I can put some distance between us.

"Colt?" she squeaks, tears streaming down her face. But I don't care if we're in the middle of a crisis. I said I was done with being manipulated and I meant it.

"We can talk about this later," I say blandly, moving over to my father. "Or never. It's really up to you. How's it going, Dad? Can you wiggle all your fingers and toes?"

It's mildly impressive how he still manages to puff up like a bullfrog while looking like a sausage that's gotten trapped under the grill fork.

"We didn't raise you to be this rude!" he blusters.

I shrug as I look over how the beam has wedged him

against the wall, avoiding meeting his gaze while I assess the problem.

"No," I finally reply. "You raised me to believe that even the slightest hint of questioning your judgement was rude. All I wanted was your approval, Dad. Your love. I thought becoming a lawyer would finally make you think I was worth something." I glance up and our eyes connect. "But it turns out that I can never win. I'll never do enough, be enough, achieve enough to warrant your unconditional love. Neither of you." I cast a look over my shoulder at my mom who's quietly watching me. "So I give up. I'm not going to try anymore. I'm going to live my life the way I want to, and if we ever get out of this mess, you can decide if you want to be part of that life."

"Of course we're getting out of here," my father says indignantly.

I sigh and shake my head. "Out of everything I said, *that's* the part you're going to focus on?"

"Shh!" Portia hisses suddenly with a frown. "Did you hear that?"

"Honestly, I don't know—" my father begins to grumble, but Portia and I both shush him this time. I strain my ears, not sure what I should be listening out for. But if Portia's thinks it's important, I'll try.

"Maybe I imagined it," she whispers a few moments later.

I shake my head as I place my bucket of fish on the floor and press myself as close as I dare against the rubble. I don't want to shift anything and have the fake tree or more of the ceiling crush us. But if there's anyone looking for us...

"Fire department, call out!" I hear faintly through all the debris.

"IN HERE!" I holler back as loud as I can, not sure if they'll even be able to hear me. "WE'RE IN HERE!"

"Who is it, Colt?" my mom asks in a trembling voice.

I crouch down to hold her hand. She's pale and shivering, eyes red and wet. "Firefighters are looking for us," I assure her. "I bet they'll have us out in no time." My heart leaps to think Zahir might be part of the rescue team, but it could easily be one of the San Clemente crews. Damn, I want to hug him, though.

Maybe finally tell him I love him. Nothing like a little near-death experience to make me realize how dumb it is I'm still afraid to do that.

My mom sniffs. "And will you still be mad at me then?"

I sigh, frustrated with going around in circles. "Mom, I'm not mad at you and Dad. Really. I'm just telling you this is who I am and nothing's going to change that. Believe me, I tried." I laugh hollowly. "So, I *am* afraid that means you're going to be disappointed in me and love me less, maybe not even want to see me anymore. If that's the case, I'll have to accept it. But I can't pretend for another damn day to be someone I'm not. Don't you want me to be happy?"

"Well...yes," she says slowly, wiping her face with her good hand. "But..."

Whatever objection she was going to try and convince me with, it'll have to wait. We only get a split second's warning as a different kind of rumble shakes the ground. Then an explosion fills the air and knocks me off my feet for a second time. I cry out and fling my arms over my head as more chunks of the ceiling and walls dislodge, the cherry blossom tree lurches down another several feet on top of us, and the rest of the glass around the fish tank shatters.

That's when the flames erupt.

"*Get back!*" I scream at Portia and my mom before scrambling over to my dad, trying to shove the structural beam off his chest. "It's okay, Dad, it's okay," I utter.

He whimpers. "Colt, I...hurry."

Portia settles my mom farther away from the flames then

rushes to join me, throwing her weight under the other side of the beam. "On three," she grunts. "One, two—"

"THREE!" we cry together, managing to budge the post just enough that my father can wriggle out from underneath.

But much like a game of Jenga, by moving one piece, we disrupt the rest, and chunks of flaming concrete start crumbling free of the rubble wall like a mini avalanche. Portia pulls my father to her as I tumble away from them, hitting the ground.

"COLT!" my mom screams as pain shoots through my left leg as well as the back of my head. The light from the fire gets blocked out by the debris mounting up. I hear bottles smashing and more smaller explosions popping, and metal, concrete and wood snapping.

Then the throbbing in my head gets too much. Blood runs into my already stinging eyes. I cough and splutter, but consciousness slips away from me.

Then there's only darkness.

CHAPTER 24

Zahir

"ZAHIR, MAYBE YOU SHOULD STAY BACK," LIEUTENANT FLORES says, raising his hands as if to try and stop me.

Wild horses couldn't drag me away.

I barely even register him or what he's saying as I dash past, racing toward the back of the restaurant where we'll hopefully have better access.

What I don't expect to run into are two of the waiters and what looks like a couple who'd been in the middle of dinner when the earthquake hit. All four of them are in what's left of part of an office and a corridor that leads to a door that's no longer there. They're heaving chunks of stone and lumps of wood away with their bare hands.

"Thank god!" the man yells when he sees us, pausing to wipe his brow. "There are people under there!"

"We'll take it from here," the lieutenant says as he and Dray usher the good Samaritans away from the unstable area.

"Are any of you injured?" I ask, doing a quick visual assessment as they fumble their way through the debris littered all over the ground.

The man takes the woman's hand as they and the waiters allow the firefighters to jump in and take over where they left off clearing the rumble. "We're all okay, right?" he checks with the group.

They all nod, but one of the waiters points to the worst area of collapse. "Table twenty-five got caught between the wall collapse and the tree falling," he tells us earnestly. "I saw it! They were fighting, so I was keeping an eye on them. We got this couple out," he says, indicating the man and woman currently clinging to each other. "But they're still under there!"

"How many people are there, sir?" Lieutenant Flores asks.

Teddy is opening up and shaking out emergency foil blankets to hand out. That would normally be my job, but I'm grateful no one is stopping me from attacking the rubble with Dray in this moment. If Colt isn't out front and he isn't with these guys…

"Four," the waiter says, gratefully gulping down some bottled water, also from Teddy. "An older couple and a younger man and woman. It wasn't so bad a few minutes ago. But then there was some kind of explosion and everything fell down some more, and…"

He trails off, but we don't need him to explain. We saw the kitchen turn into a fireball. The rest of the team should be tackling that blaze now. Hopefully, they'll get it out soon if they haven't already. Judging by the sirens filling the air, another station has come to offer us backup.

All's not lost, yet.

"Foster," the lieutenant says to Teddy. "Escort these people to the triage area. Once they're taken care of, get back here." I glance over my shoulder to see him grip Teddy's arm. "If there's anyone to spare, bring them back with you," he mutters.

"Yes, Lieutenant," Teddy says with conviction.

Then Flores rushes over to the other side of me, working with Dray to keep digging our way through, bit by bit.

"Fire department!" I yell, my voice hoarse. "Anyone in there? Call out!"

"Hello?" a woman's muffled voice comes through the rubble.

"Hold on, ma'am!" the lieutenant instructs as we alter our direction toward where it sounded like she was. "This is the Redwood Bay Fire Department, we're here to help. Are you injured?"

"No," she replies with a cough. "But my friend is under some of the crap that fell just now and he's not responding. His parents are with me. His mom's arm is maybe broken. Should I keep digging toward you? I'm worried about the structural integrity, but I didn't want to just sit here."

"Let us do the digging now, ma'am," the lieutenant says. My arms are aching but we're tearing through what's left of the roof, getting closer to the Sakura tree poking out through the cracks, reaching for the heavens. I can't see any flames, so hopefully that means the rest of the squad have gotten the fire out.

One less problem to deal with is appreciated right now.

"Please hurry," she says. "I'm worried about my friend."

"The cavalry is here!" Lili yells from behind us, and my heart leaps as I turn to see her running toward us with almost all of the rest of the One-Thirteen. She, Teddy, Lochlan, Sawyer and Anton all dive in without needing to be told, helping with the excavation. Captain Valentine is bringing up the rear, keeping a little distance as he assesses the big picture.

He can tell us to fall back if he thinks it's unsafe. Of course he needs to protect the team if shit goes sideways.

But if Colt is the man unconscious under the fresh load of rubble, the only way I'm leaving this scene is in a body bag.

I can't lose him. I *can't.* I only just got him back. This can't be the way our story ends, not after so long living separate lives. It's not fair. I won't *stand* for it!

"What's your name, ma'am?" the lieutenant asks.

"Portia," she replies. The volume of her answer tells us we're getting close, and almost a dozen pairs of hands converge on the same spot, all working to shift enough rubble to finally get a visual confirmation.

"Portia, I'm Rico," the lieutenant says. "Just hang on. We're almost there. Can you see any daylight?"

"Yes…uh…"

To my right, several stones cascade down, then suddenly four fingers wiggle their way through the crack.

"Got you!" I yell, covering her hand with mine. She squeezes me as best she can.

"That's fantastic, Portia," Lieutenant Flores calls to her. "Can you make sure you and the people you're with please move back? We're going to come through now."

"Gotcha, Rico."

We give her a few moments to get out of the way, then the entire One-Thirteen attacks that spot with determination. My heart is in my throat, and I don't trust myself to speak as the hole begins to grow, revealing the three people trapped underneath. As soon as there's a shoulder-width gap, two of them push the older woman forward.

"Please, help my wife!" the man cries, and I instinctively reach for her.

And then I know. I might not have seen Angela Ross in over fifteen years, but I still recognize her immediately. And I only saw Fredrick Ross a few weeks ago.

Colt must have been with them.

He must be the one that's still trapped.

"I'm here! I'm here!" Yara yells, practically skidding to halt beside us with a gurney and her supply bag swinging across her body.

"Possible fractured arm," I tell my partner, easing Mrs. Ross into her arms.

"I'm okay," she sobs, pointing shakily with her uninjured arm. "My son! Please help him! He could be crushed!"

There goes any last trace of doubt.

Ice sweeps through me and I squeeze my eyes shut briefly, saying a silent prayer.

La hawla wa la quwwata illa billah.

"Male victim reportedly under more rubble," I force myself to tell Yara quietly. Then before I can stop myself, I add, "It might be Colt."

Yara jerks and stares at me. "Colt? *Your* Colt?"

"It's you!" Mr. Ross splutters as he climbs out from the rubble. As if my appearance is somehow a more outrageous shock to his day than an earthquake.

"Wait, you know Colton Ross?" the second, very attractive woman asks as she clambers her way out, ignoring Sawyer's hand as he tries to help. She must be Portia. For some reason, she's clutching a wine bucket to her ample chest. I try not to wonder why she was having lunch with Colt and his parents.

His life is literally on the line. Him making it out of this alive is all that matters. Not if he was on a date. That's ridiculous. However, my poor, tattered heart isn't exactly listening to reason right now.

"He's my..." I go to answer Portia. But then I falter, watching as Sawyer and Anton dive through the opening, already tackling the area where the only man I've ever loved is apparently languishing underneath.

Even now, I can't out him to his parents if I don't have his consent.

"Delacroix," Captain Valentine shouts. I snap my head to

look at him. "What are you waiting for? Get in there and assist."

Gratitude washes through my entire body as I lock eyes with him to make sure I heard him correctly. He nods once, his expression serious.

"Thank you," I rasp before forcing my way through the narrow space. That's why Valentine is such a great captain. He doesn't need to understand everything to see that this isn't any ordinary rescue to me.

The guys have already uncovered feet in a pair of once shiny brogues and a hand. "Sir, can you hear us?" Anton calls as I position myself to lever away a long slab of plasterboard.

"His name's Colt," I utter, putting my back into moving the debris. "Colton Ross."

I try and brace myself for the possibility that we might be working to uncover a lifeless body. But I can't accept it. There's still hope. There's always hope until we know for sure.

With a guttural snarl, I finally shift the chunk of wall out the way.

Revealing Colt's slack, bloodstained face and torso.

"We have him!" Sawyer cries to the rest of the team. Half of them are still digging, and the other half are securing the structure with support beams and air bags so the rest of the building or that Sakura tree don't crash on top of our heads as well.

"Is he alive?" Mrs. Ross sobs.

My fingers are already jammed into his neck as I stare at his chest. "He has a pulse!" I shout as his lungs inflate. "And he's breathing!" I almost pass out myself with relief. Yara drops by my side, ready with an IV bag to get some fluids into him. "Colt! Can you hear me? It's Zahir."

Yara slides the line into his wrist without issue as I stimulate his sternum.

He moans.

"Colt?" I utter, aware that Dray has joined Sawyer and Anton in the widened space, helping to get the rest of the crap off Colt's body. His right pant leg is torn, and his shin is bruised several colors, making me worry about a break.

He moans again, his limbs twitching. I use some bottled water to rinse the blood from around his eyes. Judging from the small red pool under his head, it seems he's hit the back of his skull in addition to the cut on his forehead. They could both be superficial.

Or they could both be very serious indeed.

"Colt?" I say more urgently before dropping my voice and leaning closer to him so hopefully nobody else hears me.

I don't care if I'm being unprofessional.

I'm desperate.

"Colt…please come back to me. I…I love you."

Now might not be the most appropriate or romantic moment to say it out loud for the first time.

But it also might be my last chance.

His eyes flutter open.

The collective gasp flies around those crammed in the space with him. "He's awake!" Sawyer reports to everyone else.

"Baby?" he mumbles, his hand pawing groggily at me.

I grab it and kiss his knuckles, not bothering to even try and stop the tears streaming down my face. "I'm here," I tell him. "I've got you." I really hope his parents can't see us right now, because I don't think I can let go of his hand any time soon.

He peers at me through his wet lashes and manages a small smile.

"Love you, too," he mumbles.

My heart trips. He probably doesn't mean it. We're in the middle of a crisis, after all, and he's barely conscious.

Although…I meant it. So who knows?

"We need the backboard in here!" Yara yells. Teddy appears in a flash with it. Mr. and Mrs. Ross push their way into the space again behind him. Reluctantly, I place Colt's hand gently down. I need to work on him, anyway.

"What's happening?" Mr. Ross thunders. "Is he all right? We need to see him!"

"You need to step back and allow my team to work," Captain Valentine insists kindly but firmly.

"His vitals look good," Yara says.

"Leg hurts," Colt mumbles.

Yara smiles at me. "Already administering pain relief. I think you're going to be just fine, Mr. Ross."

I manage not to sob in relief as Mrs. Ross crouches down next to me and does that enough for the both of us. She practically shoves me back so she can grab Colt's hand and press it to her bosom.

"Oh, my darling boy," she wails. "It's okay! You hear that? The nice lady said you're going to be all right."

"Watch out for his IV," Yara warns her, proving she's not always nice if someone gets in the way of her treating a patient.

But Colt is woozy and he's only looking at me, smiling at me, pulling his hand free from his mom and reaching for me. "You're really here," he murmurs, his gritty, sweaty palm cradling the side of my face.

For a second, I bask in his touch. Then I remember where we are and who we're with, so I carefully push his arm back down with an awkward cough.

"The pain meds will already be working," I explain truthfully to his parents. "And the adrenaline will be making him disoriented. We need to get him to a hospital right away to check him over more thoroughly and treat his leg and head wounds. You can all ride together, so—"

Colt suddenly grabs my wrist, eyes blazing with intensity. "I told them," he says to me, his face then splitting into a beautiful, dopey grin. "I really told them."

"Told who what?" I ask. I'd like to guess, but I'm too afraid to get my hopes up.

"We don't have time for this," Mr. Ross snaps. "My wife and son need proper medical attention. I want—"

"I told them I'm gay," Colt says over his father's protests, causing the other man to stutter to a halt. "I told them I'm never going to marry a woman even if Portia *is* awesome, and I don't even want to be a lawyer anymore. I'm freeeee."

His expression is certainly blissful as he giggles, not taking his eyes off mine. I'm so stunned, words fail me. Surely he didn't do that?

Sure enough, Mr. Ross is harrumphing again. "He's delirious, just like you said. He has no idea what he's saying. It's pure nonsense!"

"Actually," the younger woman—Portia—says, moving in closer now that the One-Thirteen have cleared a path. She's still holding the wine bucket for some reason. "That's exactly what he said." She smiles knowingly at me. "Specifically, that I'm awesome. But also, the whole 'I'm gay and I'm off to live my own life now' bit, too."

"See, baby?" Colt says. "No more hiding, I promise. I'm alllll yours."

"Him?" Mrs. Ross shrieks. Of all the alarms and horns and sirens that have gone off in the past hour, that sound manages to hurt my ears the most. She's looking at me aghast, and my heart sinks.

Of course I'm still going to be the issue.

"Yes, *him,* Mom," Colt slurs before blowing a raspberry. "It's always been him. So you're not allowed to mean about him ever again, okay? It's a new law." He giggles some more to himself, but then his eyes land on me once more. "You're my ocean, baby."

"You're my sunshine," I reply breathlessly.

"Oh, hell fucking yeah," Portia says. I turn to look at her and she sighs happily. "Who'd pick me when he's already got you, huh?"

I don't know who this woman is, but it's clear to me she has Colt's back, and that makes me want to open my heart to her as well. Before I can thank her or even look back at Colt, though, Mr. Ross is off again.

"This is wildly unprofessional behavior!" he bellows from under his dusty, trembling mustache, shaking a pointed finger at me and turning a rather alarming shade of purple. "I demand this man be removed from my son's care immediately so he can be treated for his injuries without some hack encouraging his delusions!"

The entirety of the One-Thirteen goes very still, including our newest member, Drayton Hendrix. But the last thing I want to do is jeopardize Colt's health. "It's fine, I'll just—"

As I try to stand up, a small but very strong hand lands on my shoulder, keeping me in place. "Zahir Delacroix is our lead paramedic," Lili says, sounding dangerously amused. "There's no one better that could be treating your son, expect maybe his partner, Yara Ortiz. You know, the two people who just revived young Colt here."

"Don't go," Colt whimper, pawing at me.

"I'm right here," I assure him, because apparently, I'm not going anywhere.

Mr. Ross puffs up like a pigeon. "I don't have any problems with the girl. But this boy—"

"This *man* is a member of the One-Thirteen firehouse," Captain Valentine says firmly. He removes his helmet as he steps forward to square up with Colt's father. "The station that just saved your family's life. If you have a problem with the service we're providing, you are more than welcome to make your own way to San Clemente General."

"I'm not leaving him all alone!" Mrs. Ross shrieks. "He's upset!"

Behind me, Portia tsks. "He's quite clearly *not* alone, Mrs. Ross. And the only people upsetting him are you two. So either shut up or get out, because Colt's in good hands, and he needs to get his injuries seen to ASAP."

She crooks an eyebrow, not blinking until the Rosses lower their gazes.

"See," Colt says in a sing-song voice. "Portia's awesome. Oh! Portia! The Nemos! I—"

"Right here, buddy," she says warmly, holding up the mysterious wine bucket. "I'll keep them safe for you. I assume you'll want to take them home?"

"Belong to the restaurant," he mumbles, looking sad.

She scoffs. "I'll speak with the manager. If you want them, I'll buy the place some new ones. I reckon these guys will have trauma bonded with you by this point."

He blinks happily at her. "Zahir, I made a new friend, and I love her." He frowns and looks back at me. "But I love you the most, I promise."

I chuckle, and before I can stop myself, I lean down and kiss his forehead. If he's going to repeat it, then I will as well. "I love you, too. Hospital, now. Come on."

I can feel people shuffling behind me and speaking in low tones, but I ignore them all as Yara and I focus on rolling Colt onto the backboard so we can extract him. As we move him, though, he winces and jerks his hand to his left hip.

"What's wrong?" I ask, immediately going to palpate the area.

But he smacks mY hands away. "That's from before the earthquake." He grins drunkenly. "It's a surprise."

"I've had enough surprises today," I grumble. "Show me."

He chuckles and lifts his shirt up while pulling down the waistband of his pants. "I was tired of doing everything I was told," he says. "So I did something spontaneous. Maybe a bit crazy. Is it crazy, Zahir?"

I can't answer him for a moment, because my throat has temporarily closed up, and my eyes are burning with tears.

"You got a tattoo?" Yara asks, obviously also seeing the same clear medical grade adhesive covering the brand-new art on Colt's hip. "Neat! What is it?"

"My signature," I manage to croak out.

It's where I signed him during our insanely intense and amazing art sex in my new studio a couple of weeks ago.

He looks smugly at it. "I couldn't believe it didn't come off when we…you know." He waggles his eyebrows at me, and I try not to blush. Thankfully, everyone else seems to have moved farther away from the collapsed area, and don't seem to be listening in. "And I was just, like, overcome with the knowledge that I *had* to make it permanent. So I took a bunch of photos so I could recreate it and had an appointment yesterday. Because I'm yours, Zahir. I never, ever, *ever* want you to doubt that again. I'll never leave again or treat you like shit. I hope it's okay and not weird. Maybe I should have asked your permission to use your autograph like that, but—"

I can't stand it any longer. I lean down and kiss his mouth hard right there on the damn backboard. "It's beautiful," I say wetly as I laugh against his lips. "You're beautiful."

"Because you make me beautiful," he tells me.

Apparently not everyone has quite moved out of earshot. "Okay," Portia says very seriously. "I'm calling shotgun right now. I'm going to be the flower girl at your wedding." She indicates Yara. "This one's clearly going to be maid of honor, and you've probably got a dozen groomsmen over there. So that makes me the flower girl."

I laugh and so does Colt, who grips my hand despite the IV in his wrist. "Sounds like a plan to me."

Shaking my head, I brush his hair back. "You're high on pain meds."

He scoffs and rolls his eyes. "You want a more romantic proposal than this? Such a diva."

Something strange travels down my spine. I know he doesn't mean it...but whatever final reservations I had lingering within me that Colt wasn't all in finally and completely dissolve.

He's come out to his parents.

He's possibly giving up law.

He's staying in Redwood Bay.

He loves me. He might even want to marry me.

What is there now standing in the way of our future other than my fear? Nothing could be as terrifying as the possibility of losing him forever like I faced just now.

Forever *with* him sounds like exactly what I want.

"Do it again properly some time, and you'll find out if I'll say yes," I say, my skin burning and my head light as I feel in my bones just how much I mean that.

Colton Ross has been the love of my life since he breezed into my life at fourteen and even after we were eighteen when he slipped through my fingers like grains of sand on the beach. Now that he's washed back up on my shore and proven to me just what kind of man he is under the façade, I'm never letting him go again. I'm never letting him hide again—neither of us will.

We wasted fifteen years apart. As of today, that period of our lives is officially over.

"I told the guys you were my boyfriend when I thought you were dead," I confess as we lift him onto the gurney.

He laughs and reaches for my hand again. "Happy to be your alive boyfriend, Boyfriend."

I glance around at the rest of the squad who are very obviously pretending not to be listening. "You know the entire One-Thirteen just heard that, right?" I ask him with a wince.

But he just grins harder.

"They were meant to, baby," he says.

CHAPTER 25

Colt

SIX WEEKS LATER

"Coming!" I shout as I hobble as fast as I can to my front door. "Just a sec!"

When I open it, Zahir is waiting on the other side, smiling and looking as ridiculously handsome as ever. "You didn't have to rush," he says, shaking his head as he leans in to kiss me. "In fact, as a medical professional, I stringently advise against it."

I grin against his lips and kiss him some more. "I was excited to see you," I say in my defense. "And—look!" I point to my leg as he steps inside.

He raises his eyebrows. "The boot is gone!" he says happily.

"Well, not gone," I admit, shutting the door behind us. "But it's in a closet rather than on my foot full time now, yes. And the knee brace will probably stick around for at least four months," I add with a sigh. "Who knows when I'll be able to surf again." I'm grateful that both my head injuries turned out to be minor, but the broken tibia has been a bit annoying.

Still, when I think of how much worse it could have been, things don't seem so bad.

"Hey," Zahir says kindly, ensnaring my fingers with his and pulling me in for a hug. "You'll get there. You said PT was going well, right?" I nod. "So just be patient. It's more important you heal the right way now so you don't have complications down the line."

I gasp in fake shock. "Wow, you almost sound like a medical professional."

He rolls his eyes at me. "I do get that you hate being cooped up," he says sympathetically as he rubs my arm. "So much has changed recently, yet you've spent most of it in this place."

"At least this place is looking good, right?" I say as we wander slowly toward the kitchen area so I can pour us some iced tea.

He grins and squeezes my hand. "It really is," he agrees.

Not only do I have his beautiful tryptic paintings hanging on the wall now, but the large piece from our senior year is the main focus of the living room. At a glance, it doesn't *look* like us making love on the beach, and after so long hiding my true self away, it gives me a thrill to have it out in the open when people visit.

Because people do visit, especially while I've been recovering. So I got brand new forest-green sofas for them to sit on. There's *color* in my apartment now. I have lampshades and art and trinkets all over the damn place that speak to who I am and bring me joy. There's also a rug on the floor and bowls of potpourri on the windowsills.

Who even am I?

Of course, Zahir has been here the most, but a couple of times he's brought Yara or a few of the other guys from the One-Thirteen. It's crazy to me that they've just accepted me as Zahir's boyfriend after everything that happened in our past, but they have. And now I'm apparently part of the One-Thirteen family, which makes it sound like a cult you can't escape from, except I love it.

I love them.

Even Farah has forgiven me, it seems, because she's been over here at least once a week, filling up my refrigerator with home-cooked meals I either just need to put in the oven or the microwave. She calls me her bad boy and pinches my cheek and tells me that having a broken leg is no excuse for socks all over the floor.

I think I enjoy when she gets cross with me the most. Because it means she really cares.

My own family...I'm not so sure what's going on there. My parents have visited exactly one time since the earthquake, and even though they said nothing, it was clear they were embarrassed by my 'tacky' new décor. That just validates my choices, if I'm honest.

My mom is still tearful and dancing around the issue of my sexuality. My father is furious I really went through with handing my notice in at the firm. I can see they're *trying* to find a way to still connect with me, though, so I'm willing to keep the door open for them.

At least for the time being.

I've been mostly working through my notice period remotely, which suits me just fine. My father might hate it, but I think he has forced himself to acknowledge that I've been phoning it in since I arrived, and he'll be much better off appointing a managing partner that actually wants the position. It's pretty obvious to me that Preston Windward would be a perfect fit.

A few more weeks of handover work, and I'll be free. To do what...I'm not sure. But I can figure that out once I've got two fully functioning legs again.

Speaking of the only friend I made at Ross & Associates,

Preston has also been a regular visitor. His version of feeding me is chips and dip, but he brings his boxer, Jack, with him who likes to put his big head in my lap and lovingly stare at me, as if that will make me heal faster.

I actually think there's some science to that, if I'm honest.

Portia has genuinely become a good friend, too, and has kept me company on several evenings when Zahir's been working. I'm ashamed to say she's got me hooked on some truly terrible reality TV shows.

And then there's Elizabeth and the kids, who came over with little Rebecca and all three of her parents for a playdate last week. That was kind of intense, but weirdly in a really fun way. I thought having children in my home would be an awful experience, but they weren't the hellions I was envisioning they'd be. They played a board game on the floor while the adults talked for an hour, and the older girls were fascinated when I showed them my miniature Zen garden and how to use the little rake to make patterns in the sand.

I bought that as a present to myself so I'd never forget the day I dared to come out to my parents. The day I said out loud that I love Zahir and was his boyfriend. Yeah, it's also the day I almost died, but nothing's ever perfect, and you can't have the light without the dark.

My other reminder of that day is a little bigger, but I needed more feature pieces in this bland, empty apartment anyway.

In the aftermath of the earthquake, the owners of the Jiyū Sushi Bar cared way more about rebuilding the restaurant than they did about me keeping the two koi carp I rescued. In fact, they were concerned with how they were going to care for the ones in the tanks that didn't break, so having two less was a small relief for them.

Eventually, my plan is to move somewhere with a pond in the back yard. But for now, my girls Umi (sea) and Sora (sky) have a bigger tank than before, with all kinds of plants and miniature Japanese buildings to hide and play in. I've never had a pet before in my life, but with everything that's been happening over the past few weeks, I've genuinely enjoyed and appreciated having a couple of living creatures depending on me to get out of bed and care for them, especially on some of the tougher mental health days.

I know what Zahir's trying to say about being patient. I've thrown myself into this recovery and am determined to do everything I can to heal the right way. But it's difficult for me not to feel like I've wasted half my life already, and now I've finally made some huge, significant changes, I'm impatient to get going. Being cooped up in this apartment hasn't been the best.

That's why I'm not waiting anymore. There's something I've wanted to do for a while now, and even though I'm extremely nervous, I'm going to make it happen today.

Finally.

"I have a surprise for you," I say, trying to slow my heart rate down a little.

Zahir pauses then raises his eyebrows. "Yeah?"

Damn, this is going to be harder than I thought. Not trusting myself to speak, I put down my empty iced tea glass on the counter and pluck his from his fingers to do the same. Then I slip my hand against his and tug it so he starts following me back through the apartment toward the bedroom.

Anyone else would probably make a joke in that moment about how now I've gotten my foot out of the moon boot I'm ready to get my freak on (which isn't entirely untrue). But because it's Zahir, he just quietly follows me, probably picking up that this is an important moment. I push open my bedroom door, but step back a little to let him enter first.

The decision to focus updating my apartment's décor in

the living room area was a conscious one. I hadn't done anything with my bedroom.

Until now.

Since the last time Zahir came over, I've swapped the dark gray bed covers for light blue and changed the blinds from black to white. There's now a wooden slatted head-board where before I didn't have one. I even got some decorative white throw pillows and a linen runner thing that serves no purpose other than to make the bed look a bit fancy.

In front of the blinds, I've also now hung a floor length gauzy white curtain, and the same material has been pinned in strips above the bed, giving an effect like waves rolling onto the shore. It's still light out, so we can't really appreciate the effect right now, but there are fairy lights hanging among the gauze as well that will twinkle in the darkness.

I'll admit that I wasn't able to do any of this manual labor over the past few days. However, Portia and Preston were very good at bringing my vision to life. I *was* able to add touches like the jar of seashells on the dresser, the new wicker laundry basket, and the paperweight on top of the pile of books on my nightstand that looks like thick chain links from an anchor.

Portia hung a floating shelf for me specifically so I could display some framed photos of me and Zahir. We only have a couple of selfies so far, but I plan on adding a lot more. The important thing for me is that I declare to anyone who visits that we're a couple. I want pictures of us in every room of wherever I live, whether that's this rented place or the house we're undoubtedly going to buy together in the near future.

Ideally, I want all the art in my home to be Zahir's. But I just couldn't resist getting a print of the famous Great Wave off Kanagawa by Japanese artist Katsushika Hokusai. We used to talk endlessly about going on an adventure around the world with our surfboards when we were teens. But ever since our lives were changed in just one day surrounded by Japanese culture, I've felt Asia calling me. Like destiny stepped in and told me that my life could be so much more than it had been so far, and that life could really be with Zahir.

Japan has a thriving surfing scene, you see.

"Colt," Zahir says, looking around the room.

"The plants are from your teta," I explain. Farah truly spoiled me, insisting I take over half a dozen pots filled with beautifully variegated leaves and colorful flowers.

"And the rest?" he asks, probably referring to the twenty or so candles in hurricane jars I placed around the room and all the cherry blossom petals strewn over the freshly made bed. Or maybe the sea breeze incense I've got burning and the peaceful ocean sounds quietly playing through my Bluetooth speaker.

I can't stop the smile spreading onto my face as I move around in front of him. Now it's happening, the nerves are melting away. I squeeze his hands in mine, then take a deep breath before my next words.

"The more permanent changes are because I'm done being hard and masculine all the time. I can be soft and feminine too if I want. This is my sanctuary, and I wanted it to reflect my soul. My soul is where the sun meets the sea. It's with you, Zahir. The less permanent additions are because I thought about taking you down to the beach to do this. But as much as I'm done hiding away, I do think some things should be private, so I brought the beach home." I grimace and move to sit on the edge of the bed. "Sorry about this next part, but I've only got one knee functioning at full capacity right now."

His warm brown eyes go wide as I manage to get my

hand in my pants pocket and pull out the ring box that's been burning a hole there ever since he arrived.

"I know I did this once before," I say thickly. My eyes are already burning as I open the box to reveal the gold band with several raw sapphires ensconced at the front. The rough, uneven finish on the polished metal makes me feel like it's something a mermaid found at the bottom of the ocean just so I could give it to my man in this moment. "But I have a feeling you didn't believe I was serious?"

Zahir's eyes are also brimming with tears as he cradles his hands under mine, staring at the ring. "I told you if you asked me properly, you'd find out if I'd say yes," he whispers.

I've wasted enough time when it comes to Zahir Delacroix. So I don't hesitate now.

"I've loved you my whole life, Zee," I tell him truthfully. "I want to spend the rest of it by your side. You make me the man I know I was always supposed to be, and I'll spend the rest of my days lifting you up to your highest heights so you can be your very best, too. Will you marry me?"

He places his hand on his chest as the tears splash down his cheeks. "Are you sure?" he utters. "We don't have to rush this."

"I damn well do," I tell him with a frown. "I should have done this years ago. Unless you don't want to?" Suddenly the nerves are back. "In that case—"

"YES!" he cries, then laughs at his own outburst. He grabs the box from my hands, plucks the ring from it and tosses the box aside before slipping the band over his finger. "There," he says shakily with a grin. "You can't take it back now."

I grin and throw my arms around his waist, dragging him onto the bed and peppering his face with kisses. "I would never take it back," I assure him. "The contract is binding. I belong to you now, and that's a fact."

He pauses as we lay side by side to stare at his hand. "It's beautiful," he marvels.

"You're beautiful," I remind him, then caress it with my fingertips. "Gold and blue for the sunshine and the ocean," I explain.

He exhales and shakes his head. "I think a part of me was always waiting for you to come back to me. I'm so happy you did, Colt."

"Me, too," I tell him truthfully. "Make love to me, please?"

"I was already planning on it," he says, smirking as he rolls me on my back. Because of my broken leg, he's been riding me the last few weeks, and it's been amazing.

But that's not what I meant.

"No, baby," I say softly. "I want *you* to make love to *me*." He crooks an eyebrow in confusion, and I chuckle wryly. "I want to bottom."

Unsurprisingly, he pauses. "You haven't done that since you came back…"

"I haven't done that with *anyone*," I clarify. "Not since the last night I was with you in Redwood Bay. No one ever, Zee. Just you. I want that now. I'm ready. And I mean that literally." I waggle my eyebrows and laugh until he catches my drift.

"Oh…*oh!*"

He blushes. I love it.

I lean up to kiss his mouth and slip my hands under his shirt. "I have to be careful sill, but can we do it like this? Face to face with you on top?"

That seems to wake his brain up again. He starts kissing me back with the fiery passion I love so much from him, his hands threading through my hair. I feel his new ring against my scalp, and it sends shivers down my spine.

"Of course," he says, repositioning himself to take more of

his weight on his knees as he straddles my hips. "Anything you want, Colt. I want to make you feel so good."

"You always do," I assure him.

Normally, it's my pleasure to take care of us both in the bedroom. But my banged-up leg has made that tricky of late. It's actually kind of nice to be a bit of a pillow princess for a change. I can't see myself doing it all the time. But letting Zahir undress us both helps me get into a more submissive mind frame.

I want to mark this occasion by giving myself over to him completely. It's important to me that I show with my actions how much I trust him with my body and soul—that I trust him with our *forever*.

I'm at least able to grab us the lube from my nightstand. It was such a relief to ditch the condoms a while back, but now's my first time experiencing that from the other end of things.

The nerves come back a little, but only because I want this to be amazing for both of us. The danger with missing fifteen years of casual interactions together is that I'm aware I'm overcompensating sometimes by hyper fixating on our experiences now being perfect.

Although there is something I've realized recently that's put so many things into perspective. Yes, I'm ashamed for how I acted at eighteen and wish I hadn't caused Zahir so much pain. But on the other hand…would we really have survived together all this time if I hadn't gone away and understood just how much I don't want the life my parents mapped out for me? The break-up was awful for both of us. However, there's a part of me now that wonders if that time apart wasn't necessary—essential even—for making us the men we are today.

The men that both of us are going to spend the rest of our lives with.

Zahir's on top on me, our warm stomachs rubbing together as he kisses me through his smiles. "Are you really all mine?" he asks.

I take his hand and place it over the fully healed tattoo on my hip. "Forever, baby."

He shuffles down and kisses the spot sweetly. Then he moves his mouth over to my leaking cock, and suddenly the vibe is more sinful than sweet.

"Oh, baby, oh," I utter, threading my fingers through his silky hair. He hums and looks up at me through his dark lashes, knowing exactly how much he's turning me on.

Despite me telling him I'd already stretched myself, he still pops off my length, then kisses down, nuzzling and sucking my balls, licking my taint, before pulling my cheeks apart and feasting on my hole. I groan and pant, lifting my knees up as much as it's comfortable to do so with the brace on.

In that moment, my recently broken tibia doesn't seem to be an issue one way or another.

"Fuck, fuck, *fuck*," I grunt.

I haven't been rimmed in…well…fifteen years. I never trusted anyone else down there. But Zahir doesn't hesitate to pleasure me, probing his tongue and fingers inside where I already worked myself before he arrived. The last thing I wanted was to hold us up because my body might fight us.

I should have known it wouldn't do anything else but welcome Zahir back with open arms.

"Please," I whimper, pawing at his shoulders and tugging at his hair. "Please, baby. I'm ready. I need you now, so badly."

Mercifully, he immediately listens to me, pulling back and finding the lube to drizzle over his hard length and into my crack. I don't need this to last all night. We have the rest of our lives together. But I do I need him now and I need him *hard.*

That's why he's my person, my soul. He knows exactly what I'm craving, and he gives it to me. Within moments, he's thrusting deep inside me, nailing my prostate the perfect way to make me scream and lose my mind. The intrusion is almost too much for my body. I'm so full, so overwhelmed. But I know it's Zahir and I can trust him with my heart, body, and soul, so I let go, allowing him to drive us toward our bliss.

"Colt," he mutters between kisses. He's being careful of my leg, but that doesn't mean he isn't digging his fingers into my ribs and biting my lower lip.

"Yes, yes, yes!" I chant. "Are you close? I need...I'm going to..."

He wraps his hand over my cock and tugs. I wail, knowing it's not going to take much.

"I want to see you come, beautiful," he murmurs in my ear.

How can I refuse?

My knee brace reminds me not to dig my heels into the mattress, but I still arch my spine as my climax crashes through me like a great wave. I cling to Zahir, loving how he bellows with his head dropped back, shooting his load inside me like he wants to mark me and claim me.

Like he wants to breed me.

After we've collapsed into a heap of sweaty, tangled limbs, he eventually pulls out of me and stumbles to the en suite to fetch us a warm, damp cloth to clean up with. Again, that's usually my job, but since my injury I've accepted that it's quite nice when Zahir does this job, and today in particular I bask in the role reversal. There are cherry blossom petals stuck all over me and despite my best efforts, my shin is aching like a bitch.

The moment couldn't be more perfect.

Once the essentials have been mopped up, I pull my *fiancé*

back down with me on top of the duvet and kiss his forehead. It's funny that the breeding image isn't shaking from my mind. I don't think I've uncovered a new kink. Rather, it's jostled up something I've been pondering for a while now.

"Zahir," I say seriously as I stroke his back. He hums to show he's listening. "Before we get married, there are a couple of things we might want to check."

He lifts his head and smiles sleepily at me. "You want to negotiate the contract?" he teases.

I shrug, but he's not wrong. "I was hoping we could move in together. Whatever I end up doing, my salary will probably take a big hit. But I still have an insane amount of savings for a deposit."

He nuzzles our noses together. "I don't need a big house," he says. "We will probably need a pond for the fish, though. And maybe space for a dog?"

I smile. "I was pondering that, too. But, um, the house. How many bedrooms?"

My heart is racing again as I watch his reaction. Initially, he just looks curiously. "Well, one for us and one for guests, I suppose?"

"What about more bedrooms for not-guests?" I ask, my mouth dry. "What if I was thinking about…kids?"

In all the years I've known Zahir Delacroix, I don't reckon I've ever seen his eyes go so wide, not even just now when I proposed. "I didn't think you wanted children," he whispers.

I take a deep breath and cup the side of his face. "I didn't. To me, kids were a burden, or things you created to manipulate. But I feel differently now. I think…I think we'd be amazing dads. But I keep going and over it, and I don't care about bloodlines or whatever. In fact, ego's the thing I hate most about the whole idea. If you're open to it, I'd want to adopt. There are so many kids who aren't loved enough, and

I just know we could give that to them. I'm not talking right now, obviously, but…someday. That's where I see us down the line. I just thought I'd check that fit with you."

For several moments, he simply stares at me as his eyes fill with tears. Eventually, he sobs as his face splits into a beaming smile, then he gathers me up in the tightest hug imaginable.

"That would be the greatest honor of my life, Habibi."

I'm not ashamed to say that special little word makes me lose it. I cling to him and laugh and cry until I feel sick.

Zahir Delacroix is going to be my husband. He wants to have children with me. And for the first time in our long history together, he dared to call me his habibi, his darling.

Nothing in my life has turned out the way it was planned.

And yet it's absolutely perfect.

Epilogue

ZAHIR – ONE MONTH LATER

"I don't really know what I'm doing," Captain Lucy Padilla whispers to me, her eyebrows raised.

I lean closer to her. "You're the only qualified person we know. Do you want to stop?"

She huffs, blowing a tendril of brown hair off her forehead. "Nah. I guess we're all here now, huh?"

"You've got this," Colt whispers back to her.

"Debatable," she says with a wink. "Let's give it a try, though." She clears her throat and steps back, raising her voice for everyone else gathered on the beach to hear. "Dearly beloved," she begins.

"Uhhh…" I glance around. From the second row, Sawyer shakes his hand in a 'so-so' motion. "Maybe something less boring?" he suggests in an exaggerated whisper.

Captain Padilla arches an eyebrow. "Hey there, all you gays, theys, and girly pops," she tries again, completely deadpan.

That gets a raucous cheer from the crowd and two thumbs up from my ever-helpful colleague. I chuckle and roll my eyes, looking back at my fiancé, who's also grinning. So long as he's having a good time, that's all that really matters.

"Excellent," Captain Padilla says, shaking her head as she looks down at her notes. "Okay, we are gathered here today to celebrate the marriage of Zahir Delacroix and Colton Ross. An event, I'm assured, that has been close to twenty years in the making and not, as it might appear, one single month."

"Shotgun wedding!" Lili coughs into her fist.

I sigh. "I'm applying for a transfer," I mutter.

Colt squeezes my hands. "I think you're stuck with them, baby."

Isn't that the truth?

I have to act disgruntled by their heckling, because that's what will make the One-Thirteen happy. Well, some of them. Yara and Lochlan are already weeping joyfully into their handkerchiefs. Captain Valentine is beaming with pride. Lieutenant Flores is diligently filming everything. And young Teddy is watching the whole event unfold in awe.

That's pretty much how I feel.

I have to hand it to my husband-to-be. When he sets his mind to something, there's no stopping him. It really did only take him a month to put together a dream beach wedding for us, declaring that he'd wasted far too much time already, and he wasn't going to wait a minute longer than was necessary before making an honest man out of me.

Once we realized the police captain was a licensed wedding officiant, all we needed was to book a time and date with the town council, hire a bunch of chairs, and organize a flower arch to complete our ocean backdrop. Caterers will arrive shortly to provide drinks and a BBQ so we can party the night away as the sun sets.

It couldn't be more perfect.

All I really cared about was having the most important

people attend. We picked a Saturday when the first watch of the One-Thirteen wasn't working, obviously. But I was thrilled when our new honorary member, Drayton Hendrix, made time in his schedule to join us as well. As predicted, Yara agreed to be my maid of honor, and all the guys—including Lili—declared themselves groomsmen. As we haven't bothered with any formal attire, that basically just meant their only responsibility was to throw me a messy bachelor party.

I think that suited everyone just fine.

Colt's new friend Portia really did mean it about being the flower girl, and took great pride in walking down the aisle, scattering a whole tree's worth of Sakura petals to guide my way. She was gracious enough to share the attention with the littlest members of the wedding party, though, allowing Nevaeh and Dashel Adams and Rebecca Quick to walk down before her, holding hands and waving to a chorus of 'Ahhhh's.

Of course, Teta was the one to give me away, with my parents and a few other family members sitting proudly among my rowdy work family. Before taking her seat, my grandma kissed my cheek and told me how happy she is for me and Colt.

"True love always finds a way," she whispered into my ear.

I've basically been fighting back tears ever since.

I think Preston was very touched when Colt asked him to be his best man. It warms my heart to see him thriving in Redwood Bay and building the kind of friendship group he never found in all his time on the East Coast. Although, I have noticed Portia and Preston making eyes at each other. Colt calls them his 'two Ps in a pod.'

That's either going to result in the most spectacular power couple this town has ever seen or a disaster to put even earthquakes to shame. There won't be any in between.

His parents are here, which I'm moderately surprised by. Although, I did hear Mrs. Ross say more than once earlier that this just wasn't what she'd ever imagined for her son, dabbing her eyes like she's at a funeral instead of a wedding.

Mrs. Bloom replied that she understood. Of course, most parents aren't blessed with a son-in-law as handsome, kind, and talented as me, so she must still be so overwhelmed with gratitude. Mrs. Ross didn't have much to say to that, and Miss Margot Fonteyn growled until the other woman scuttled away.

I'm not sure things are ever going to be smooth between us and the elder Rosses. But at least Colt still has some kind of relationship with them. The fact they're here means they're trying, so that's a start.

It's clear to see, though, that since rejecting their grand life plan, he's never been happier. The wedding isn't the only project he's been putting his mind to. We've also been house hunting, not considering places with less than four bedrooms, and on a mission to visit the animal shelter once we've moved in together so we can start growing our family right away. Colt saved up a truly staggering amount when he was in New York, so we're in the extremely privileged position of having enough for not just a deposit, but we can also pay part of the sum upfront, leaving us with a very reasonable mortgage.

That way, he won't have to worry about the drop in his salary. After some consideration, he's decided not to completely walk away from law, after all. He has already left his father's firm, which I'm sure will be a bone of contention between them for a long time to come. But that's Fredrick Ross's cross to bear.

Colt's plan is to open up a small practice with the sole intention of providing legal advice at reasonable rates to local businesses and charities. I know he feels like he abandoned Redwood Bay when he fled to the East Coast, and the idea of giving back to the community has breathed new life into his career. It's obvious his dad pushed him into becoming a lawyer, but he is amazing at what he does, and when he's representing people he actually cares about, he knows it will bring him joy.

He also knows now how important a balance between work and the rest of his life is. No more fourteen-hour days to bury who he really is. A regular nine-to-five won't just leave room for me and the family we hope to build, but other pursuits as well.

Once his leg is fully healed, Colt absolutely intends on obtaining the necessary certifications so he can officially start teaching surfing to kids. He's already got three guaranteed students, after all.

And we're finally going to travel.

We spent so many hours on this beach, talking about the future. I think a part of me clung to those childish daydreams, and that's why I put my own future on hold for so long. I shouldn't have, but now it doesn't matter. We've got our bucket list of places to visit, not just to surf at, but that's definitely where we're starting.

The honeymoon won't be for another couple of months. We're waiting until the fall because by then his leg should be back to full strength, but that's also the best time of year for surfing in Japan.

It might seem a little strange to some people that a themed restaurant where he almost died should now be such a source of comfort and inspiration to him, but that's Colt. After spending most of his life repressing anything his parents deemed as frivolous, he's now embracing joy wherever he finds it. There's something gentle and deeply spiritual about Japanese culture that he wants to celebrate in his everyday life.

To him, Japan has become a symbol of his rebirth, but he's very conscious of not becoming one of those Westerners that fetishizes the country. So we're planning on immersing ourselves there for several weeks to learn all we can, starting with surfing on the shores of Miyazaki before traveling to the Sakurayama Park in Gunma to see the winter cherry blossoms, visiting Osaka, Kyoto, and Tokyo in between.

He's already started learning the language, which the staff at the Jiyū Sushi Bar have been greatly amused with helping him practice. As much as his recovery will allow him, he's been volunteering with the restaurant's clean-up operation after the quake. And he won't admit the amount, but I know he also made a substantial donation to their repair fund that's going to help cover what their insurance didn't.

Because that's the kind of man he is. The man I'm whole-heartedly choosing to spend the rest of my life with. He's curious and sweet and caring, willing to put others before his own needs at almost every opportunity. I still catch him referring to himself as a selfish, manipulative bastard some-times, but that's all part of the image his parents tried to mold him into. He's still carrying some guilt around as well for the way he behaved when he was eighteen, which again, really wasn't his fault.

I don't care how long it takes. If I have to spend the rest of our lives proving to him that he's a good man who has been completely forgiven, that's what I'll do. It's why one of my only requests for the new house is to hang my charcoal study of him up in our bedroom. I know that's asking a lot of him to be vulnerable like that, but the world deserves to see how beautiful he is, inside and out. By displaying the work in our bedroom, it will still be private. But I want him to see himself every single morning the way I do.

His response to my request was to strike a bargain, because as previously stated, he's still a damn lawyer. I kind of love that, but when he said he'd hang that charcoal study in our house so long as he could put on a long overdue gallery showcase of my work in public...I knew I was in trouble.

Everything significant I've ever painted since I met him has been about us and our relationship in some form or another. My natural instinct has always been to keep all of that completely private, just in case anyone ever worked out some intimate detail they shouldn't. It's taken me several days since his proposition to realize that's just not our reality anymore. There's nothing left to hide, and all my man is asking to do is be allowed to show me off.

Action is his way of showing love, after all. It's not enough for him to say the words or marry me or *tattoo my name on his skin*. He needs the whole world to see it. Or at least Redwood Bay. So I've cautiously agreed to a little display at the town library to begin with. But he's already talking about organizing a charity auction for the pieces I'm not interested in keeping as well as any I'd like to create specifically for the purpose of displaying and selling.

Is it terrible to be excited that strangers might want to donate money to good causes in order to hang pieces in their homes that are snapshots of my soul? Works that are my truest, messiest, most earnest representations of how Colt and I previously existed in this world?

I hope not.

We deserve to be seen after all this time cowering in the shadows. Which is why throughout the rest of our future home, I want photos of us everywhere. We might have missed fifteen years together, but now that Colt and our relationship are finally out of the closet, we're going to make up for lost time. We've even started a couple's Instagram account that I'm sure is entirely nauseating, but I couldn't care less. On my own account, I never even showed my face.

But life is for living and when my time comes, I want a million memories to look back on and smile at.

In the meantime, I finally freed the dogeared strip of photos from the pages of my high school yearbook, gave it a frame, and displayed it in my living room. I didn't even have to ask—Colt has already demanded the strip gets pride of place in our new home. I look at those two naïve kids, knowing they had no idea what was to come, but so incredibly grateful that they made it in the end.

When I think of all the heartache we both suffered over so many years, it's hard to believe we finally arrived here. The odds were against us from the very beginning. But I think that only proves how strong our love truly is, and that we were destined to be together. Colt likes to talk about a thread that always bound us, even when we were on opposite sides of the country. Neither time nor distance could keep us apart forever, though, and now forever is what we're committing to spend together.

The past haunted me for so long, and the future didn't seem like it was going to be much better, so I was just floating through the present like driftwood from a shipwreck, bobbing aimlessly on the waves. Now my soul has been reunited with its other half, I can't wait to sail through life with Colt by my side, ready to face anything the world throws at us. There's nothing we can't overcome so long as we remain honest and true.

No more hiding.

Of course, we have to finish getting married first.

"Right," Captain Padilla says, looking warily around the congregation. "If there's anyone here who knows something we don't and thinks this marriage is a bad idea, speak up now. Otherwise, this train is leaving the station."

I wondered earlier why Mrs. Bloom had situated herself beside Colt's mom. As I glance their way, I see her subtly place her hand over Mrs. Ross's. Miss Margot Fonteyn wags her tail. I grin and look back at my man. No one says a thing. Even the One-Thirteen know when not to joke around.

"Phew," I whisper.

"I wasn't worried," Colt murmurs back, making my heart ache even more. Of course he wasn't.

"Fantastic," Captain Padilla says with genuine relief. "In that case, I now pronounce you two husbands for ever and ever! You may now celebrate with a kiss. But keep it PG-13, guys. We've got kids present."

Our little corner of the beach goes feral as the music from the speaker starts to play and I kiss Colt as my husband for the first time. It's difficult to accomplish with how much we're both grinning, but somehow we manage it.

Technically, we still have to fill out the paperwork. But little does my new husband know, I've already had the most important thing signed. With everything we've had to authorize recently, his autograph was easy enough for me to steal a copy of.

I can't wait until later when I reveal my present to him, the one I snuck out to organize last night. A matching tattoo of his signature on my hip, declaring to the world that I'm his for the rest of time, just like he's mine.

Our love is the greatest masterpiece I could ever imagine. A lifetime in the making, and yet somehow, we still have a lifetime yet to celebrate it.

He's the sunshine sparkling on my ocean. For so long, I thought our love had been lost. We just had to find our way back to each other to reignite the spark. After that, our shared destiny was free to rise from the ashes, stronger than ever before.

The earth can shatter, and the sky can fall. But nothing can stop us now.

This love is going to last for all eternity.

———

Thank you so much for reading Zahir and Colt's story! Next up in **Redwood Bay Fire**, we have Teddy Foster, our adorable young probationary firefighter, and his celebrity crush, former pro-football player, Cassius Garda. If you don't want to miss out on their age gap romance, pre-order **Striking the Match** today!

Turn the page to discover box sets of more heartwarming small town and found family series from HJ Welch, and contemporary fairy tale adaptations from Helen Juliet.

———

Thank you to my team!

Cover Designer: Jacqueline Sweet

Editor: Meg Cooper

Love, Support & Inspiration: Ed, AK, Charlie, Sarah, Hubby & our kitty cats

Also Available

REDWOOD BAY FIRE #1: IGNITING HIS FLAME BY HJ WELCH

Love makes us all brave

DARIO

After escaping my controlling ex-boyfriend and moving to Redwood Bay, I swear off men for good. The only company I need is my new rescue dog, Queenie. Meeting gorgeous firefighter Lochlan Bell at puppy training class doesn't count because he's straight, yet for some bizarre reason he's decided to become my friend. When he suggests *pretending* to be my boyfriend for Thanksgiving to stop my concerned family from worrying about me, the lines start to blur. Even if Lochlan suddenly realizes he likes men, though, he'd never be into a nerd like me. Right?

LOCHLAN

Who knew that pulling a trembling puppy from a burning building would lead to meeting my new best friend? Dario Garcia-Perez is so cool and smart, I'm surprised he puts up with a dumb jock like me. But I can tell he's running from something that hurt him real bad. Or some*one*. It takes me way too long to realize that all these protective feelings I have for him might mean something else. Something more. Something amazing. Just as we start getting closer, though, Dario's past comes back to haunt him. The difference now is that he has me, and I'm not going anywhere.

__Igniting His Flame__ is a red-hot, standalone MM romance. It's the first book in the found family __Redwood Bay Fire__ series. Join the members of the One-Thirteen house as the heat turns up and they find true love! This book features a completely oblivious bisexual himbo, two four-legged best friends, a childhood bedroom with only one bed, a shared obsession with all things sci-fi, a disaster at the amusement park, an ex with a dangerous vendetta, and a guaranteed HEA with absolutely no cliffhanger.

Content Warning: This book deals with a past domestic abuse situation between Dario and his ex. No violence occurs on page.

Click here to get the Igniting His Flame eBook

Also Available

PINE COVE BOX SET BY HJ WELCH

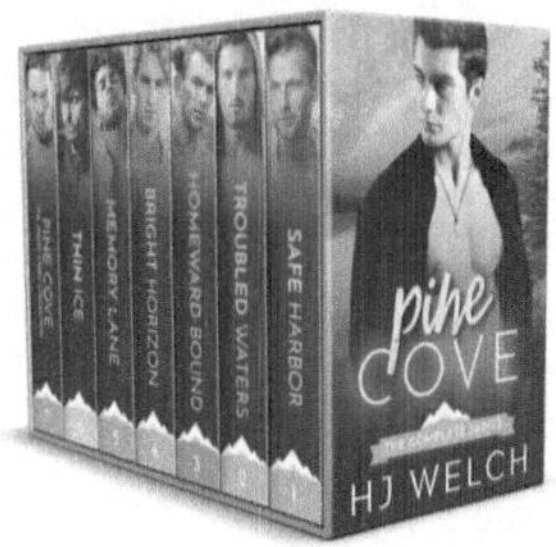

Welcome to Pine Cove, where true love lives happily ever after! **This 2000 page box set contains all six novels as well as all five companion short stories.**

Click here to get the Pine Cove eBook bundle

Click here to get the Pine Cove audio bundle

———

Safe Harbor

Robin Coal needs a fake boyfriend for his high school reunion. He asks his housemate: a gorgeous, totally straight ex-Marine. What could go wrong? There's only one bed, and Dair might not be so straight after all... When Robin's past threatens their future, only Dair can save him.

———

Sweet Spot

It's Halloween and Robin has prepared a sexy little surprise for his boyfriend Dair when he gets home from work. Hold on to your horses, Marine!

————

Troubled Waters

Bodyguard Scout Duffy doesn't know what's worse: the fact that his scorching one-night-stand, Emery Klein, is his bratty new client, or the fact that he doesn't even remember Scout. But Emery's life is in danger thanks to his out and proud charity work, and once he finally recognizes Scout, their chemistry in undeniable.

————

Homeward Bound

Swift Coal just found out he's a father, and his daughter (and her cranky cat) are coming to stay. His best friend's younger brother, Micha Perkins, has nowhere to go and a wrongfully tattered reputation. He's relieved when Swift asks him to be a live-in babysitter. He just has to hide his lifelong crush. Easy, because Swift is straight—right?

————

Bright Horizon

With sixteen years between them, baker Ben Turner and lawyer Elias Solomon have no idea their crush is mutual. But when Ben inherits his long-lost family's estate and becomes an overnight millionaire, Elias swears to protect the innocent younger man from the vultures circling him. To unravel the mystery of the inheritance, they must go to England to confront Ben's estranged relatives…and their feelings for each other.

————

Crossed Paths

Raj Bhat is done living in the shadows. It's time for him to take charge of his own destiny and tell the man he's fallen for how he really feels.

———

Midnight Sky

It's the night before New Year's Eve. Taylan Demir is all alone, and he's just lost his dog. Except when his handsome customer, Hudson Perkins, comes to his rescue, Taylan doesn't just get his dog back. He's suddenly got a hot date, and maybe someone to kiss when the clock strikes midnight.

———

Memory Lane

Angel Shields saved Jay Coal's life in high school, and Jay has secretly loved his straight best friend ever since. Now Angel's back in town with amnesia after a suspicious work accident and it's Jay's turn to rescue him. He pretends to be Angel's fiancé to see him in the hospital, but with his scrambled-up memory, Angel's not sure it's fictional after all. He just knows he loves Jay more than ever.

———

Thin Ice

Kamran's ex broke his heart, tricked him into aiding a bank robbery, and now he wants him to do one last job. There's only one way to say no: seek the protective custody of the biggest, grumpiest FBI agent ever, Lee Marshall. And pretend to be his boyfriend for a week-long family reunion in their giant mansion. Wait, what?

———

Calm Shores

Gorgeous, sophisticated Dante walks into Oliver's bar and orders…a boyfriend?! Dante needs a man to keep his mother from setting him

back up with his awful, cheating ex, and Oliver is up for the
challenge.

———

Fresh Snow

Emery Klein is throwing the best Christmas party ever, but his
fiancé, Scout Duffy, and all their friends have something more
exciting in mind.

———

*Each Pine Cove book can be read as a stand alone and has its own happy
ever after. But if you read the whole series, you'll see a lot of familiar faces!*

Click here to get the Pine Cove eBook bundle

Click here to get the Pine Cove audio bundle

Also Available

HOMECOMING HEARTS BOX SET BY HJ WELCH

Meet the five members of Below Zero, a boy band who have just been dropped by their record label and have to find their way back home again. Join Blake, Joey, Raiden, Trent, and Reyse as they each discover their happy ever afters! **This 1500+ page box set features all five original novels as well as three bonus epilogues that catch up with the guys after their HEAs!**

Click here to get the Homecoming Hearts eBook bundle

———

Scorch

Blake Jackson just wants to open a dance school now his pop star days are done. But his life is turned upside down by a reality TV show, and an old school friend the director has made into his fake boyfriend. Blake isn't gay, but he's happy to reconnect with barista Elion Rodriguez. However, Elion is gay, and has been secretly in love with Blake since freshman year. As the lines between fake and reality begin to blur, an obsessive stalker shadows Blake. Can he save Elion from getting burned?

Spark

The last thing Joey Sullivan wants is to go back to his homophobic family, but he's penniless and has no choice. Recently single and heartbroken Gabe Robinson loves the town Joey hates. As a librarian and voluntary firefighter, he's used to helping people. When Joey gets a lucky break out of state, Gabe doesn't hesitate to take him on a road trip. The sparks that fly between them have to be just temporary, though. Joey can't wait to leave town and his family are eager to kick him out the door. Can Gabe's love save him from ending up on the streets? *Contains bonus epilogue.*

Burn

Songwriter Raiden Jones never thought he'd need a bodyguard. But when a malicious hacker starts destroying his career and threatening his life, he finds himself desperately in need of protection. That means ex-Marine Levi Patterson is stuck on tour with the bratty Raiden, their friction quickly turning sexual. Bisexual Levi is firmly in the closet and Raiden's never thought of being with a man before, but the chemistry is too fierce to ignore. Will the hacker ruin everything before they can work through their differences? *Contains bonus epilogue.*

Steam

Bad boy movie star Trent Charles is in need of an image makeover. Ashby Wilcott wants some peace and quiet after his ex-boyfriend cheated on him. They both find themselves in a remote ski resort, but Ashby refuses to fall for hot-as-hell Trent. Good thing Trent is straight, because Ashby is done with trouble makers. Except when Trent rescues Ashby from a sleaze, they find themselves pretending to be boyfriends for a wedding weekend. Ashby awakes a longing in Trent he's never felt before, and Ashby realizes Trent has a heart of gold. But can this fling last longer than the melting snow when there's a creep determined to tear them apart?

Blaze

Reyse Hickson might be an international pop sensation, but he's also forced to remain in the closet thanks to his homophobic record label. When gorgeous Corey Sheppard saves Reyse from a mugging, Reyse can't resist falling into his bed, if only for one night. However, a family emergency calls Reyse home, and it seems like the perfect chance for him and Corey to steal some secret time together. But it can't last. Reyse's label would never allow it. Can Reyse and Corey walk away from the best thing that's ever happened to either of them? Or is this love worth going down in a blaze of glory? *Contains bonus epilogue.*

Each Homecoming Hearts book can be read as a stand alone and has its own happy ever after. But if you read the whole series, you'll see familiar faces returning, and enjoy the spectacular ending of Blaze even more!

Click here to get the Homecoming Hearts eBook bundle

THE FAIRY TALE COLLECTION: CONTEMPORARY MM RETELLINGS BY HELEN JULIET

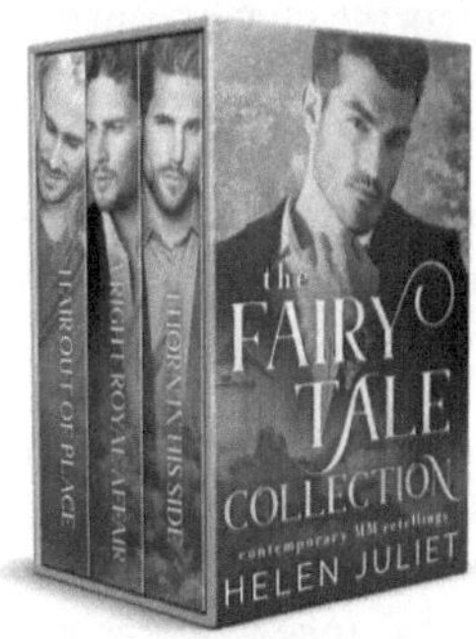

Experience Beauty and the Beast, Cinderella, and Rapunzel as you've never seen them before in this thousand page box set of contemporary adaptations! Available together for the first time, each book is a standalone with its own HEA, but watch out for familiar faces!

Click here for the Fairy Tale Collection eBook

Click here for the Fairy Tale Collection audio

———

Thorn in His Side

Beautiful, innocent Joshua Bellamy finds himself in an arranged marriage to the older, brutish, and scarred Darius Legrand. But in Darius's secluded mansion, Joshua begins to see that Darius isn't so scary after all. In fact, despite being a little grumpy, he's actually very protective and caring. When danger comes knocking on their door, will Joshua and Darius's blossoming love be strong enough to save each other?

––––––––––

A Right Royal Affair

Nobody knows that Prince James of the United Kingdom is bisexual, and as he's sixth in line to the throne, it needs to stay that way. But when he meets the cheeky, outrageously gay Essex boy, Theo Glass, everything could change. Against his better judgement, James asks Theo to help him put on a royal charity ball to remember. Can they resist their mutual attraction for a whole week alone in a picturesque castle, or will true love bloom?

––––––––––

Hair Out of Place

Raphael d'Oro is a secret prince who has spent his entire life exiled in a London penthouse. But now he's in a race against time to get back to his tiny European nation to claim the throne that's rightfully his and save his people. Good thing he has his insanely hot older bodyguard to take care of him. But Griff Thompson would never want someone as inexperienced as Raphie, would he? Even *if* they keep finding themselves in places with only one bed…

Click here for the Fairy Tale Collection eBook

Click here for the Fairy Tale Collection audio

About the Author

HJ Welch is an author of contemporary MM romance series, including the international bestselling Pine Cove series. She lives just outside of London with her husband and three balls of fluff that occasionally pretend to be cats. She began writing at an early age, later honing her craft online in the world of fanfiction on sites like Wattpad. Fifteen years and over half a million words later, she sought out original MM novels to read. By the end of 2016 she had written her first book of her own, and in 2017 she achieved her lifelong dream of becoming a full-time author. When she's not writing she's usually dancing, singing, filming music videos, taking long walks, working on jigsaw puzzles, drinking prosecco, or talking about Taylor Swift.

She also writes contemporary British MM fairy tale adaptations as Helen Juliet.

———

You can contact Helen via the following:
Newsletter: https://www.subscribepage.com/helenjuliet
Website – www.hjwelch.com
Facebook Group – Helen's Jewels
Instagram – @helenjwrites
BlueSky – @helenjuliet.bsky.social
Book Bub – @HJWelchAuthor
Facebook Page – @HJWelchAuthor

www.ingramcontent.com/pod-product-compliance
Lightning Source LLC
Chambersburg PA
CBHW060534190726
48283CB00003B/723